MW01137609

Text Copyright © September 2013 Alec Peche, revised July 2017, January 2022

Published by GBSW Publishing

Photograph: Rachael Paulsen Photography

ACKNOWLEDGMENTS

I owe a very special thanks to: Emma Davis and Balagi for their endless encouragement to write this novel. To my editor, thanks for fixing my grammar! Many thanks to Rob Kientop for designing a sinister cover for the book. To my family, for providing expert opinion on the Coast Guard and other research. To Grace for being a first reader, and finally to my circle of friends who are a daily source of kinship and support.

CHAPTER 1

*J*ill Quint sipped her steaming chai tea basking in the morning sun. She marveled that all was right with her world. She'd just returned from a much-needed vacation the night before and had no real plans for the day other than gazing at her small vineyard.

It was spring, and the grapevines were in bloom. The air was fragrant with their scent. Jill had lived in Palisades Valley for six years, and this year's Muscat crop would produce the first bottles of wine from her land.

As an undergraduate, she'd dabbled in viticulture classes offered at the university, while focusing on biology as her entry to medical school. It had taken her fifteen years to put that education to good use.

After finishing medical school, she'd found herself fascinated by forensic pathology. Forensic pathologists examine a corpse to determine the cause of death. Working in the county crime lab had provided her with extensive knowledge about the endless methods by which one human being could hurt or kill another. That, together with countless hours spent testifying in court about her findings, had caused her to re-evaluate her job.

After much soul searching, she'd decided to move to Palisades, build her own lab in a vacant barn, and grow grapes. Jill's specialty was toxicology, the study of the effect of chemicals on living organisms, Or, in her case, humans. That toxicology passion also served her vineyard, as she worked to refine organic processes to control pests and experimented with the sugar content in her grapes.

When she left her position as a forensic pathologist with the county crime lab, she'd planned to just grow grapes. The lab was an afterthought that she thought was more relevant to pest control than forensic toxicology. However, she soon found her forensic pathology services sought out by law enforcement agencies across the state. Her consulting reputation grew from there as she was requested by agencies outside of California as well as private citizens.

Fees from her consulting business kept her dog in high-quality dog food and allowed her to keep current on the latest chemical analyzers for her consulting cases. Just prior to her vacation, she'd solved a homicide related to toothpaste on the east coast. She well knew the hidden dangers found in the average home medicine cabinet.

Trixie, her beloved Dalmatian, returned to the porch with a saliva-saturated ball. Trixie was happy to be home too, as she knew where the squirrels hid in the vineyard. Maybe this would be her day to finally catch one. Jill hoped that she would fail at that mission. She'd found Trixie at a crime scene a few years ago and had adopted her, and they had been best friends ever since. Trixie had an excellent nose, and Jill had trained her to recognize the ten most common chemical causes of death in humans. Jill considered Trixie's nose to be just another chemical analyzer in her lab.

Maybe once she finished her tea, she would go for a run. While she got considerable exercise each week, there was always room for improvement, and certainly, Trixie would appreciate loping over the gentle hills of the region.

Just then she felt her cell phone vibrate. Pulling the phone out of her pocket, she glanced at the unfamiliar number before answering, "Hello, this is Jill."

A female voice on the other end of the line asked, "Is this Dr. Quint?"

Jill replied, "Yes, this is Dr. Jill Quint."

"Hello, this is Emma Spencer. I live in Woodport, a suburb of San Francisco." With a sob, she continued, "my fiancé, Graeme St. Louis died yesterday. We just returned from Puerto Rico on a scuba diving trip and while underwater Graeme was scratched by some coral. By the time we returned to San Francisco International Airport, he was sick due to an infection in his right leg, and four days after the initial scratch he died. We were due to be married next month."

Jill gave the woman a few moments to gather her composure as her last few words had been released through sobs of grief.

Jill decided to ask a question that might move Emma beyond her fiancé if only for a few seconds, "How did you get referred to me?"

"A close friend," That friend had heard Jill's name mentioned on a news report when Jill had offered a second opinion on a case in Texas. The town was very small, and the cause of death had originally been determined by the deceased's physician. While the deceased was in his seventies and had a history of heart disease, his death was unexpected.

One of the deceased's children had hired her to give the family a second opinion on the cause of death. From her investigation, she'd determined that one of the other children had overdosed him on blood pressure medication by grinding it up and putting it in a protein shake. It had made national news at the time, as the victim was the retired CEO of an oil drilling company, and his heir had grown impatient while awaiting his turn at the helm of the company and had decided to hurry his death along.

Jill was intrigued with the case as the San Francisco Medical Examiner had determined the cause of Graeme's death to be from necrotizing fasciitis, but she knew through her experience in the crime lab that murder was sometimes hidden in seemingly natural causes. She arranged to meet Emma that afternoon. Graeme was due to be buried in two days, and Emma knew she could only hold off the mortician from embalming Graeme for another twenty-four hours. Jill would need to gather any blood samples prior to his embalming.

While Graeme was already dead, and necrotizing fasciitis was known to kill a quarter of its victims, it was unusual in someone so young and healthy. The worst-case scenario in someone that young should have been the loss of his injured leg. Maybe he'd waited too long to get care. She would know more after she took some blood samples, reviewed his hospital records, and the medical examiner's autopsy report.

Jill looked at her cold tea and then at Trixie. She had four hours before she needed to leave to meet Emma Spencer. She would have to give some thought to preparing the specimen containers that she would need to do her analysis. She'd only one shot at collecting evidence from Graeme's body. The family was understandably on a timeline to bury him, and she would need to obtain any usable evidence this afternoon from Graeme. She decided to go for a run, as that would give her time to think about this case.

Jill remembered that she had a date planned with Nathan for this evening, and she might have to push that back a few hours to accommodate her roundtrip drive to San Francisco. He was used to her erratic schedule, and as he always had work to do for his wine label design company, she hoped that he would not mind the time change.

They had been dating for a year. She'd met him for the first time when she began exploring a wine label for her own vineyard. He was in great demand worldwide, as vintners recognized the power of the label design to attract buyers.

Nathan had helped her settle on a name and a label for her winery. This fall, her wines would be sold under the name Quixotic Winery, and she would feature a picture of an Italian villa typical to the Asti region, representing her romantic pursuit of creating the perfect Moscato wine. Jill had a considerable sweet tooth and had loved Moscato for its sweetness. The chemist in her thought that she could improve upon what was available currently on the market. She just needed this year's crop to begin the journey.

She put her cup in the sink and returned to her bedroom to change into her running clothes. After lacing up her sneakers, she put her long mane of blonde hair in a braid and fetched Trixie's leash. They started off at an easy pace, on a rarely traveled road. On one hand she hated running, she felt sure that she lacked the genetic design to do more than a one to two-hundred-meter distance. She was more of a sprinter. Alas, to stay fit she tried to run three to five miles several times a week. Trixie's heritage as a fire truck running dog guaranteed the dog to be the faster runner of the two of them, and it always took Trixie the first half mile to slow down her speed to that of Jill's pace.

To keep her mind off her dislike of running, Jill contemplated Graeme St. Louis. The hospital where he had expired had an excellent reputation and utilized cutting edge technology in the keeping of complete electronic records. She would be able to review his entire hospital course, including all special studies performed on him. The medical examiner would not be happy to see Jill, as that would mean that someone doubted his determination of the cause of death. Jill thought that Dr. Meyers was an excellent coroner, with a reputation among law enforcement personnel for accuracy in establishing a cause of death. Jill also had an excellent stature, both from her stint at the crime lab and from her growing body of work with friends and families of the deceased. No ME relished having Jill come into his or her jurisdiction, as that typically meant that his or her professional judgment was being questioned. Jill worked on a dozen cases a year, while the average big city coroner might do that same number in a week. She simply had more time to review each case in greater depth and puzzle over any loose details.

Jill's record of concurring with an ME's cause of death was running at slightly over seventy percent. Smaller counties across the country without a full time ME used a physician or a nurse practitioner to determine cause of death.

An ME and a patient's personal physician operated from different paradigms. The ME was suspicious, as that was his or her line of work, whereas the patient's own physician expected a person to die someday. They might be surprised that a patient of theirs was deceased, but they could always rationalize a heart attack, blood clot, stroke, or fall because these things happened in the everyday lives of their patients.

Most of Jill's cases originated with grieving friends and family members, and she offered a second opinion confirming the ME's cause of death. People found her when they searched for private autopsies. Jill was selective in the clients that she took on. She turned down cases where friends or family members suspected medical malpractice. There were plenty of pathologists who could provide a second opinion for a medical misadventure instead she focused on accidental or expected deaths that might genuinely be homicide.

So far, she'd always agreed with the San Francisco medical examiner in prior cases, but that didn't stop Dr. Meyers from naturally resenting her review of the case. There would be a slight tussle from his office regarding proper paperwork to gain all of his information and findings.

She planned to take various test tubes to collect blood

samples. In addition, she would grab another twenty to thirty agar molds to collect tissue samples from the area around the leg wound. Finally, she would take some large, long-needled syringes to collect tissue specimens from the liver, kidneys, lungs, and brain. She would also check her digital camera to make sure that it was charged and had an empty memory card.

Necrotizing fasciitis was an interesting condition from her view. The public thought that a Pac-Man like bacteria ate a victim's flesh. It was far more complex than that. Bacteria released chemicals that dissolved tissue, sort of like an acid bath from a bad horror movie scene.

Necrotizing fasciitis was first discussed in the United States by the medical profession during the civil war, where it was known as gangrene. While new methods to treat the condition and stronger antibiotics had been created, mortality remained high. The condition was on the rise worldwide, as diabetics were more prone to this complication. The media had intense interest in dramatic cases, mostly young people who might lose one or more limbs if they survived. Beyond the sensational cases, ordinary people died every day from the condition. It was very likely that Graeme had died from necrotizing fasciitis, but she would find the investigation interesting.

Jill saw the entrance to her vineyard half a mile down the road. Thankfully, she was nearing the end of her run. Trixie looked barely winded, whereas she was red-faced and soaked with sweat. The run had given her time to organize her thoughts in advance of her upcoming meeting with Emma. She released Trixie from her leash and headed into the house to shower and change. On her way inside she jotted down a list of the supplies she needed to take with her into the city. She kept a kit in her lab for these investigations, but she liked to re-check her supplies, as she usually had only one shot at getting specimens from the deceased.

She had a ninety-minute drive into San Francisco, and her

car contained her kit for collecting specimens and gathering a lot of paperwork. It would require permission from Graeme's family to get his records from everyone who had provided care to him as well as the records from the medical examiner's office. She'd asked Emma to bring documents proving that Graeme had given his authority to her to give Jill permission to review the records. It would be unusual for a fiancé to have that authority in a couple so young, but Jill was grateful that she wouldn't have to contact Mr. St. Louis's parents. That would take time and emotional anguish that she wanted to avoid.

She made an appointment with the funeral home for late afternoon and hoped to be back home by eight tonight. That would allow her time to clean up and get the smell of death out of her head prior to dinner. Despite nearly twenty years of examining the dead, she had never gotten immune to that smell. She'd planned to dine with Nathan at a local pizza parlor and wanted only to smell pepperoni at that time.

After dressing in a casual pantsuit, she packed her supplies into the trunk of her 1956 Ford Thunderbird, a pearly white beauty of a car. She'd been its owner for fifteen years and loved the unique, sporty car that was a sheer joy to drive. If she'd been staying in the central valley, she would have put the top down, but San Francisco had unpredictable weather, and the road noise after ninety minutes could be deafening. She was meeting Emma Spencer at the home she had shared with Graeme St. Louis on the outskirts of San Francisco. She programmed her GPS, set her radio to pop music, and prepared to enjoy the drive, which wouldn't be as nice on the way home, as she would be in peak commuter traffic.

CHAPTER 2

She pulled up to the long-gated driveway at the late Graeme St. Louis's home. The house couldn't be seen from the road, and in this part of the real estate world, she knew that she was approaching an eight-figure dollar house. She presented to the gatehouse, gave her name, and the gates opened. As she continued up the drive, she considered that Graeme St. Louis had achieved success at an early age to have such a large mansion. As she approached the stone steps leading to the beautiful Ionic columns aligning the front door, the tall, ornate door opened, and a young woman stepped out. Her face was pale and her eyes red rimmed, the picture of grief.

She put her hand out by way of introduction. "Dr. Quint, I'm Emma Spencer, thanks for agreeing to meet with me."

Jill responded with a warm handshake. "Please call me Jill. I'm so sorry for your loss."

Fresh tears threatened, and Emma took a deep breath and straightened her backbone. "I ordered lunch for us. We'll go into the library to dine, and we can discuss the reason I called you."

Jill followed Emma across a wood floor covered with Turkish rugs. It was a gorgeous house with stunning views of the Pacific Ocean. They entered a handsome two-story wood-lined library filled with books. A leather seating arrangement the color of mahogany made for a cozy area to read a book. Emma approached a parquet card table, where lunch had been set up.

"Jill, there is lentil soup, turkey or vegetarian wraps, soft drinks, coffee, and tea. There are also vanilla bean cupcakes for dessert. Please help yourself."

Vanilla bean cupcakes were Jill's secret weakness. In private, with no one watching, she could devour three of them and then be blissfully high on sugar until a crash an hour later. Since she was in the company of a client, she restrained herself. She had a small bowl of soup and a turkey wrap.

As they ate their lunch, Emma filled Jill in on the house, its history, and some of its contents. Jill could see that it was a helpful emotional break for Emma from the constant weight of grief. They finished their lunch and then took their drinks to the seating section, and Jill sank into the wonderful leather. She took out her notebook and settled in to interviewing Emma.

"Emma, why don't you start by telling me about your relationship with Graeme? How did you meet? It's very helpful to know as much about an individual as possible."

"I owned my own design company, and Graeme hired me to renovate this house. I was one of three bidders that he interviewed, and he found my concepts to be the most aligned with his vision. The house had sat empty for nearly a decade in an estate probate proceeding, then a bankruptcy proceeding. Prior to the probate, the house, while occupied by the previous owners, had not been maintained or upgraded for two decades. It was nearly falling down on its columns by the time Graeme closed escrow on the property."

Emma paused, taking a few sips of the tea that she'd carried to the sofa.

"It took me nearly a year to paint, upgrade the electric and plumbing systems, renovate the garden, and otherwise pull the house into the 21st century. During that year I had many meetings with Graeme, checking in with him about color and fabric choices. Those business meetings became dinners that were part business and part pleasure. Toward the end of the project our relationship had become more friendship than business. We dated after the house was finished, and almost a year ago, Graeme proposed to me. I moved in with him six months ago."

"Describe your vacation last week for me."

"Graeme had a client who had requested his presence in Puerto Rico three weeks ago. Graeme figured that he could meet the client's needs and give ourselves a brief break from the wedding madness. It was to be a four-day extended weekend trip. He would meet with his client, I could explore San Juan, and then we would have time to scuba dive, golf, and simply relax at the resort close to Old San Juan.

"We arrived in the early afternoon on Friday, and after checking into the hotel, Graeme went off to meet with his client and I headed for the interior décor stores of Old San Juan. We met up again in the hotel suite to change clothes and leave for dinner. Graeme was somewhat distracted over dinner, as he was occasionally after meeting with a client. We retired to our room where we both did some work, answered emails, and simply relaxed.

"Saturday morning, Graeme met again with the client, while I visited the local museum. We met for lunch and were excited to experience the scuba diving trip that the hotel concierge arranged for that afternoon. When Graeme booked the trip, he asked the resort to have the concierge arrange a scuba trip to his specifications. Apparently, that is something that the resort frequently does for guests. We had not been to Puerto Rico, it was a short trip, and Graeme thought it more expedient to allow the hotel to arrange activities for us.

"We arrived at a Fajardo scuba shop to board the boat that

would take us out to the Sandslide reef. Graeme had done some quick research before we left and knew that this was where he wanted to go scuba diving. We tried to scuba dive whenever we visited a part of the world that offered a body of water to explore. We had scuba-dived together at least twenty different dive sites. We kept a bag packed with our scuba gear, wetsuits, masks, fins, regulators, underwater cameras, and other items. It also contained a second copy of a current dive certification for both of us."

Emma paused a moment to take another drink of her tea. The pause gave Jill some time to catch up on her notes.

"We took the boat out to the reef and put on our wetsuits. We went through our usual pre-dive checklist, and then something peculiar happened. The tanks are always supplied by the dive shop. Obviously, you can't fly tanks on an airplane. Graeme's tank was unusually light. The regulator read that the tank was full, but given that it was so light, we asked for a different tank. We got a little argument from the guys operating the boat, but in the end, Graeme was unwilling to use that tank, so another one was supplied. We continued with our pre-dive procedure without any further incident.

"We got in the water, and the divemaster indicated that he would join us in ten minutes to show us where Sandslide was located. He gave us general directions about which way to swim."

"Emma, I have only been snorkeling. I have never been scuba diving. Was it unusual for the divemaster not to immediately be in the water with you?"

"Yes and no. Graeme and I were very experienced divers. We could have been certified as divemasters, but we never had an interest in completing the coursework. As we always seemed pushed for time, often the divemaster was helpful in getting us to a particular reef so we could spend the most time exploring the reef, rather than sometimes losing time finding the way to the reef. This is most important at deeper dives. We also like the safety of having a divemaster in case of an equipment problem or sharks. Sandslide is fifteen to seventy-five feet deep. Recreational divers can go up to one hundred thirty feet, and beginners can go to sixty feet, so we were well within our limit. This was not a deep dive, so we were not concerned or surprised by the divemaster's delay.

"Graeme and I swam in the direction the divemaster had pointed. We were happy to be in the water heading for a reef. We could see the edge of the coral and briefly waited for the divemaster to catch up to us. Once he joined us, we began our descent while he directed us around the reef. We shot some pictures and made slow progress around the reef. The fish were vivid blues, greens, and yellows. We videoed a school of tiny seahorses and a turtle swam with us for a few minutes.

"The divemaster led us in the beginning, and then he directed us and followed behind. We had been diving for thirty minutes and were wrapping it up and traveling back the way we had come. I led, Graeme followed, and the divemaster brought up the rear. As we neared the end of the reef, we had one last constricted coral fissure to go through. As we did, the divemaster banged Graeme's lower leg pretty hard against the coral, tearing his suit and causing a small gash on his leg."

Jill felt like she was underwater with Emma and Graeme, Emma's description of the dive, coral, and fish was so detailed and vivid.

Emma stayed with her story, "The divemaster apologized profusely and motioned us to continue to the surface. We surfaced and returned to the boat. Graeme gingerly removed his wetsuit, and we examined the gash. It was not deep enough to require stitches and looked like it would soon heal. The divemaster provided his first aid kit, and Graeme put ointment and a Band-Aid on the cut. Despite the accident, we were in good spirits, as we had enjoyed the dive and had taken some great pictures.

"We returned to shore and then to our hotel. We cleaned up, had dinner, sat on our balcony sipping wine, and retired to bed at an early hour.

"At about four the next morning, Graeme awakened me. He was hot, not feeling his usual self, and the leg was slightly swollen, red streaks already running up from the gash. He was able to change our flight to a seven a.m. departure that morning rather than returning the next day. We packed and made it to the airport for the flight. Graeme was walking fine, but he was tired. During the flight, the leg swelled some more, and the red streaks moved up to his knee. We decided that we would go straight to University Hospital from the airport."

Emma paused again and took a few sips of her iced tea.

After the brief break, Emma continued with her story. "Upon our arrival at the emergency room at University Hospital, we explained the injury and the symptoms since returning to shore to the doctor. The nurse took Graeme's pulse, respirations, and blood pressure, as well as some blood. His blood pressure was low and his temperature elevated. The nurse took a swab of the wound. The physician started him on antibiotics within thirty minutes and made arrangements to admit him to the ICU. Both Graeme and I were alarmed until a team of physicians gave us an explanation. It seemed that Graeme's wound was in the early stages of necrotizing fasciitis. We didn't immediately understand what this was, so the team provided us with answers. It was scary that so bad an illness could be connected to a wound that was so minor that it didn't even require stitches.

"Graeme's prognosis was good as we had gotten to the hospital quickly, and powerful antibiotics were being pumped into him to counteract the infection. A surgeon numbed Graeme's leg and removed the dead skin around the wound and cleaned it out with an antiseptic solution. This all happened very fast and caused Graeme's lawyer mind to think of his own mortality."

Emma sighed, "Naturally, we had planned to re-do our Wills and other legal documents after we got married, but after the conversation and paperwork that Graeme had to sign so that the hospital staff could tell me about his condition, he arranged a lawyer associate of his to come to the hospital and draft a new Will and healthcare power of attorney. I had no idea what was in either document. I hadn't wanted to intrude on the conversation, and to be frank, I thought that Graeme was overreacting, despite the seriousness of his condition. Graeme spent about an hour with his associate, who then left to draw up documents on his computer. He returned several hours later with a notary and a video camera, wanting to make sure that the documents couldn't be contested. That was completed, and everyone left. By then Graeme was exhausted. The day and the infection had really taken a toll on him. I left to go home, planning to return in the morning.

"The next morning, I returned to the hospital. Graeme and his leg appeared much better, and there was talk of transferring him to a regular bed later that morning. The wound cultures had come back from the laboratory, and the antibiotics that he was on appeared to be fighting the infection. The red streaks were disappearing, the leg swelling had gone down, and his temperature and blood pressure were normal. This was good news. In fact, the doctors planned to discharge him to home care the next day if he continued to improve. The physicians felt that they had started antibiotics early enough, and Graeme was young and healthy, which pointed to a good prognosis.

"Graeme's friends and family stopped by the hospital to visit him after he was transferred to a regular bed. Again, that night, I returned home, planning on going to the hospital the next day to take Graeme home. However, at around six in the morning, I received a call from someone at the hospital who said that Graeme was being transferred to the ICU, as his blood pressure was unstable, and he had a fever."

Emma paused again, got up, and paced the library. Jill could see how this situation, which had happened so fast, had been a real roller coaster ride for Emma. After more pacing, while Jill quietly reviewed her notes, making additions where necessary, Emma sat back down.

Emma said, "I drove fast to the hospital and was shocked by the decline in Graeme's condition. He was in and out of consciousness and seemed to not always recognize me. The leg was puffed up some, and the red streaks were back.

"The surgeon wanted to take him to the operating room and amputate his leg below the knee. While the surface wound looked worse compared to the previous day, I did not see the rationale for removing the lower leg. The surgeon explained that the leg infection was releasing powerful toxins into Graeme's blood and that his prognosis was poor. The only way to halt the disease at that point was to remove the original source of the bacteria."

"I desperately wanted Graeme's input and asked the surgeon to give me an hour to either get a decision from Graeme or make it myself. He gave me just a little time. Graeme's parents were in the air flying back from a vacation in Russia. I couldn't reach them in time to make the decision. I leaned over the bed and explained the situation to Graeme, looking for some hint of what he would want."

"All I got from him was mumblings that someone was trying to kill him. First, a shove down the stairs at his office building, then a gentleman who pulled a knife on him the day before we left for Puerto Rico, the regulator on the tank, the gash from the coral, and finally, he murmured that someone was in his hospital room in the middle of the night with a vial of something in their hand. It took him several attempts to tell me all of this, and at the time I thought it was the fever talking.

"In the end, I let the surgeon take him to the operating room to remove his lower leg. By mid-day, he was back in his room. He was weaker and more confused for the rest of the afternoon, and then he seemed to lapse into unconsciousness and never recovered. His heart stopped working by early morning yesterday, and despite the best efforts of the doctors at University Hospital he was gone," Emma broke into soft sobs.

Jill looked around her for help. Emma needed support from someone other than a consultant. She'd seen many a grieving family in her role as the medical examiner, and she'd always felt awkward trying to comfort the strangers that passed through the coroner's office. In her role as someone who gave a second opinion in the cause of death, she still had grieving relatives to deal with, and since they employed her, she felt honor-bound to provide comfort, but really all she felt was hugely uncomfortable at a time like this.

Death was so clinical to her. She never got attached to the dead; rather she did what she could by bringing them justice. She made sure that in the rare case of a covered-up murder, she found justice for the victim and their family. What happened to the killer was beyond her control, and she did her best to stay away from the courts. Sometimes she was dragged into court by defense attorneys, but she did her best to give her findings to the local medical examiner so the case could be closed from a death certificate perspective. This tactic allowed her to smooth any affront felt by the ME and to avoid testifying in court about eighty percent of the time.

Jill waited for Emma to regain her composure. She had a few more questions about Graeme's deathbed mumblings, and she'd forms for her to sign. She would then drive to the mortuary to evaluate Graeme. Jill asked Emma to repeat what Graeme had said before he was taken to surgery. She re-told the story twice, and Jill thought she had enough new information to perform some additional tests on Graeme. Emma signed the release of information paperwork for the hospital, the medical examiner, and the mortician, as well as Jill's consultant contract.

She informed Emma that she usually spoke with clients at least daily until she was able to reach a conclusion. Most cases took two to three weeks depending upon the complexity of the analysis.

Some specialized DNA tests were beyond the capability of her lab, and outside labs could take a week to get results back to her. Occasionally, those results directed her to further testing. Frequently it took time for the hospital and medical examiner to provide copies of their records to her. She would need to take many blood, skin, and tissue samples. She would photograph a variety of body shots at various magnifications. Finally, she had micro goggles to examine the deceased.

She would check with the hospital to see if the lower leg that had been removed in surgery was still available for her to examine. Typically, something like that would be sent to the hospital's pathologist for examination. This was routine in order to confirm that the surgeon had made the right decision in recommending amputation.

After the pathologist's examination, the tissue was often sent to medical waste. Depending on the disposal schedule and the pathologist's workload, the hospital might still have the leg, or it might have been sent along with the body to the ME.

CHAPTER 3

*J*ill called the mortician to see if he had the leg. He indicated that the leg had not come with the body. He'd contacted the ME, but neither had he received the leg. She could only hope that the hospital still had it.

As she pulled up to University Hospital, she paused to make a list of every possible part of the medical record that she would need a copy of to review. She wanted to collect all the information as if she'd been at Graeme's bedside during his entire hospital stay. She would likely have to wait a few days to get the requested information, as it would probably take the information clerk a while to find everything on her list. She would leave pre-paid overnight delivery envelopes so that the hospital could mail the records to her in bundles.

The leg was going to be difficult to locate. Jill knew that it would do no good to ask the record clerk, so she headed to the Pathology Department to determine if someone still had the leg. If they did, she thought she might be able to get them to release the leg to the mortician. As it was getting later in the day, she wasn't sure that it would get moved today. She might have to make another trip back tomorrow to separately examine the leg.

Jill fortunately had an old medical school classmate in the University Hospital Pathology department. She prevailed upon her classmate to locate the leg. It took a few minutes, but she found it within the department. She would press the funeral home to make arrangements to transport the leg and reunite it with the body. If the funeral home fetched it today, she would just stay late in the city and re-schedule her date with Nathan.

The San Francisco medical examiner's office was within walking distance of the hospital, so Jill set out at a brisk pace to deliver her request that all findings related to the autopsy be provided to her. She needed more than the death certificate. She wanted the weight of every organ and all of the findings that the ME had regarding Graeme's cause of death.

Her visit to the ME's office complete, Jill drove to the funeral home. In her role as consultant, she visited too many funeral homes. She was often perceived by morticians as delaying a funeral. They could not embalm, dress, and other-wise do the hair and make-up of the deceased until after she completed her review. She hoped that this mortician was busy enough not to hover over her while she did her examination, collected specimens, and took pictures. If nothing else, she would put pressure on the mortuary to transport the leg. That would avoid having her in the way for two days in a row.

Luck was with her. The mortician was busy elsewhere, and he would transport the leg today. That meant that she could wrap up her tasks in San Francisco today.

She called Nathan. "Hey, I'll be occupied in San Francisco longer than I thought. Let's re-schedule our pizza date for tomorrow."

"Okay, babe. If you feel like it, drop by my house for a glass of wine on your way home."

They said their goodbyes. Jill returned to thinking about the case and Graeme's final comment to Emma, someone is trying to kill me. If her second opinion on the cause of the death matched that of the ME, then this would be a straightforward case.

If Jill found anything suspicious, she might need to enlist the aid of her three closest friends, Jo, Marie, and Angela. Jo was a CPA and a fabulous forensic accountant. She could always make sense of any individual's or company's financial activities. Jo wasn't certified as a forensic accountant, but she was hugely curious about cash flows. From Jill's non-accountant view, Jo was almost psychic about knowing where to look for illegitimate financial transactions. Money was so often the reason for a covered-up homicide that it was frequently where she started her investigation if she had to move beyond a simple cause of death opinion for the family.

Marie performed candidate reference checks for a multinational company. She had many tools at her disposal to investigate an individual, both in the United States and throughout the rest of the world. It was all public data if you knew where to look. She was as good as a private eye and generally had a complete picture about anyone in less than two hours of computer work. She'd spent twenty years in human resources and performed hundreds of searches of employee candidates while working for a manufacturing company. She was fabulous at investigating candidate backgrounds. Jill rarely used her services, as usually, the killer was obvious.

Angela had a knack for pulling information out of people in a totally disarming way. Who needed a Sherlock Homes when Angela could gain information in the softest, most compassionate, and subtle manner? People never realized the information they gave to Angela, as she was so mesmerizingly nice.

The services of Jill's friends had been written into Jill's consultant contract with Emma as potential additional charges. She was often able to save clients money by using her friends.

They charged a lower hourly rate, as it did not have to meet an evidence standard. Her friends deposited their consultant fees into a special vacation account, and they had been able to fund their vacations from the account for the past couple of years. She would drop them an email later that night as an FYI in case she brought them into the investigation.

Jill parked her Thunderbird in the mortuary parking lot and went inside to meet the mortician. She would need to evaluate the area where she could examine Graeme. She might need additional lighting, protective clothing, or medical waste disposal containers depending on the setup inside.

She noted that she would have optimal working conditions.

The lighting was excellent, medical waste containers were available for her use. Protective clothing was also available. She would wear the mortician's protective coveralls but would supply her own mask and gloves. Since she dealt with bacteria in all bodies that she examined, she never took risks with inferior latex gloves or poorly fitted masks.

She returned to the car and gathered her test tubes and agars, her camera with multiple lenses, and her microscopic eyepieces. Since the ME had performed a full autopsy, there was no need for her to weigh the organs. She could gather all of her information without making further cuts to Graeme's body.

The first task Jill performed when approaching any body was to crank up the lighting. She then put on protective clothing and her micro goggles. She always liked to start with a close examination of the entire exterior of the body.

Graeme had an athletic build. His skin was a light brown, suggesting a biracial heritage. She would have Emma check the death certificate. Some of her tests were race-specific, so she would need to have a better handle on his heritage. During the examination, she noted an irritated appearing IV site with skin discoloration on the right upper arm. She spent considerable time photographing that arm and the leg above the amputation.

Next, she used swabs to culture the skin discoloration and the right arm IV site, and various other parts of the skin. She removed a number of long-needled syringes and a hand-held ultrasound device. Using ultrasound waves Jill determined the location of the needle inside Graeme's torso. She aspirated a sampling from the heart, the lungs, and the marrow in his hips, his liver, and his kidneys.

She then used the ultrasound to determine where the arteries were and took blood samples from those locations. Two hours later as she finished her examination, someone from the funeral home brought the leg into the room. It was nice that the leg could be buried with the rest of Graeme's body.

Personally, Jill had put in her Will that she wanted to be cremated, but still, she would want all of her parts with her when she entered the oven.

The leg was a mess, as one would expect. It had been diseased before it was removed two days ago, and it had not improved with time. The amputation was about two inches above the scuba diving injury. Again, she took many pictures, cultured different parts of the gash from the coral, and took blood samples from the foot. She spent another thirty minutes with just the foot.

It was interesting that the leg hadn't been passed over to the ME, but then the pathology lab wouldn't necessarily be aware that Graeme had died or that his body had been moved to the ME.

When Jill finished, she packed up all of her equipment and samples into special cases. Those cases could survive a car crash or be dropped from a height of eight feet. She felt she owed it to her clients to protect her findings and samples. Sometimes, her specimens were the only physical evidence that law enforcement had for a case.

She removed her protective clothing and then wiped down her micro goggles and face shield. Finally, she did a surgical scrub on her hands to ensure their cleanliness. She thanked the mortician for the help, indicating that he could proceed with preparing Graeme for burial. She went outside, securely packed her cases in her car, and noted that dusk had settled over the sky.

Traffic had greatly improved since rush hour. Jill was over the Bay Bridge heading for home. She loved looking north toward the Golden Gate Bridge, barely visible, cloaked in fog. It presented a romantic view of the world.

As she drove home, she speculated about the possible tests that she might run on the samples she'd collected. How could someone be murdered by necrotizing fasciitis? Furthermore, if she wanted to prove that this case was murder by necrotizing fasciitis, how would she go about validating such a finding? Since becoming a consultant, Jill found that the best path to follow was to assume that the deceased had been murdered.

It was her hypothesis. She then performed a series of tests to validate that theory. Jill found that rather than trying to decide if she agreed with a medical examiner's finding, it was more expedient to assume homicide, than try to build a case as though she was a defense attorney.

CHAPTER 4

She contacted Nathan once she got beyond city traffic. She explained her case to him and what specimens she'd collected and her impression of Graeme and Emma.

She asked him about his day, and he spoke of a new client. Like Jill, Nathan's new client would be a first-time vintner with this year's crop.

Unlike Jill, she had no education or feel for the vineyard. The client had brought a Merlot sample with her when they met, and he thought it had tasted sour. He hated putting his label design on her bottle. He had two label templates that he worked with, one that had his signature somewhere in the picture on the label and another that did not. Some vintners objected to him working his signature into the scene on the label. With other vintners, while he appreciated the label commission, he disliked their wine and thus did not want his name associated with the contents, so he purposely left his signature off the label.

After more conversation, they agreed to dinner tomorrow to make up for the canceled date. An hour later, Jill pulled into her driveway and unloaded her equipment and samples. Trixie was excited to see her, with a ball in her mouth. Jill worked off Trixie's excess energy with a good round of chase-the-ball in the lights of the driveway. She then settled in her favorite chair with a glass of Moscato and her case notebook.

After her second case, she'd taken the time to organize her thoughts as a consultant, and she designed a standardized plan. She took her forms and filled-in data on the case. Some of the data fields would have to wait until she reviewed the records from the hospital and the medical examiner. Now she gave focused attention to her testing plan: How would she prove a homicide? With a few more hours of work, she fell into a deep sleep after the long day.

With her plan in hand, Jill spent the next morning organizing her samples and began some of the testing. She recorded her results and had a series of timers set for when some of the agars would be ready. She reviewed pictures she'd taken and moved them to file folders. She studied the leg at length, as well as the odd tissue around the IV site that she'd noted during her examination.

She also did some online research to refresh her memory on necrotizing fasciitis, other cases resulting from coral gashes, and the bacteria identified by the hospital as having been cultured from Graeme's wound. This case generated an uneasy feeling in her. It was too damn perfect. Perfect fiancé in a perfect house engaged to a perfect man dying of a textbook perfect sensational disease. Jill often had an intuitive sixth sense regarding cases in which she offered an opinion, in addition to the medical examiner's ruling. As impossible as it had seemed at the start of this case, she had a feeling that she would eventually convince the medical examiner that it was a homicide.

At lunch, she decided to take a break from her testing and her thoughts. She and Trixie had engaged in a rousing game of catch that morning, but now it was time to examine her vineyard. She would view the size of the grapes, taste a few, and try to detect any signs of pests. Just strolling through the grapes would clear her head for a while.

An hour later she returned to her lab. Some of the agars were reaching the first time in which she could run tests on what had grown there. These initial tests were fascinating. Graeme's death had clearly been caused by septic shock, an overwhelming blood infection. The infection spread rapidly in the blood causing major organ failure and eventual death. However, Graeme's infectious agent was a mystery. She'd never before seen anything like these agars. The bacteria that had caused the initial necrotizing fasciitis in Graeme's lower leg was exactly the same as that at the IV site in his arm. Yet the growth of the bacterial colonies was different. This could not have been a break in sterile technique on the part of hospital personnel.

Based on the reproduction of the bacteria, it was as if someone had a vial of bacteria that first was spread on the leg wound and then a few days later injected into the IV site. Jill had seen her share of strange homicide methods, but this method, if proven, was very sophisticated. The killer would have to have knowledge of and access to microbiological agents. If, as Graeme had stated on his deathbed, there had been several attempts on his life, then this was an organized effort with likely more than one person involved.

She'd many more tests to run and still awaited the copies of the hospital and medical examiner's reports. Jill planned to speak with Emma this afternoon, but she would not reveal her thoughts as yet since she had one to two more days of testing in her lab, and she also sent out two specimens for additional testing to another lab. While she had a high-tech laboratory in her barn, she maintained a contract with a reference lab for some costly and rarely performed tests.

Nathan had canceled their evening pizza date due to a meeting with a customer from Europe. They had rescheduled for the second time in two days. Although the delays had been unavoidable, she swore that she would have pizza regardless tomorrow. She missed being with Nathan, but a pizza craving had to be uniquely satisfied.

After a quiet evening, she awoke early the next morning, the day of Graeme's funeral dawned sunny and bright. She would not call Emma today, as she thought that it was the wrong thing to do for many reasons. She returned to her laboratory reviewing data as test results became available. A tentative conclusion of homicide began to form in Jill's mind based on scientific results. She'd a few more agar growths she needed to check as well as the results from the reference lab that would not be available for a couple more days.

She wrapped up her findings so far and consolidated the data onto her forms. She would enter it into her computer tomorrow. She left her lab with the agars set up to run her final tests in the morning. She took the paperwork with her to the house so she could reflect on the case. She changed clothes, before driving to the pizza joint for her date with Nathan.

CHAPTER 5

*J*ill sat in her favorite booth sipping a glass of Chianti when Nathan strolled in to join her. After an exchange of an 'I missed you kiss,' he settled into the booth.

Jill reminded herself how lucky she was to have found Nathan. She loved his tall, lean frame, glossy black hair, and gorgeous blue eyes. His artistic personality was a nice pairing to her scientific nature, rather like Chianti and pepperoni. She loved being in his company and their conversation. She tended to get wrapped up in her consult cases, and his very presence diverted and relaxed her brain thus balancing her world.

She thought that he might be the one man suited to her. They were taking it slow, as they had both exited long-term relationships within a year of meeting. They simply felt that there was no hurry to figure out that next step of living together or perhaps even getting married. They both liked their respective houses and functional outbuildings on their property. In her case, Jill had her lab and her winery to begin the production of Moscato.

Nathan had his studio where he met with clients and

designed labels. For some clients, beyond the label he provided branded marketing materials and signage relating to the label. His studio had a drafting table, CAD software, and a variety of industrial printers. For most clients, he also served as the printer of the labels they would affix to their bottles. He had an assistant who did a production run of several thousand labels at a time. If he had branding materials larger than a legal-size document, he appropriately sized the graphics and had the materials printed elsewhere.

Jill had Trixie, and Nathan had Arthur, a sleek grey cat. The pets did not get along. Trixie viewed Arthur as prey to be chased; Arthur behaved as though Trixie was beneath his contempt. He stared down his nose at her, just out of reach, while grooming his paws. They provided endless entertainment to Jill and Nathan. Thus far, neither of them had found sufficient reason to give up their homes, and their pets followed that same direction.

They, fortunately, had a shared passion for pizza and wine. They lingered over their wine after consuming a medium pizza. Jill gave Nathan a brief outline of her current case and her suspicions. She left out the names of the deceased in the normal course of conversation with anyone. She needed to keep a level of confidentiality for her clients.

"It is the most intriguing case I have investigated in the past several years. I am a snorkeler, so the whole scuba thing is beyond my knowledge."

"Since I'm a scuba diver, I'll describe the preparation for a dive from start to finish."

Jill strictly went for snorkeling. She found the ocean depth a little scary and preferred to stay on the surface. Nathan had used a concierge in the past to set up a quick scuba trip, so he helped her better understand the procedure for arranging an excursion.

They were going to her place after dinner, and she would

share her notes with him. Nathan would be of real help to her investigation on this case. They wrapped up their discussion, paid the bill, and walked to their cars. She pulled out onto the highway to head home and could see Nathan in her rearview mirror.

Jill pulled into her driveway fifteen minutes later. Something was not right, but she couldn't put her finger on it. Trixie ran up to her car agitated. Nathan parked behind her car on the driveway. She got out of her car to calm Trixie, but the dog didn't want to be soothed. Instead, she tried to get Jill to follow her to the barn where her lab was located.

As Nathan exited his car, she said to him, "Nathan, something is not right, and Trixie is leading me to my lab."

It was then that Jill noticed the unlit exterior lights and the darkened yard.

Jill went back to her garage for a flashlight.

She murmured, "Now I know what was wrong when I pulled in. It's dark by the barn, which is normally lit up. Let me go see if there is a circuit breaker that has been tripped or something."

Nathan followed her with a second flashlight that she handed to him. As she approached the barn, she hoped that her generator had kicked in. When she'd designed the layout of her lab and the winery, the barn was specially wired for backup power. Her barn was better prepared for a loss of power than was her house. But the lights she'd left on in her house were working, and her neighbors had electricity on their properties.

She had temperature-sensitive agars growing, and her results would be invalidated if there was temperature variation outside the normal range. She couldn't hear the generator running, but it was on the opposite side of the building so she might not hear it. As she reached the door handle, she noticed that the lock was damaged and the door ajar. She felt uneasy and was glad Nathan was with her.

They walked in, and Jill noted the damage to her lab with the flashlight beam. She pulled out her cell phone and called the Sheriff to report the break-in. Meanwhile, she went back outside and around to where her generator was located. The generator had been switched to the off position. She moved it again to the on position, and the exterior lights flickered on. Whoever had done this was long gone, as she'd been off the property for half a day. She didn't think that this was a random burglary or a typical residential break-in. Her valuables were in the house. The lab's specimens and computers were the valuables in the barn at the moment.

No wonder Trixie was agitated. She must have heard the activity earlier. She was relieved that the dog had not been injured or killed by whoever had done this damage. She now had a second source of evidence that there was something suspicious about Graeme's death.

She paused to hug Nathan. She was so glad to have him by her side at this moment. Jill felt apprehensive and afraid of being the target of some unknown person. After the brief but heartfelt hug, she gathered her inner spine and returned to the entrance of the lab.

"I don't want to disturb any evidence," she said as she handed sterile gloves to Nathan from a spare box she kept in her garage.

She turned on the interior lights, but they stayed off. Jill went to the circuit box and moved the switches, and the overhead lighting came on. Dismayed, she surveyed the mess. Broken glass littered the floor and counters.

"Nathan, can you lift Trixie and take her outside?"

Trixie weighed over sixty pounds and she didn't like being lifted, but Jill wanted to make sure she didn't step in an infectious agar or lab chemical or slice her paws on broken glass. Once Nathan got her outside, they took her up to the house and then returned to the lab to resume examining the damage. Jill had toured Nathan through the lab several months ago, but it had been a neat and clean space at that time. Meanwhile, a Sheriff's deputy officer arrived.

Nathan and Jill introduced themselves to Deputy Davis. She was a tall African American woman with a cool, competent air about her. Jill felt safer in her presence, and the gun holstered at Deputy Davis's waist relaxed her further. Outside the entrance to the lab, Jill explained her role in consulting on homicide cases and gave the deputy an overview of the kind of instruments she had in the lab. Jill then explained the details of her present case to Deputy Davis.

While they could do some fingerprinting of some key surfaces like the doors, the generator, and the fuse box, neither Jill nor Deputy Davis had much hope of finding the person that caused the damage. The destruction inside her lab seemed pointed at her current case. This was the first time in her consulting career, indeed in her forensic pathology career, that an as yet unidentified person had attacked her property.

Deputy Davis completed her report and gave Jill a copy for her insurance company. She didn't know yet if any of her expensive analyzers had been damaged or if it was strictly the specimens. Deputy Davis also gave her the names of a few security companies that protected other businesses in the Palisades Valley. Jill had been thinking about increasing her security once she started producing wine, but now she had a more urgent need to protect her lab, her property, her dog, and herself.

After Deputy Davis drove away, Jill straightened her shoulders, and said to Nathan, "Well, I guess I better go clean up this mess and see what is salvageable."

Nathan sighed, "Jill, you're tired. Why not wait until the morning to clean this mess up."

Jill responded, "I'm too revved up on adrenaline to relax at the moment. I may as well use that energy for something positive. I'm racking my brains trying to figure out who thought I might be getting close to new information on my current case. Besides, I might find something to salvage."

"Nathan, would you mind staying the night? Until I can get some security in place, I'm uneasy about staying here by myself. I need to clean this mess up. I can't lock the lab since the lock is damaged, and at this point, I need to see what specimens and records are recoverable."

Nathan, without hesitation, agreed to stay and help Jill clean up. He'd never seen her self-confidence dented like it was at the moment. He was a third-degree Master Black Belt in Hapkido and could defend her in hand-to-hand combat. He was working on his fourth degree, and he was pretty handy with swords, canes, and sticks. Jill knew of his love for Hapkido, but she'd never seen him in competition, and thus she was unaware of the degree of personal protection he could provide.

He sure hoped he wouldn't have to do a live demonstration, and in the end, he wasn't much help against a gun loaded with bullets.

Jill returned to the lab with the lights blazing. She'd let Trixie loose in the yard in case someone attempted to return to the scene of the crime. Trixie would at least bark to alert them. She gave Nathan a refresher on her lab and put yellow sticky notes on any potentially infectious waste or hazardous chemicals. For Jill, it was years of practice that guided her on the handling of substances in the lab, but Nathan was a novice and she needed him to take precautions inside her lab. She gave him a water-proof coverall and gloves just in case he accidentally touched the wrong thing, and she did likewise as they got to work.

Jill started with the actual samples. The blood, biopsy fluids, and agars that she'd collected from Graeme's body in the funeral home had all been contaminated or destroyed. Broken glass and plastic littered the floor. All that remained of the specimens that she'd spent hours collecting was either in the package on the way to the outside reference lab, or if she had luck, she might have a usable syringe or two in the sharps container. If the person that had done this damage hadn't thought to look there for syringes that she used to extract tissue and fluid from Graeme's body, she might be able to re-start her specimen testing.

She walked over to the container, and her luck held as it contained some of the original specimens' tubes with fluid still in them that she could re-use. She was even luckier that she had a syringe from the leg wound and another from the IV site in the arm. The third syringe held a sample that she'd taken from the non-infected arm, and it also had its uses. She could reproduce some of the key agars that had been destroyed.

Jill and Nathan made significant progress cleaning the mess up. She then moved on to her analyzers. They would need to be recalibrated but otherwise seemed in working order. The person that attempted to destroy her lab seemed intent on dumping all specimens on the floor and smashing them, not smashing the equipment.

Next Jill and Nathan explored her computers, both those within the analyzers and the desktop computer she had on one workbench. Nathan was far more computer literate than was Jill. She showed him where to locate the interior computers for most of her analyzers, and then she went to her desktop computer. She powered it up and found that it had been reformatted, with all of her data on Graeme destroyed. But fortune shone on her here. She'd kept her backup paper copy of all findings on the forms that she kept with her until a case was closed.

Early in her consultant career, a virus had destroyed the computer on which she entered data. Even back then she'd kept paper backup. She'd been disorganized and scattered with her paper at that time, and it had been painful to reconstruct the case after the computer virus. This time she'd only lost her data entry time, as her forms kept the data in a ready format.

This was the first (and she hoped the last) case that Jill

ALEC PECHE

seemed to be under attack from someone who did not want her to find the truth about the cause of Graeme's death. She would discuss with Nathan how she should secure her data going forward with all cases. She would contact Emma early in the morning to discuss all of tonight's activity.

Nathan and Jill finished cleaning up the lab, and they left the lights blazing everywhere but her bedroom as a meager attempt to keep out any additional intruders. She'd put the sharps container in Nathan's trunk for now. She would process some more agars tomorrow and send a duplicate set to the university. She had a friend in the pathology department seeking interesting cases for her students. Jill would love to get their feedback on the samples.

Jill settled into her bed, her head on Nathan's shoulder. With Trixie on the floor by the bedroom door, she promptly fell into an exhausted slumber. Her adrenaline rush had run its course, and she didn't stir until morning.

CHAPTER 6

*A*s a morning person, Jill awoke with a surge of energy to get out of bed and celebrate the sunrise. She left Nathan asleep, as he was a night person, and it was best not to disrupt the grumpy artist until he awoke later in the morning.

She had a to-do list. Check with two security system companies and get an estimate today. Call Emma and discuss the case and the vandalism. Check that her samples had been received by the reference lab. Re-calibrate her analyzers to assure they were in working order. Contact her pathology friend at the university and mail the agars from her three remaining tubes of blood. Prepare her agars to restart the analysis of the bacteria. Find a safer place than Nathan's trunk to store her blood tubes. Set up a call with Jo, Marie, and Angela to brainstorm over the next steps.

Best of all, Jill had a great excuse to avoid jogging through the countryside for a few days. She rather thought that her personal safety might be at risk until this case was passed on to law enforcement. Jill was quite pleased with herself for thinking of this excuse not to go running. Trixie wouldn't be happy, but she could pacify her with some frequent fetch time. She also planned to stick close to Nathan for a few days. She needed someone watching her back.

On her second cup of coffee, Jill set up appointments with the security companies for that morning. She wanted to secure her winery and her lab for the years ahead. She needed to balance those long-term needs with the panic she felt now to surround her property with a security guard every twenty feet. If these security companies knew how vulnerable she was to buy the top-of-the-line system, she would be taken to the cleaners.

After completing her calls with the security companies, she put her thoughts in order for her conversation with Emma Spencer. It had been an interesting thirty-six hours. Jill was going to brief Emma on the preliminary findings from the destroyed lab tests in her lab as well as the vandalism to her lab. While Emma had hired Jill strictly to offer an opinion on the cause of Graeme's death, the damage to her lab made it personal, and she was going to take the case a step further to see if she could figure out who was trying to destroy evidence that might prove that Graeme had been murdered.

Yesterday had been Graeme's funeral, so she expected Emma to be exhausted from that experience. She didn't want to telephone her too early, but given her evidence, she felt she needed to warn Emma to get additional security for her home.

Jill felt confident that she could cross Emma off her suspect list. His death had already been ruled an accident, and if she wanted to hide the murder, the easiest path would be to simply accept the medical examiner's cause of death.

She planned to discuss with Emma the possibilities of who would want Graeme dead. Once the medical examiner accepted her test results and changed the cause of death, then the case would be turned over to the San Francisco Police Department. However, with the evidence destroyed and new evidence not available for another thirty six hours, she felt she needed to alert Emma to her vulnerabilities.

Jill and Emma spoke about the funeral before Jill launched into an explanation of her preliminary findings and the lab vandalism. Emma was horrified. She'd really thought that Graeme had died of an accidental overwhelming blood infection. Her hiring of Jill had been her final act of love for Graeme to verify the cause of his death. Now she had to grieve all over again. To know that they could have had a long life together, but that it had been cut short by his murder, was almost too much to bear.

Jill waited as Emma coped with this latest news, answering her questions concerning the science of the bacteria and why she thought it was not natural infection growth. When Emma had all her questions answered, Jill moved on to her security. She asked Emma to think of her own surroundings as well as the security at her home and business. Without having a clue as to the identity of the killer or vandal, Jill had no idea if Emma was in harm's way. Better to be safe than sorry on that issue. They set the appointed time for more conversation the next day.

She then checked on her FedEx package and noted that it had arrived at the reference lab in the last hour. She spoke with her contact in the lab and asked that a few tests be added to the ones originally requested. While she was hopeful of running the same tests in her own lab, due to the fact that there was potentially a break in the chain of custody, the reference lab specimens would serve to verify her findings after the case was turned over to the SFPD once they opened their investigation.

Jill had her first appointment with a security company. She toured the estimator through her property and discussed her business needs as far as securing the vineyard, the wine production area, the laboratory, and her home. She also mentioned that she'd been vandalized the previous night, and she wanted to know what the company could have in place today. While she didn't think her lab would be wrecked again, she rather thought that she might be the next target of the unknown assailant. Whoever had arranged Graeme's death thought that the evidence from her lab was destroyed. If they destroyed her next series of tests, the cause of death couldn't be overruled. With Graeme's body embalmed and buried, the evidence was gone, except what was in Jill's head, or so the killer would think.

An hour later she followed the same routine with the second company. Both companies verbally suggested similar strategies for about the same price. The second company could actually have installers at her house within the hour, so she signed a contract and heaved a sigh of relief that she would have some needed security by later today.

With her personal protection being improved by the hour, Jill returned to the house to check on Nathan. He sat in her kitchen with a cup of coffee. He took a good half an hour to get going once he rolled out of bed in the morning. She offered to make him breakfast as she had the ingredients for a breakfast burrito. He gratefully accepted her offer. She made a smaller one for herself and they dined at the table.

He showed signs of achieving alertness, so she described her morning, including the work that would improve her security. Nathan offered to move his life into Jill's home. While she hated to put him in danger's way, she was rather spooked at the moment and welcomed his presence.

They went over to his house to collect clothes, Arthur, and his other stuff, and the materials Nathan needed to continue work at Jill's house. Fortunately, Nathan could rearrange his work to shadow Jill for the next few days.

She thought she would be able to deliver her findings to the San Francisco medical examiner's office soon. The ME would in turn notify the SFPD. Jill figured that once her test results were made public, it would take the heat off her, and then she and Nathan could go back to their normal lives.

They arrived back at her house and settled Arthur in. Trixie was not happy, but Jill rather liked the thought that Arthur would keep Trixie occupied and close to him. She was worried that Trixie would get hurt in the current circumstances.

Nathan and Jill headed over to her lab to re-calibrate her analyzers. Jill started her agars again and set the timers. Nathan had re-set all her analyzers and sat down at her desktop computer to see if there was anything he could recover. He considered himself good with computers, but this was beyond him. He spoke with a friend in town who was his go-to person for the rare computer problem that he couldn't fix. In the end, they decided that it would be just as fast for Jill to re-enter her data.

This act of vandalism was a lesson for her. In the past, she'd kept her case consultant data on the desktop. The rare time that she lost data, she pulled up her backup copy. Now that Nathan had seen her process for collecting data on a case, he would develop a process with built-in redundancy for her to follow with back-up to the cloud.

Early in his design career, he'd lost a design he'd spent weeks working on. He had recreated the design, but for some reason, he never felt that the duplicate design artistically matched the original. After that experience, he had set up an elaborate backup system so that he would never again lose a design.

Jill sighed and glanced around her. She'd restored order to her home and to her lab. That feeling of control lessened her panic about Graeme's killer. What she really needed now was a good workout.

She turned to Nathan and asked, "Did you bring your kick-boxing gloves with your stuff this morning?"

Nathan smiled at her with a gleam in his eye and stated, "Yes, do you want to burn off some excess energy from the stress of the last twenty-four hours?"

Jill responded, "I don't know how to kickbox, but I sure want to kick something at the moment, and just one kick won't be enough. I need at least half an hour of kicking to clear my head."

Nathan said, "Then let's go back to your house, change clothes, and I'll get the equipment. Do you have an exercise mat?"

She'd chased a few fitness passions over the years that had caused her to accumulate an exercise mat or two. They changed their clothes, gathered up Nathan's equipment, and strolled over to an unused barn where she stored the mats. She'd never tried working out with Nathan before. Nathan wanted to teach her a few self-defense moves given her current precarious situation.

CHAPTER 7

*T*hey spread the mats out in the empty barn. Nathan insisted that they stretch before the rigorous work as he wanted to go over the self-defense moves before the cardio workout.

Nathan demonstrated how to fend off various forms of attack. Next, he showed her where to strike for maximum impact. After he was satisfied that Jill could protect herself with the basic tenets of self-defense, he moved on to some kickboxing.

He showed Jill how to shift her weight to kick for maximum power. He put on gloves to deflect her kicks and then proceeded to goad her into the most physical workout she had ever done. After forty-five minutes, every hair on her head and every piece of clothing she wore was soaked with sweat. She dropped to the floor. Nathan had barely broken a sweat. This was another reason not to jog. In the end, she wasn't as fit as she thought she was. It was all very depressing.

Jill and Nathan returned to her house. She planned to drink a large glass of water, shower, and lure Nathan to her bed, in that order. She'd been totally turned on for the last hour and a half by Nathan's body and movements. He had the upper hand then, and now it was up to her to wrestle with him for the upper hand in bed, and she looked forward to the contest.

A few hours after the workout, Jill was both energized and calm. Thanks to Nathan, she felt prepared to deal with any intruders. She'd also burned off her mad. Her attitude was completely re-adjusted into a much more positive state of mind. She thanked Nathan profusely for helping her get there. She felt refreshed and renewed and ready to apply all of her considerable brainpower to solve the mystery surrounding Graeme's death.

She returned to the lab. Her re-started agars had reached their first checkpoint of growth. The results were exactly the same as the first agars that had been destroyed. She also had an email from the reference lab, giving her highly specific DNA results. She needed the results of just one more series of tests, and then she would be able to prove that Graeme's infection was not the result of his body's weak immune response, but a deliberate exposure to an infectious agent.

Jill sat down at her desk to plan her next steps. She would summarize her findings and turn them over to the medical examiner, who would then give them to the SFPD. However, the vandalism in her laboratory had made this personal. She was both mad and scared. She wanted the killer caught and soon. She didn't like her property, her dog, and her man at risk.

She decided that the case would be solved faster if she stayed in the game. It would take her another day or so to gather additional evidence to give to the ME to try to convince him to re-evaluate his cause of death before the police would officially be brought in on the case.

Depending on the caseload of the SFPD homicide unit, it would take the detectives some time to get up to speed on the case. As Graeme's death had been an elaborate scheme, she was sure the police would work the case. As it involved both California and Puerto Rico, the homicide investigation would be complicated and the case cold as it had been nearly a week since Graeme's death.

Jill studied Nathan working at his temporary drafting table. She would love to run her thoughts by him, but maybe she would contact her friends and bounce ideas off them. They had partnered with her on other cases and would be worried when she gave them all the details about this case.

They lived in Wisconsin but had on occasion taken time off from their day jobs to work on one of her cases. As the hourly consulting fee was more than their normal jobs paid, it was not a financial hardship to consult on her cases. They could do significant Internet search work to assist Jill in closing a case. In this case, Angela would have to come to California and potentially go to Puerto Rico to help her solve the case.

She was confident that Emma would agree to her consulting plan, as her friends' fees were very reasonable, and it would help her get resolution sooner.

She texted them to check their availability for a conference call. It was early evening in their time zone, and she might luck out and catch them at a good time. She was texted back almost immediately and was fortunate to get them on the phone. First, she dialed Jo, then Marie, and finally Angela. They quickly caught up on each of their personal lives. Jill then moved into the reason for the call.

"Let me update you on my current client, Emma Spencer, and her recently departed fiancé, Graeme St. Louis."

Jill proceeded to explain her case findings so far, including the vandalism of her laboratory. Her friends were glad to hear of Nathan's presence. They had worked on other cases of Jill's over the years and were amazed to hear that her lab had been broken into. Jo and Marie couldn't get away, but the vast majority of their work was Internet research, so they could still actively contribute. Angela's work was more hands-on, as she needed to strike up conversations with people involved in the case in person. She could leave for California tomorrow.

Angela was a professional photographer, and her photoshoot for the next four days had been canceled because of the weather. She was supposed to do an outdoor shoot, but the weatherman had projected record rainfall and thus the shoot had been re-scheduled at the last minute. While it rained buckets in Wisconsin, Angela would come to California to assist Jill.

Jill arranged a meeting with Emma for tomorrow with Angela after she picked her up in San Francisco. She would have the use of Angela's skills for almost a week between photo shoots. In addition to the four-day photoshoot, she'd allocated three days for processing the pictures. After Angela and Jill met with Emma, they would get Jo on the phone to strategize their areas of research.

She'd another eight hours to wait for the third batch of test results that would definitively prove homicide. The security company was finished with its first day of installation, so Jill had more protection tonight and a sign on her property adver-tising the new security. She looked at Nathan to see if he was deep in thought on a design.

"Nathan, I'm finished for the day. I'm going to return to the house to see what I can find for dinner tonight. I'd like to stay on my property until the final agars complete their growth tomorrow morning."

Nathan looked at Jill, somewhat scared to have her in the kitchen. Not because he feared for her safety, but rather because he feared for his stomach. In the year they had been dating, she'd never cooked anything for him other than breakfast, and she had been quite clear that she didn't like to cook. He had a tall frame to feed, and the afternoon's activities had worked up his appetite. He was at a point where he could break away from his work.

"Jill, why don't let you let me see what I can find to cook in your kitchen?"

Jill viewed Nathan with amusement. She knew what had him worried. He was trying to politely decline her cooking.

"Nathan, as your host, I feel that I should cook for you, but you appear rather queasy at that thought. I guess I should clear the air. I can cook. I have actually never poisoned a friend with my cooking. It just tends to be rather bland. As good as I am in chemistry; I am clueless when it comes to spices. I can't tell if a dish would benefit from some mustard or some rosemary. Mostly I don't enjoy cooking, but I can make a reasonable effort in the kitchen."

Nathan had never heard such a weak evaluation of someone's cooking ability. Jill had not had him over to her house for a meal that she cooked from scratch. It was good to know that she wouldn't kill him with her cooking, but he rather thought that a trip through the drive-through at In and Out Burger would be a better culinary experience than her cooking.

"Let me explore your kitchen, and I'll see what I can create for dinner. You've had dinner at my house, and you know I like to cook. I just need to assess your supply of spices and other ingredients."

They slowly walked hand in hand to her house, playing fetch with Trixie as they went. Arthur waited on the front stoop twitching his tail. He looked angry to have been relocated to Jill's house. Nathan paused to scratch his ears, and Arthur hissed at both a bounding Trixie and Nathan. Nathan picked Arthur up on the way in, knowing that if he put him on a stool in the kitchen, he would settle down. As this was his first overnight stay at Jill's, the cat was justified in his anger.

CHAPTER 8

$\mathcal{N}$athan started with reviewing the contents of Jill's refrigerator and freezer and then her pantry. He was pleasantly surprised at the fairly wide collection of ingredients. Jill had a great kitchen. Beautiful granite countertops, a large center workspace, a six-burner stove, and a double oven, and it was all wasted on her. She'd had the kitchen re-modeled with a thought toward resale value of the house not for its daily usefulness. He thought he was really going to enjoy cooking here.

He gathered the ingredients for a chicken penne pasta, salad, and sautéed winter vegetables. He searched her wine cellar for a bottle to accompany the meal. Arthur watched all of this activity from his perch on Jill's bar stool. Nathan offered him a piece of chicken, which the cat ate with relish. He proceeded to clean himself and finally settled on the back of a couch for a nap.

Jill had watched the whole entertaining show between man and cat. She opened the bottle of wine that Nathan had selected and poured two glasses. She was still smiling as Trixie settled against her leg and managed to look down her nose at the cat and the man. Nathan appeared to be very comfortable in her kitchen while Jill relaxed and thought about the case, her friend's arrival, and the defense moves Nathan had taught her that afternoon.

After a delicious and relaxing dinner, she loaded the dishwasher and took a second glass of wine to the couch to settle down close to Nathan. They watched some TV, and then headed up to bed. Last night had been exhausting, and she couldn't wait to fall asleep.

Sometime later that night she woke up with Nathan's hand over her mouth.

When Nathan noted that she was awake and alert, he whispered very quietly to her, "Someone's in the house. I heard boards creaking."

They both held their breath and listened. After half a minute they distinctly heard footsteps in the house. Jill looked around the room and noted that Arthur was still asleep, but Trixie had her head up, her ears alert.

Jill stared at Nathan and murmured, "What should we do?"

Nathan thought for a moment and said into her ear, "I want you to stay here with Trixie. You know from this afternoon that I know martial arts, and can defend myself. I'm going to walk around, see who's here, and how many of them there are, and then I'll make up my mind what to do next." Jill looked at Nathan with alarm. She didn't like him risking himself over her business, but at this point she had no other solution.

Nathan got up from the bed and put his pants on. Jill looked around the bedroom for weapons and encouraged Trixie up onto the bed and grabbed her collar. Dalmatians weren't known for defending people. She was worried that rather than being helpful, Trixie would hinder Nathan with the intruder in house. Nathan had thrown her robe at her on his way out of the room. She wrapped it around herself and gathered several objects that could be used to hit someone in case the intruder entered the bedroom. She strained to hear for noise coming from the house.

She again heard those creaky floorboards on the first floor. She didn't know whether it was Nathan or the intruder making those sounds.

Jill picked up the house phone to call 911 and found the line dead. Her cell phone was downstairs plugged into the kitchen outlet. She was restless and anxious, so she decided to get out of bed to see if she could help Nathan or reach the cell phone to call the Sheriff. After securing the dog in her bedroom, she crept downstairs.

Just as she began descending the stairs, she heard a crash and grunts coming from the first floor. Then the front door opened, and somebody ran out. Jill reached for the hallway lights, but like the phone line, nothing happened when she flipped the light switch. Nathan returned silhouetted in the front door.

She yelled to him, "Nathan, what happened? Are you hurt?"

Nathan looked up the stairs at her, "No, I'm fine. I chased him off but got in a few excellent kicks before he left."

She couldn't see his face in the dark, but his voice sounded like he was smiling. She shook her head. Trust a Hapkido Black Belt to enjoy confronting someone in the dark.

Jill exclaimed in a panic, "The phone lines have been cut, and the electricity is out, so I can't call 911 until I get to my cell phone in the kitchen."

She ran down the stairs and gave him a quick hug and then proceeded into the kitchen. She found her cell phone and called 911. She told the dispatch person that she'd had an intruder in her house, that her friend had chased him off, and that her landline and electricity had been disabled. The woman at dispatch stated that she was sending an officer to her location.

Jill reached into a kitchen cabinet and grabbed her flashlight. She used it to light her way across the house, as she lit candles in various rooms. She and Nathan made their way upstairs to finish dressing. It was going to be a long night.

Within five minutes, Deputy Davis from the previous night

drove up to the house. Jill and Nathan met her outside and gave her an overview of what had happened. Deputy Davis returned to her squad car and retrieved a powerful flashlight. She used the flashlight to examine the entries to the house. There were markings that indicated that the back door had been forced open. Jill relayed that she'd had the security company protect her lab first and that someone was to return today to set up the alarm system for the house. She made a mental note to make sure that the new security system functioned without electricity. This was the first time in her years as a consultant that her personal property had been vandalized. She was a bit afraid, but mostly the break-in just made her mad.

Deputy Davis questioned Nathan at length. When she thought she had all the details of the break-in described for her report, she did a final walk-through of the house. She speculated for what purpose the unknown assailant might have. In her opinion, the intruder was not looking for something in the house, rather he or she wanted Jill. None of the house's contents were disturbed, and Nathan had caught the intruder on the stairs. The intruder had not been carrying a gun or a knife. Oddly enough, Nathan thought the intruder appeared to be carrying a syringe. They thanked Deputy Davis for her time and escorted her out to her car before returning to the house to discuss the night's activity.

Jill and Nathan debated whether to stay at her house with no electricity. Their alternative plan was to pack Arthur, Trixie, and some clothes and return to Nathan's house. In the end, they agreed with Deputy Davis. Prior to leaving she'd theorized that the intruder would not return tonight.

Jill was dead on her feet, so they decided to stay at her house for the rest of the night. They returned to the kitchen where she retrieved her flashlight and cell phone, then continued through the house extinguishing the candles.

Nathan teased Jill, "I've never had such an exciting girlfriend before. This is the first time I've used my martial arts skills to chase an intruder out of the house. Despite the danger, I'm having a good time."

Jill squinted at him, rolling her eyes, "I'm glad my life provides you with amusement."

He just chuckled and strong-armed her into bed. She was asleep within minutes. They had no more interruptions that night.

For the second day in a row, Jill and Nathan awoke sleep-deprived. Jill left Nathan in bed. She needed to make calls to the security company and to an electrician. She would have to get electricity connected soon, or she would lose the contents in her refrigerator.

Jill stared at her kitchen assessing what she could cook for breakfast. Her stove was gas, and she checked to see if it would ignite. She was in luck. She looked at her coffee pot and decided that she would boil water and slowly drip it through the coffee grounds and the filter. She tried that experiment, and the coffee tasted reasonably good.

With caffeine surging through her system, she set out to make her calls. An electrician would be there within the hour. For all the homes he'd serviced in his electrician's career, he'd never repaired a house with electricity that had been purposely cut by an intruder. He seemed delighted with the new experience when she explained her problem.

She had a long conversation with the men at the security company. Like the electrician, he'd never served a customer who was having security challenges like those on Jill's property. He thought he could set up a redundant battery-operated alarm. If in the future, someone cut her power, the loss of electricity would activate the system alarm siren.

Just as she finished the call, Nathan entered the kitchen. She greeted him with coffee and proceeded to make their breakfast.

After two nights of disrupted sleep, they were both dragging this morning.

By the time she finished breakfast and cleaned up, the electrician had arrived to fix the power. He quickly located where the lines had been cut, made the repairs, packed up, and was on his way thirty minutes later.

After she showered and dressed, Jill went out to the lab. She was pleasantly surprised to find the power working and nothing destroyed. Even though she'd backed up her test results and specimens, it was still a relief not to have to clean up another mess.

She left the lab to greet the man from the security company as he arrived on her property. She showed him the back door to the house and where the power had been cut. He would address both issues and add them to her bill.

Jill took a few moments to compose her thoughts about the case and the intruder prior to her scheduled call with Emma.

She phoned Emma primarily to discuss the case findings with her. Jill's late-night uninvited visitor eliminated the last of any doubt that Emma might have had concerning Graeme's death being a homicide. She was in a haze of grief, and she hadn't completely understood Jill's scientific explanation for the intentional spread of bacteria in Graeme's body.

"Jill, I never expected your investigation into Graeme's death to result in a determination of homicide, and now you have a madman after you. I am tempted to advise you to leave the case to the SFPD, but I don't know that'll make a difference."

Between her own lab and the reference lab, she had evidence that someone had introduced staphylococcus bacteria at the site of the wound caused by the coral. Additionally, someone had crept into Graeme's hospital room and injected it into an IV. There was just no other explanation for the growth pattern. Bacteria always evolved inside the human body, so that exact

DNA and that exact growth pattern had to have occurred from intentional human intervention.

She finished her call with Emma and called the medical examiner to schedule an appointment for later that day to discuss her findings with him. Her first step would be to convince him that her conclusions were correct.

Jill went outside to check in with the security man to see when he would finish with her full installation. She wanted the system up and running before she left for her appointment in San Francisco. Next, she went to talk to Nathan. She hated to be a wimp, but the events of the last two nights had unnerved her.

"Nathan, I'm spooked, so will you go with me to San Francisco?"

"Actually, I was going to suggest that I accompany you. I've drafts of a new label for a client in the city. It would save my client traveling here. I don't blame you for being spooked. Let's just be careful and cautious. Come here and let me give you a hug."

After a much-needed hug and a very pleasant kiss, Jill went to her lab to put her thoughts together for her conversation with the medical examiner that afternoon. While she'd had meetings like this in the past, this was one of the most unusual methods of murder she'd ever seen. She gathered her photos, her test results, and those of the outside reference lab and put a solid case together. She figured that once the medical examiner had changed the cause of death, the assaults on her lab and on herself would stop. At least, she hoped they would.

As they would be picking Angela up at the airport while they were in the city, they decided to take Nathan's car, which had more room. They discussed what to do with Arthur and Trixie, as both were worthless at their own self-protection. In the end, they decided to leave the animals at Nathan's house.

After the stop at Nathan's, they set forth for the drive into the city. They had twenty minutes of driving on country roads, and then they would hit the Interstate. Jill was very uneasy and kept an alert eye for any car following them. She spied a four-door silver sedan about five minutes after pulling out of Nathan's driveway. Both she and Nathan watched it in their mirrors all the way to San Francisco. Nathan pulled up to the medical examiner's building and saw her safely inside with her paperwork.

As he left the building, he noted the silver sedan parked down the block. As he'd some time before his meeting with his client, he decided to probe the sedan. He drove around the block and parked four spaces behind the sedan. He got out of his car and walked toward the sedan. It abruptly pulled away from the curb just as he was reaching for the door. Nathan wrote down the license plate number in case that information was useful in the future. He waited another ten minutes, but the sedan did not return. He pulled out and drove to his client's office.

CHAPTER 9

*J*ill sat in medical examiner Meyers's office and went over her case findings. They both knew from their training that bacteria morphed inside the body. However, DNA testing was critical now in linking bacteria to their source. In tracking hospital-acquired infections, a lab could conduct sophisticated testing connecting the bacteria of one patient to that of another who had occupied the same room three weeks before. That same type of testing showed that the bacteria was exactly the same in two different sites in Graeme's body. It had not morphed at all. As the first exposure had occurred in Puerto Rico, there was no other explanation for the bacterial genetic pattern other than an intentional exposure.

Dr. Meyers had not had the amputated leg at the time of his examination of the body. It was pretty clear-cut that Jill's test results and photographs provided the evidence to change the cause of death. He'd had two other cases hit at the same time, a drug overdose of a celebrity athlete and the fifth homeless-person murder of what seemed like a serial killer.

"There's no excuse on my part for missing this. We had a

celebrity drug overdose and a potential serial murder victim here at the same time. The press and the SFPD were distractions. This seemed like a routine case of hospital death by septic shock started by necrotizing fasciitis.

"I worked the opposite hypothesis as you did. This was a death by natural causes unless proven differently. I saw the toxic release of bacteria and confirmed the septic shock as the cause of death. This has been a learning lesson for me."

"Before you completely beat yourself up, remember that you had many cases to process at the same time. You also didn't have the story from the fiancé. Frankly, when I took the case on, I absolutely expected to confirm your autopsy findings. I was as surprised as you are at what these test results pointed to. I even did a literature search to see if it had been done before, and the answer was no."

"You're too kind, Jill. I bet there have been other similar cases and other MEs who missed the evidence."

He completed a revised certificate of death and contacted the homicide division of the San Francisco Police Department.

In his twenty years as an ME, he'd not seen or read of a case of homicide by necrotizing fasciitis. He asked Jill if she would be okay with him submitting the case for publication. She readily granted permission, as she was pleased that it would get discussed in professional circles, but she had no desire to publish it herself.

While they awaited the arrival of the police, Dr. Meyers and Jill discussed theories regarding the murder weapon. They settled on the initial infection being caused by the ointment and perhaps a middle of the night visit by someone in the hospital.

Detective Carlson arrived at the medical examiner's office half an hour later. With both the medical examiner's and Jill's explanations, the detective agreed that she would open a homicide investigation into Graeme St. Louis's death. Jill did not know Detective Carlson, but she was impressed with her competence. Within the hour, she had the investigation underway.

"I have a contract with Graeme's fiancée, Emma Spencer, to offer a second opinion as to the cause of Graeme's death. The contract includes optional work to be done by my experts, Angela, Marie, and Jo, as part of that opinion process. Over the past four years, they have worked several cases with me to identify who wanted the loved one dead. They each have different skills to cover different parts of research for a case."

"Dr. Quint, I believe that you should leave the homicide investigation in the hands of the SFPD. We're better prepared to solve a case quickly and have access to more computer systems than you as a civilian do."

She spent a solid fifteen minutes trying to convince Jill to leave matters in the hands of the SFPD. In prior cases, Jill might have left the case in the hands of the authorities, but she was mad after the incidents in her home and her lab. The detective cited sections of the penal code that would impact Jill and her friends if they interfered with a police investigation. Jill promised to keep her informed of any and all findings. The detective knew that she couldn't legally stop Jill and her friends from proceeding with their own investigation.

Jill phoned Nathan indicating that she was ready to head to the airport to pick up Angela. She waited inside the medical examiner's building until she saw Nathan's car pull up to the curb. She got in and they drove to SFO. She updated him on her meeting with Dr. Meyers and Detective Carlson. He told her about approaching the sedan, and he agreed to call the detective with the license plate number.

She met Angela in the baggage claim area. After a hug, she introduced Nathan to Angela. They liked each other on sight. Angela was amazed at all that had happened in the past twenty-four hours, and she was glad that her friend had Nathan to provide the protection she needed.

They headed home to the Palisades Valley, stopping by Nathan's house to pick up Arthur and Trixie. Angela had been to Jill's house previously and loved the relaxed feel of her vineyard.

After Nathan prepared dinner, they sat down for a conference call with Jo and Marie. They were shocked to hear about the visits from the intruder. They had been helping her with cases for at least five years and Jill had never before been a target. They were glad to know of her newly installed security system, and Angela still had goosebumps upon hearing her describe the events of the previous night. She also relayed to them her conversation with Detective Carlson and the fact that the SFPD did not welcome their assistance with this case.

They had heard a reporter state on the news that night "that the medical examiner had changed the cause of death to homicide for prominent San Francisco resident Graeme St. Louis."

Jo had performed an initial search on Graeme. While he'd done very well in his practice of law, most of his wealth had come from two other sources. He'd inherited three million dollars from a great aunt nearly a decade ago, which he had used to be the funding of an angel investment in a wildly successful Silicon Valley company. His net worth was estimated to be one hundred million dollars. He practiced law because he loved his job, not because he needed the income. Her research also showed that he was a generous man, having made several large private donations to charities in the San Francisco Bay Area. As he was an estate attorney, he'd set up a trust that contained all his assets.

Jill saw two possible reasons for Graeme's death: he could have been killed for his net worth, or he could have been killed because of what he knew about the estate plans for one of his clients. The question was who would benefit from his death? Either the killer wanted his money or wanted him to take information to the grave. According to Emma Spencer, he'd changed his Will while he was in the hospital. However, there had been several attempts on his life prior to the scuba diving trip. So, they would need to look at the original beneficiary of the trust. Ms. Spencer likely did not know the answer to that, so Jill would have to request someone at his law firm to release the information to her.

Since people at his law firm knew that he'd changed his Will in the hospital, Jill thought that ruled out his partners. She also thought that she could rule out Emma Spencer, as she did not benefit from the Will until after the change was made. If he'd been killed in those earlier attempts, she would not have been the beneficiary. Her line of reasoning sharply pointed at the need to send Graeme to his grave with some particular piece of information.

Angela asked Jill if she'd checked with someone at the law firm to see whether Graeme had ever mentioned the previous attempts on his life. Given that two of them had been in and around his office, he might have commented to his associates. That would corroborate Emma's statements about the previous attempts on his life. Jill's gut said that it wasn't Emma, but Angela was right in that she should verify her feeling with evidence.

They chatted for a few more minutes about the case and then decided to all turn in after another long day for all three of them. Angela would join Jill in a face-to-face conversation with Emma Spencer and Detective Carlson tomorrow. She had high hopes that Angela would elicit new information from Emma. She also thought a trip to Puerto Rico might be in their near future so they could trace the arrangements for the scuba diving trip. She would have to check in with Emma on the budget for this case.

Jill wasn't sure how far she would go if Emma did not want to fund further investigation. She didn't think she could leave the case alone since her home and her lab had been invaded over the past two nights.

The three of them headed up to bed, having ensured that the security system was set. Jill hoped that she would finally get a good night's sleep. Today had been a very busy day, and she dropped off instantly into a dreamless sleep.

She awoke the next morning and walked to the kitchen. Angela joined her a few minutes later. She'd been awake for an hour due to the time zone difference and had spent that time formulating questions for Emma Spencer. The two discussed the questions over coffee and tea in the breakfast room, which was where Nathan found them an hour later.

As there had been no further visitors to Jill's property, Nathan planned to return home with Arthur and complete some of his own work that had taken a backseat to Jill's safety. He felt comfortable knowing that Angela would be with Jill all day. They agreed to meet at Nathan's house at seven that evening for dinner and the latest update. Trixie would be on her own for most of the day, but at least Jill wasn't worried about the dog's safety.

Nathan left for his house and Angela and Jill made the journey to Emma Spencer's house in the '56 Thunderbird. They thought they had a good plan to work for resolving the case. Jill hoped that Angela would glean new information from Emma. Furthermore, she hoped to get the approval of a reasonable budget to solve the case. They also had a list of financial documents to give Emma that Jo wanted to review. Emma would either have to provide the documents or provide written permission for Jo to access the documents.

Angela was amazed by Emma Spencer's house. She'd never before been in such a grand private home in her life. Emma answered the door and escorted them through the house to the library where she and Jill had originally met several days ago. Angela immediately had Emma at her ease, asking her about several of the objects d'art she'd seen in the house. Some of the contents reminded her of displays she'd seen in museums she had visited throughout the world.

Jill brought Emma up to date and she was happy to hear that Jill had no further late-night visitors on her property. Detective Carlson had reached Emma late in the afternoon yesterday. She had interviewed Emma early last evening and shared with her a press release announcing the opening of the homicide case.

"I called Graeme's parents and members of our families to give them advance notice of the change in the death certificate before they heard it on the news. That change to homicide is like a punch in the gut. As I had to do two days ago when you first gave me the news, my family had to grieve all over again knowing that he didn't die of septic shock."

Emma looked wiped, as it had been the worst week of her life.

Angela gently launched into a series of questions for Emma. "Emma, do you have any pictures of the boat or the crew on the boat? Was anyone else on the boat with you?

"I should have some pictures on my memory card. We used a special underwater camera, and I haven't looked at the images since we returned to San Francisco. I'll look at them after you leave and email you all the pictures on the camera. There were two other couples on the boat with us, but they were snorkelers, and I don't have their names."

"The pictures would be great. When Graeme told you about the previous attempts on his life, do you remember any other details? Between which floors in the building was he? On which street in San Francisco was the knifed pulled on him?"

"I don't remember any additional details about the stairs, but the street was within a block of his office near a coffee house."

Next Jill shared with Emma the list of financial documents Jo wanted to examine. Emma was not sure who would provide that information, but she'd a couple of starting points, and she would keep them informed. Finally, Jill brought up the delicate conversation about the budget. She was immediately relieved when Emma indicated that they had an unlimited budget to solve the case. Emma also volunteered to accompany them to Puerto Rico, but Jill was able to convince her that she would be of more help here gathering the financial documents.

Jill and Angela left Emma standing at the door of her house as they drove away. Once out of sight of the house, they pulled over to the curb.

"So, what do you think of Emma? Is she the murderer?"

"I'm afraid I have to agree with your gut that she did not kill Graeme."

They worked on a game plan based on the new information they had gleaned from Emma. They agreed that they would stop in at Graeme's office, and then visit the location where someone had pulled a knife on him. The perpetrators were long gone, and they expected to find no evidence, but they wanted the visual of what Graeme had described. They also booked a two-night trip to San Juan, Puerto Rico, leaving the next day. The scuba accident trail might be faint at this time, but they felt they had to pursue it first.

Jill put the car in motion, and they visited the alleged crime scenes. Graeme's building was a conservative-looking three-story office building. They looked at the stairways, but all they could conclude was that someone had to be purposeful if they pushed someone else on the stairs since the stairs were wide. A quick conversation with the office manager revealed there were no cameras on the stairs or the doors leading to them. The security needs were relatively minor and more related to documents and computers than people.

Next, they found the street where the coffee shop was the location of a knife having been pulled on Graeme, and again there were no cameras or any other sign of evidence that anyone had been threatened in that location.

Then they left San Francisco and headed back to the Palisades Valley. After making this drive three times in the last week, Jill was glad that she didn't do it daily.

They were leaving around eight the next day and would get into San Juan close to midnight tomorrow night. It would be a long, boring day of flying through too many time zones. They would update Jo by email, as they had no real new financial information for her to investigate.

Jill swung by her home on the way to Nathan's to pick up Trixie so Nathan could dog-sit her while Jill was in Puerto Rico. They had a nice dinner at Nathan's and used the time to strategize their probe into the scuba diving trip.

So much for romance. Nathan was being a good sport about Jill being focused on the case rather than on him. They were both comfortable that her fancy alarm system would protect her tonight. Jill and Angela needed to leave at around four in the morning to reach the airport by departure time.

Jill and Angela went back to her house to pack and make sure that they were ready to leave at that hideously early hour tomorrow. At least, because it was a last-minute purchase and because Emma had suggested it, they were flying in first-class all the way to San Juan. They would have a chance to catch up on their sleep on the plane. Angela spoke Spanish which would come in handy when they began questioning people about the scuba trip.

For the second night in a row, the house remained quiet. They left for the airport before dawn and flopped in their airplane seats for another couple of hours of sleep. They awoke with about two hours to go on the first leg of their travels. Sharing a delicious bottle of wine and the better food of first-class, they talked about the case.

"This sure is the way to travel. I would book our next girl-friend vacation in first class, but I'm just too cheap at heart. First-class gives you more space and you're at the front of the plane, but we all arrive at the destination at the same time give or take an extra ten minutes to get off the plane," said Jill.

"I have never been able to sleep on a plane, but with these seats, I could stretch out. It's nice to arrive a little more refreshed," replied Angela.

"There is the sleep opportunity that first-class affords us passengers! Let's plan our schedule on the island. We don't want to waste a minute, especially since you're best at collecting information when you can talk to someone face-to-face." Jill was known affectionately among her girlfriends as the taskmaster and she was in true form.

"Given the lateness of the hour when we arrive, I would guess that today is going to be strictly travel with a few girlie drinks squeezed in at the end of the day."

Jill continued with her planning as if Angela hadn't spoken. "In the morning, I'll book snorkeling trips for both tomorrow afternoon and the next day. I think the more time we spend with the scuba company the better. I wouldn't think the tainted ointment would still be in the first aid kit on the boat but if it is, and I can retrieve the ointment tube from the first aid kit and replace it with a new tube, I would be doing future divers a favor."

"I'd like to rule out both the resort and the concierge in the morning. Last night I also requested an appointment with Graeme's client, Mr. Lott. I might do that in the morning, depending upon his availability." Angela was confident that she would be able to learn about the nature of Graeme's appointment with Mr. Lott, although she hadn't quite decided on her approach.

"I plan to play the nervous snorkeler, and I'll see what I can get out of the various diving companies. How do they hire divemasters? Do people usually get injured banging into coral? What does it take to get certified to scuba dive? How do I know that my tank is filled with enough gas? Then let's meet for lunch back at the hotel, compare notes, and prepare for the afternoon excursion."

"Sounds like a plan. I think we need a lot of practice consuming girlie drinks, so we might have to repeat that experience several times" Angela giggled.

They would be staying at the same resort where Emma and Graeme had stayed. They wanted to take the same scuba diving trip as they had, but neither Jill nor Angela were scuba certified (nor did they want to be). Instead, they decided to approach it as a snorkeling trip over the Sandslide reef. The reef started at fifteen feet below the surface of the ocean, and they thought it likely that they could at least see the coral reef that Graeme had been slammed into during his dive.

They planned to follow the exact same route that Emma and Graeme had followed. It would be interesting to see if the concierge set them up with the same dive company that Emma and Graeme had used. They also planned to investigate the concierge, the dive company, and the divemaster to find out who they were, how they chose to use that dive company, and how much advance notice they had been given as to which coral reef Emma and Graeme wanted to go to. It seemed as though the divemaster who had pushed Graeme into the coral had to have known about that particular piece of coral in order for the coral to cut him.

It was likely that the concierge requested at the time of the reservation the reef that Emma and Graeme wanted to visit. That meant that the killer had almost three weeks to explore the reef and determine which sharp edge to shove Graeme into. Graeme and Emma had made the reservation at the hotel twenty-one days in advance of their arrival. It was doubtful that whoever wanted Graeme dead had replaced the concierge at a major five-star resort with that little notice. However, for the right price, the concierge could have been bought off to either provide a reservation for Emma and Graeme to a particular scuba diving company or to notify him as to which company was hired to take them to the reef.

They planned to check with several concierges to see how they directed hotel guests to scuba diving companies. After they determined which concierge had made the reservation, Angela would question him about what he did regarding the reservation for Emma and Graeme. The investigation would be tricky, as they were acting in no official capacity, nor were they licensed private detectives.

When this case was over, Jill planned to explore what it would take to get private investigator licenses for herself as well as her friends. It might give them legitimacy for future cases.

Jill had brought along the pictures that Emma and Graeme had taken aboard the boat they used for the scuba diving trip. The name of the boat was in one picture. In another picture, one of the crewmen leaned against the wheel. Emma indicated that none of her pictures included one of the divemaster. Jill was hoping she could find that boat and crew on this trip. She also optimistically hoped that she would find a tube of anti-bacterial ointment in a first aid kit on that boat. She doubted it would be so easy to find the murder weapon.

She'd arranged two nights in Puerto Rico as she wasn't sure how many boats and boat trips she would need to check to talk to the right people. Thankfully, she was somewhat tanned from running outdoors, and Angela already had olive skin tone because they sure were going to get a lot of sun.

Jill, Jo, and Angela had been to Puerto Rico before but had not actually spent any time in the city of San Juan. On their vacation three years before, they had flown in and immediately headed to Fajardo on the other side of the island. They had enjoyed the rainforest of El Yunque. Their favorite evening activity was a kayak ride to Vieques Island with its bioluminescent lagoon. Now Jill and Angela were there strictly to work, but they would still enjoy the warm nights, island breezes, and girlie drinks made with rum.

As predicted, by the time their plane landed and they'd retrieved their luggage, it was close to midnight when they stepped on the hotel's shuttle bus. Fortunately, they were on Pacific Time and therefore headed to the hotel bar to relax after check-in since their body clocks said it was three hours earlier. They had planned to talk to a concierge if there had been one on duty, but they were told at check-in that concierge services ended at ten pm.

Jill checked her email on her iPad as she sat at the hotel's bar. She was happy to see a huge email from Emma to Jo with many financial documents attached. Nathan sent her an email that included a funny picture of Trixie and Arthur. There was also an email from her wine supplier with pricing related to bottles, corks, grape-pressing equipment, oak barrels, and bulk grape juice. The juice is what she would use to titrate her Moscato wine to the perfect taste.

They finished the rum drinks, sent off a few emails, and headed up to their hotel room. They had a busy day planned for tomorrow, and a quick check of the weather report showed that they would be able to visit the coral reef without the threat of rain or high winds. Angela would be questioning concierges, and tomorrow with Emma's assistance in arranging an appointment, she would be interviewing the client Mr. Lott, whom Graeme had met with prior to the ill-fated scuba diving trip.

They awoke to a beautiful day in Puerto Rico. The sky and the ocean were spectacular in the morning light. Jill and Angela had a light breakfast before going their separate ways. Angela had a list of people to question, and Jill was in search of scuba diving companies. They might end up interviewing some of the same people but interviewing someone twice could result in them obtaining different information.

When Jill had determined that Graeme's death had likely

been caused by separate exposures to the same bacteria causing necrotizing fasciitis, she'd called one of her pathology associates, Dr. Anne Johnson, whose focus was microbiology. She'd spent half an hour on the phone speculating about where the killer had obtained the bacteria, how he might have mixed it in the antibiotic ointment, and finally, into a vial used to inject Graeme in the hospital. Anne had suggested that the killer had to have major knowledge of microbiology. He needed to know how to not kill the bacteria and yet not contract it himself.

Before her meeting with the ME, she'd researched where an average Joe could purchase an agar containing the bacteria. Schools and universities were a major source of purchasing such agars for their science classes. So, it was likely that the killer had been able to procure some kind of documentation that made it look like he represented the school, or he'd some connection to the academic world.

She would have to leave it up to the police to track down the supplier of the bacteria. She would contact Detective Carlson later to discuss this angle. Jill's knowledge of pathology gave her a head start in reaching a conclusion about the murder weapon in this case - bacteria. The SFPD likely had no prior experience with bacteria as a murder weapon, but in many ways, they could treat it like poisoning. Instead of a chemical destroying a human, it was the bacteria used for Graeme's murder.

Dr. Johnson offered to experiment in her own lab to evaluate how one would create the infected ointment and the infected vial. Jill highly doubted that she would ever find the actual tube of ointment or the vial. She thought that by figuring out how the ointment and the vial had been created, it would lead her to the killer. Specialized knowledge was required to create those items, and that special knowledge limited the suspect pool.

CHAPTER 10

*A*ngela approached the concierge desk.

"Hi, I need some assistance arranging a snorkeling trip for this afternoon and potentially tomorrow morning as well."

"Certainly, I can help you with that. Is there a particular area of Puerto Rico where you would like to snorkel?"

"My friends Emma and Graeme stayed at your resort a couple of weeks ago, and the concierge, perhaps it was you, arranged a great trip to the Sandslide reef, so that is where I would like to go."

"What are your friends' last name? I'll check our records to see who booked the trip and what company they used. I'll do my best to send you out with the same company."

"Their last names are Spencer and St. Louis. It was probably booked under St. Louis."

"Yes, I see their records. Peter booked the trip for them. He is on the concierge desk tonight. I see he booked the trip with our customary dive shop. Let me check its availability."

He made the call to the dive shop and was able to confirm departure times for two trips to the reef. The boat was taking other passengers, but they had not specified a location, so everyone would go to Sandslide with them.

"Thanks for your help with the trip. Have you and Peter worked here long?"

"I love my job and have had the pleasure of arranging activities for guests for nearly five years. Peter has been here even longer."

"Again, thanks for your help, and have a nice day."

It was Angela's conclusion that the hotel concierge likely had not played a role in orchestrating the accident with the coral. He'd worked there far too long, and the scuba company had been used by the hotel for the past decade, as it had rave reviews by hotel guests. So, this pointed to the divemaster. After Angela had obtained as much information as she could from the concierge, she set her sights on Mr. Lott, the client with whom Graeme had met before the fateful diving trip.

Meanwhile, Jill was at the harbor assessing the many diving companies. She stopped in a medium-sized storefront and briefly observed the people inside. They were a chatty bunch, which was exactly what she needed. She went inside and pretended to be a scared scuba diving novice. The idea of scuba diving scared her enough that she never planned to try it, so her acting was close to her real self. The owner spoke at length about how he checked the qualifications of his divemasters. She went to the second dive shop and posed the same questions. She also asked the store owner about the length of the hiring process. It seemed a long shot that someone could have gotten hired fast enough to be the killer. The resort had given Emma and Graeme's dive company less than twenty-one days' notice. All of the dive companies that she interviewed would have been pressed to hire, verify certification, and check someone out as a new employee in the divemaster role in less than twenty-one days.

Jill's final stop was the dive company that had served Emma

and Graeme. Again, she pretended to be an agitated snorkeler and asked about the experience level of all of the company's divemasters. In particular, she verified that they used the normal process to verify a divemaster's certification. She also learned that new employees were supervised by the owner for the first four dives. The owner had several lucrative accounts with the luxury hotels of San Juan, and he wanted to verify that new divemasters had good people skills for his clients. His business reputation was only as good as how well a divemaster performed. The divemaster with the shortest employment time was Luis Gonzales, and he'd been employed for two weeks.

Jill and Angela met back at the hotel for lunch. They shared what they had learned through their visits to the dive shops and with the concierge. They agreed that the hotel concierge was not involved in the homicide. Graeme's client, Mr. Lott, was genuinely saddened over Graeme's death. Graeme had been handling a routine trust update based on new tax laws for Mr. Lott. So, they crossed him off their list of suspects.

This pointed to the divemaster, who just happened to be the divemaster for their afternoon excursion. When they checked in with Jo this evening, they would have her do some research on Mr. Gonzales's bank account and criminal history.

They returned to their hotel room and changed into swimsuits, grabbed their towels and sun block, and headed for the harbor for their afternoon snorkeling trip. They got on board the boat and noticed that the crew was different than in Emma's pictures.

They greeted Mr. Gonzales and reiterated that they wanted to visit the Sandslide reef. He showed no nervousness with that request. Angela went to work on him, questioning his background, experience, and even his family.

Mr. Gonzales was happy to be working for the dive company and had been a certified divemaster for five years. He had a wife and two children at home. Jill knew that the statement about his family was a lie, as she'd asked the owner about him that morning. As time went on, he gave off a sleazy vibe. He let it be known that his services were available that evening at their hotel if they so desired. They were grateful that there were other groups on the boat, as they would not have felt safe being in the open water with this guide.

They arrived at the Sandslide reef and disembarked into the water with the other passengers. Mr. Gonzales had a waterproof cheat sheet with pictures of the fish that they would see underwater. He told them that they would have to swim about a hundred yards to the start of the reef and they were all to follow him. They set off at a slow swim pace and arrived at the reef shortly. Emma happened to have a picture of the coral arch that had injured Graeme. Jill and Angela had just wanted to see the coral, the area, and get an overall sense of the water to determine what the divemaster had to do in order to slam Graeme into the coral.

They spotted the coral arch from the surface of the water. It appeared to be about fifteen feet underwater. Angela pretended to take pictures of the fish, but in reality, she photographed the coral. There was another dive company in the area and that boat had five people currently scuba diving at the same reef. She took a picture of the boat with the intention of possibly reaching out to those divers later. They both attempted to swim down to the reef, but they lacked the lung power to do anything more than touch it and return to the surface. It was sharp to the touch, and Jill could understand how the gash in Graeme's leg occurred.

They both continued to other places above the reef. They didn't want to look too suspicious to Mr. Gonzales. On the other hand, he didn't seem to be the sharpest tool in the shed, so they were probably worried for nothing. They also managed to take a picture of him to confirm that he was the divemaster who had gone with Emma. If he was, they'd provide the SFPD with a copy of the photo. They would have Jo run him through a criminal database that she used to check out prospective boyfriends. It was not the quality of search that law enforcement used, but it would be a good starting place. After half an hour of snorkeling, they returned to the boat.

They re-applied sunscreen and chatted with the other couples aboard the boat as they traveled to shore. Jill used a safety pin to prick her finger and cause it to bleed. She then requested Mr. Gonzales fetch a first aid kit if there was one on board as she needed a Band-Aid. Angela surreptitiously took a picture of the kit. Jill asked to look through the kit searching for the perfect size Band-Aid. She hoped to steal the antibiotic ointment from the kit. She even had five different brands of ointment that she'd purchased from a Puerto Rican store to throw in the kit if she was successful in taking the tube that she found there. She trusted that one of the five tubes would be a brand match. Unfortunately, Mr. Gonzales hovered the entire time, and she wasn't enough of a magician to make the trade. She would have a second opportunity tomorrow, as they had booked another snorkeling trip aboard this boat in the morning before they would leave to return to San Francisco in the afternoon. If the tube of infected ointment was still in the kit, they would be doing future boat passengers a huge favor by eliminating the possibility of a bacterial infection. It was unlikely that the infected ointment was still in the first-aid kit a week later, but again Mr. Gonzales was not the smartest person and Jill had seen plenty of dumb criminals.

After returning to the harbor, they left the boat to return to their hotel room. It was late afternoon, and they had the evening in front of them to enjoy the tropical breezes, a nice meal, and girlie drinks, with plenty of time to catch up with Jo, Marie, and Emma.

Angela thought that she'd exhausted interviewing the people with whom Graeme had come into contact during his trip. Jill and Angela believed that likely Mr. Gonzales had been paid to shove Graeme into the coral and apply the infected antibiotic ointment. That ointment was the backup plan to attempting to get him to scuba dive with the nearly empty tank. The tank plan was lame, so likely it had been Mr. Gonzales's idea. The infected ointment plan was much more sophisticated and clearly beyond his intellectual resources.

They both had several calls to make. Jill called Emma to update her on their day. In addition, Emma confirmed that Mr. Gonzales was their divemaster by the picture sent to her from Angela's camera. Emma relayed that Detective Carlson wanted to speak with her, and so Jill planned to contact her after her conversation with Nathan.

Angela needed to check in with several clients for her photography business. She handled her own bookings for photoshoots, and there was often a fair amount of discussion about the date, time, and location prior to the client locking in Angela's services.

Jill called Nathan. "Hey, how are you doing?"

"Missing you but amused with Trixie's and Arthur's behavior. How is Puerto Rico? I was there about five years ago. There are a few wineries on the island. Mostly red varietals."

"We have mostly been interviewing so far. Of course, we have been practicing with the girlie drinks."

"Practicing?"

"It takes talent to drink a girlie drink without getting the little paper umbrella wet or dropping the cut fruit in your lap. So, we are practicing our technique!"

"Okay, that is a new excuse for drinking that I have not heard before. Hey, got to run, my client is here. By the way, your security system has been quiet. No intruders so far."

Jill called Detective Carlson next, who again told her that

she should leave the investigation to the SFPD. Jill remained deaf to the detective's advice. She told the detective about their investigation of the hotel concierge, the dive companies, and the divemaster in particular. Detective Carlson said she would run a criminal search on Mr. Gonzales, after which she would reach out to the local police in San Juan to bring him in for questioning. The detective scheduled a meeting with Jill. She wanted to visit Jill's lab to gain a better understanding of how the bacteria had been used as a weapon.

Their final call that night was to Jo and Marie. They updated them about Angela's interviews, Jill's exploration of the dive companies, and their snorkeling trip. Jo and Marie were sad to be missing the action, but things were busy at work.

As it was, Jo had barely had time to do the research they needed from her on Graeme's financials. In another day, it would be the weekend, and Jo could devote more time to reviewing the financials and doing independent research on his practice, his investments, and his estate plan. Her eyes were bug-eyed from staring at numbers all day, and she was looking forward to the break of researching Mr. Gonzales's financial background. She'd never investigated someone from Puerto Rico, and she was hopeful that she would find the same computer records as were found in the United States. She would send them an email later if she found anything.

Marie's first task was uncovering everything she could about Mr. Gonzales. She wondered if his diving certificate was real. They discussed researching the other diving boat company men, but they all had longer worker histories, and thus they were ruled out.

With their conversations complete, they left the hotel and walked to the city center to a restaurant recommended by the concierge. It was a small family-owned grill. They started with tapas and margaritas. Their main course was chicken paella, with flan for dessert. They were glad to stroll through Old

Town and the harbor after dinner. Jill wished that Nathan was with her, as for some reason she was uneasy. While eating dinner, she thought that she'd caught a glimpse of Mr. Gonzales. She was afraid that paranoia was starting to occupy her mind.

They had reached the end of the sidewalk at the tip of the harbor and turned to make the slow walk back to the hotel. It was then that two men stepped out of the shadows and into their path. On one side of their path was a breakwater retaining wall composed of large boulders. On the other side were mostly full boat slips. They looked at each other, assessing their options. They had no weapons and were wearing flip-flops. Furthermore, there was no one nearby to yell to for help. They could jump into the water, but Angela was a slow swimmer. Jill had a large handbag, and Angela had a tiny one. The men did not appear to have any weapons in their hands.

Jill remembered the recent training experience with Nathan. Angela had a good six inches in height on both men. Angela distracted them with a cheery good evening, while Jill came in from the side. She gave both men a solid thump with her purse, and while they grabbed their heads, she shoved them into the water.

They quickly headed back as fast as their flip-flops would carry them to their hotel. Once there, they requested that someone at the hotel call the local police so they could file a report. Angela had the foresight to take the men's pictures while they trod water.

After giving their report to the police, and changing their hotel room, Jill left a voice mail for Detective Carlson relaying details of their event-filled evening. Next, she called Nathan to tell him about the incident. She was grateful that his training had given her the confidence to go on the offensive against the men.

Angela loved to travel to new locations and have new experiences, but tonight's activity was beyond her desired level of excitement. She had never encountered someone who had borne such ill will toward her before. This was more than she expected as a consultant on this case.

They called Jo and Marie, as an update on the experience needed to be described verbally, rather than through email. Unloading on Jo and Marie helped calm them down considerably, and they were laughing by the end of the conversation.

They had an uneventful night and, in the morning, packed their bags for the trip home that afternoon. They debated canceling the morning's snorkeling trip, but Jill really wanted a second opportunity to get the ointment from the first aid kit. They again headed to the harbor, boarding the same boat as yesterday but with a different divemaster. Angela had found out through her usual skillful interviewing that Mr. Gonzales had called in sick to work that day. Again, there were additional passengers on the snorkeling boat, and they went to a different reef from the previous day.

Jill again tried the ruse of needing a Band-Aid to get her hands on the first aid kit. Fortunately, no one hovered this time, and she was able to switch the tubes of antibiotic ointment. She secluded the potentially infected tube into an evidence bag. She debated what to do with the ointment tube if she was successful in getting it out of the first aid kit.

As Puerto Rico was a territory of the United States, and as the successful murder of Graeme occurred in San Francisco, it was likely that any legal proceedings would follow in San Francisco rather than San Juan. Unless Graeme's and Mr. Gonzales' fingerprints were on the ointment tube, it was unlikely that the tube would play any legal role in the evidence of the case. In the end, she decided to overnight it to her home in Palisades Valley. She sealed and protected the evidence bag. While the ointment tube was not fragile, she wanted to make sure that no delivery workers would be harmed if the package was infected and if it was dropped or exploded. It really was just a tube of antibiotic ointment.

A few hours later Jill and Angela sat in the first-class cabin on the way home to San Francisco. They spoke softly of their next steps with this case and anxiously awaited the results of Jo and Marie's research.

CHAPTER 11

$\mathcal{A}$t close to eleven pm, Jill and Angela reached Nathan's driveway. He'd made a great dessert and had a perfect white wine chilled for their arrival. Trixie was happy to see Jill, and the three of them chatted at length about the case.

"Would you like me to stay with you tonight?"

"Actually, between your self-defense lessons and the encounter with the men in Puerto Rico, my confidence in dealing with this unknown assailant is high. I hate to keep disrupting your business. Besides, I have the new security system, Trixie, and Angela, so I don't feel uneasy being in the house alone."

"Trixie is a lousy guard dog. It's more likely that you'll have to protect her than the other way around. In fact, I might insult her by saying that Arthur is a better guard cat," Nathan said with a smirk.

"Yeah, but she is just about the prettiest spotted dog you'll ever see, so that counts for something," Jill declared laughingly as she hugged Nathan goodbye.

Jill turned into her own driveway and was relieved to see the expected exterior lights on at her home and lab. Jill and Angela were tired and half an hour later sunk into sleep. Jumping the time zones, snorkeling, the encounter with the men at the harbor, and the time spent in the air traveling to and from San Juan had made for three very long days.

Angela was leaving in two days to return to the Midwest. They both hoped that Jo and Marie would come up with a list of suspects as to who had killed Graeme. They had a day left in which Angela could interview subjects in person. Tomorrow Detective Carlson would be visiting Jill's laboratory. The ointment package that she'd mailed from Puerto Rico would arrive, and with any delivery luck, she could send fingerprints back with the detective for the SFPD to match.

Jill and Angela both awoke shortly after dawn after a quiet night. Jill owed Emma a call to update her on the case. She discussed the attack in Puerto Rico, the antibiotic ointment that she'd mailed, and her meeting with Detective Carlson. Emma was such a gentle soul that she had trouble absorbing the aggression towards Jill, let alone the murder of her fiancé.

Jill also wanted to check in with Dr. Johnson to see if she'd drawn any conclusions concerning where the bacteria had been purchased and how it had been injected into the ointment and the vial of solution that ultimately killed Graeme.

Detective Carlson arrived an hour later. She'd been in the SFPD's crime lab, but she knew it to be limited when compared to the county's crime lab. She was fascinated by Jill's lab, especially the wide variety of tests that she could conduct in that space. Jill walked her through the bacterial testing that she'd done on Graeme and how she'd reached her conclusions. Detective Carlson knew that the medical examiner had agreed with Jill and therefore her findings were accurate, but it greatly helped her better understand the crime after Jill's explanation. Angela joined them for a cup of tea while they discussed the case.

Detective Carlson again advised them to leave the case in the hands of the SFPD. Jill simply ignored her request. She'd done investigations for some of the other cases that she had handled. This case was much more difficult certainly because of the method of homicide. The multiple attempts on his life, an investigation in San Francisco and San Juan, and finally Graeme's complicated financial situation only added to the intrigue. Beyond everything else, the case was fascinating. She felt compelled to continue their research because she wouldn't feel completely safe until Graeme's killer was behind bars.

While they discussed the case, the overnight package arrived from Puerto Rico. Jill dusted the tube of ointment for fingerprints for Detective Carlson. As a consultant, Jill no longer had access to the computer system containing fingerprints.

"I know this hasn't been in a chain of custody, but can you run the prints anyway? Maybe we'll get lucky, and it will point us to someone that might be our killer."

The detective left with the prints and the tube of ointment. Jill had retained a sample of ointment and had swabbed the tube before handing it over to the detective.

This entire case suggested a sophisticated scheme. As yet they had not identified the reason for the murder, or the killer. Jill sampled some of the ointment to set up agars and various laboratory tests. She also sent a sample to the reference lab for a DNA match to the bacteria found in Graeme's body.

While the tests were processing Jill, Angela, and Trixie walked her vineyard. She showed Angela the wine label that Nathan had designed. Then she went to her tasting area so that Angela could sample her experiments with the Moscato blend. She thought she had a winner on her hands, but it would be good to have Angela's opinion as she have a very refined sense of taste for beer brews but also was talented with wine flavors. They spent a very enjoyable hour getting pleasantly buzzed with a variety of Moscato samples. Angela agreed with her choice of the best blend, and so Jill would be ready to go to market in the fall with her vintage.

When they returned to the house, it was time to phone Jo and listen to her evaluation of the financial records. It was amazing what information Jo uncovered. She had been able to review Graeme's law practice, his trust value, the start-up company he'd invested in a decade ago, and the value of that spectacular house. Jo could not detect any questionable financial circumstances in any of Graeme's holdings.

Jill was surprised as she'd never seen Jo come up empty before. If the murder wasn't related to money, what was the motive? The three of them discussed the case further. Money could still be the motive. It might be simply the size of Graeme's holdings. There was nothing illicit or illegal in his holdings. Perhaps just someone wanting to own those holdings?

The most obvious suspect was Emma Spencer. The problem with that idea was that Emma had not been a beneficiary until a few hours before Graeme's death. None of the earlier attempts on his life would have resulted in making Emma a very wealthy woman.

Jill would have to subtly discover who the original beneficiary of his estate had been. Angela would question Emma, and Jo would do a search on the Internet to see if there was any way to locate that beneficiary. They chatted for another fifteen minutes exploring various angles to the case. Eventually, they ran out of fresh ideas to pursue.

Jill could have walked away from the case at this time and collected her fee for the work that the four of them had performed thus far, but she was still angry at the incidences on her property, her friends, and herself. Angela agreed that she should continue to pursue answers in Graeme's death.

Jill's recent group of agars related to the tube of ointment would be available for analysis in another hour. While she finished the work in her lab, Angela was going to take time to write out her own notes and thoughts on the case. Nathan was expected for dinner in two hours, and he was taking care of cooking it. He was anxious to hear about the conversations with Jo, Detective Carlson, and the results from Jill's testing of the ointment tube.

With Trixie at her side, Jill walked down her front porch to head over to the lab. Trixie acted strangely tripping her up and slowing her down. Just as Jill squatted down, she felt and heard a bullet wiz by her head. She grabbed Trixie and made a dive for the outside corner of the lab building. She saw the wood splinter seconds after she lunged around the corner from a second shot. Huh! And Nathan opined that Trixie wasn't a good guard dog. The dog had just saved her life!

Thankfully, she wore her cell phone at her waist. She dialed the 911 operator.

"This is the 911 Operator, what is your emergency?"

"This is Dr. Jill Quint. I was just shot at, and I need the Sheriff immediately. I dived into my barn, and that is where the Sheriff can find me."

The nearest deputy was seven minutes away, but the 911 operator stayed on the line with Jill until she heard sirens in the distance. The operator had also managed to place a call to Angela's cell phone and advise her to take cover in the house.

The deputy placed his car between where Jill thought the sniper might be sitting and Jill. The sniper was probably long gone since there had been no additional shots once she dove into the barn.

"Hi, Ms. Quint. I understand that you think you have a shooter out in your vineyard?"

"I don't think. I know. Take a look at the splintered wood and the bullet in the far wall," Jill said, as she pointed to the wall behind her.

"A second unit is on its way. I'm going to use my rifle scope to see if I can spot anyone with a gun," the deputy said as they crouched beside his car.

Jill thought she caught a metal reflection in the late afternoon sun, but the deputy pushed her head down as she was the target. Jill also called Angela's cell phone to check on her. She was doing fine staying in the middle of the house, but she was glad to have the deputy there and to know that more help was on the way.

The deputy remarked that a talented marksman attempted to harm Jill. He estimated the shooter to be two to three hundred yards away, and yet he'd nearly hit Jill twice. Trixie must have sensed him in the surrounding hills, and thankfully she'd bent over to pat the dog. Otherwise, she'd be dead.

Just then additional patrol cars arrived. The officers were able to shield Jill and get her into the house. She and Angela hugged each other and then the dog that had saved Jill's life.

The officers began the search for the gunman. They found the spent casings from the rifle used to shoot at Jill. They called for a K-9 unit to do a scent search. The search dog was able to pick up the gunman's scent from the casings, and the dog followed that scent for half a mile to a side street. The scent disappeared from there, and the officers speculated that the gunman had gotten into a car and driven off at that location. There were no distinguishable shoe prints anywhere on the path to the car.

There was a wide easement on the side of the road used by biking enthusiasts to park and unload their bicycles. They were simply too many tire treads to figure out which belonged to the getaway car.

She relayed the story multiple times to the various deputies, the case regarding Graeme St. Louis, the previous events on her lab, and herself. Jill was simply puzzled as to why she was still a target. First the altercation in San Juan harbor and now, one on her own property. Clearly having the cause of death announced by the San Francisco medical examiner had not taken the heat off Jill. They discussed whether Angela might be followed by the killer to her home in Wisconsin and they agreed that it was unlikely. Jill seemed to be the only target.

Next, the officers moved on to discuss Jill's safety in the immediate future. She needed to take Angela to the San Francisco airport in the morning. Jill had called Nathan as soon as she was safe in her house. Just then, he arrived and joined the conversation after a tight hug.

"I'll take Angela to the airport, but how many officers will be here guarding Jill in my absence?

"We'll have to check with dispatch."

After a brief conversation, the deputy returned with bad news.

"Sorry, Dr. Quint, but we don't have the resources to staff deputies at your house. The best we can do is frequent drive-bys."

"That's okay. I would have been surprised if you did have spare officers to guard me."

Nathan looked very unhappy at that news, but he too knew the small law enforcement resources they had as a town.

"I can stay in the house later if I can be guarded for the next hour in my lab. I can wrap up my lab testing this evening if I can safely make it outside to the lab now."

The deputies, Nathan, Jill, and Angela moved their discussion to her lab so she could finish her testing in less than an hour. She could talk to the deputies while running the tests.

Jill, Nathan, and Angela returned to the house after closing up the lab. Palisades Valley had a small Sheriff's department that could not afford to place a deputy at Jill's house around the clock. Jill debated whether to move to Nathan's house or have Nathan move to her house, but in both those scenarios, she would put Nathan at risk. She called the security company that had installed her system to find out if they offered personal security services. It would be expensive, but it could provide such a service. Jill compromised and scheduled the security company to provide a security guard at night, and during the day the deputies would do frequent drive-bys. She could stay inside her house during the day, and her property perimeter alarm should alert her if the gunman attempted to get close to the house.

Nathan would stay the night, take Angela to the airport in the morning, and be available to help Jill run errands over the next several days. Nathan could pull into Jill's garage, and she could get in his car and get down with a blanket over her. This would be how she would get off of her property to do anything she personally needed to do in the next few days. Trixie would stay in the house with Jill, and Nathan would take her off the property for exercise.

What a mess my life has become! Being a pathologist was not thought to be an exciting occupation. The work was often tedious and redundant with far too much time spent looking into a microscope. It was extremely rare to have a pathology finding as she had in this case. The San Francisco medical examiner had been impressed with her findings, and Dr. Johnson was having intellectual fun figuring out how the killer had obtained and used the bacteria to kill Graeme. Jill had also been having fun with the case until the attempts on her life. She was no longer having fun. Now she was just plain anxious and paranoid.

It was getting late by the time everybody left. The security guard was in place. Angela, Nathan, and Jill settled into her living room, each with a big glass of wine. Jill was grateful for Angela's presence. It was wonderful to have the calming support of a friend. Still, she was grateful that Angela would be out of harm's way once she was dropped off at the airport. She owed Emma a phone call and would update Detective Carlson in the morning.

Her life depended upon her figuring out who had killed Graeme and who was targeting her. She would brainstorm with Jo about the finances and speak to the SFPD. She also needed some new angles on this case that she hoped Marie would provide.

CHAPTER 12

The next morning, Jill hugged Angela as she prepared to leave for the airport with Nathan. Angela had contributed over forty hours to the case, but when she landed in Wisconsin, she'd to go back to her regular job and then would be able to contribute very little other than moral support to the case.

Jill planned to stay indoors all day doing computer research and following up with phone calls. The first call this morning was to Emma to update her on the shooter and the preliminary results of their collective investigation of Jill's team. Emma's biggest concern was for Jill and her team's safety. From Emma's comments, it sounded like the SFPD had made little progress in the investigation into Graeme's death.

As Emma was pleased with the progress of Jill's team, she offered to modify their original contract to include the ongoing investigative work. Jill was pleased with the offer. She would've continued the case without the contract because she now felt the threat on her own life. It would be wonderful for her friends to continue to get compensated for their time and effort on this case, though they would have helped her regardless. Emma and

Graeme had a joint bank account, and Emma felt strongly that Graeme would want Jill's ongoing investigative services paid for from that account.

Jill put a call into Detective Carlson next but reached her voicemail. She left her a message to give Jill a call. The SFPD was under no obligation to share any information with Jill. However, as she'd become a second target of the killer it was in its best interest to share information, even though Jill lived outside of its jurisdiction.

While waiting for the detective to return her call, Jill phoned her friends. She left a voicemail for Angela knowing that she was in the air returning home. She also left a voicemail for Jo, whom she couldn't reach in person. This just seemed to be her day to hit people's voicemail.

Jill brought Marie up to date with everything that had happened so far. They agreed that they should start with the divemaster, Mr. Gonzales. She would also research Graeme's law partners and the executives at the tech company that he'd invested in. Marie checked her schedule and was fortunate that she could take a vacation day the next day and Jill was relieved that Marie could devote the time to her case. She really felt that her efforts would accelerate their investigation. She ended the call with a promise to email the names and whatever information she had on the people she wanted Marie to research.

The camera trained on her driveway showed that Nathan had returned from San Francisco. Trixie was restless and it was great that Nathan could take her out for exercise. When he returned, he scanned Jill's refrigerator and pantry. He thought he would be spending a fair amount of time at her house over the next few days. He made a shopping list of things that he wanted to put in her kitchen. They would go shopping after lunch. He whipped up a chicken salad, and she had a sourdough loaf to go with it. After cleaning up the kitchen, they went out to her garage.

Jill felt somewhat silly crouching below the dashboard with the blanket thrown over her as she left her house. Nathan indicated when it was safe for her to sit on the seat as they approached the main street of Palisades Valley. He'd been watching his review mirror and had not seen anyone following him. Admittedly, he was an amateur at this game. First stop was the Sheriff's office. Jill wanted to know if he had new information on the shell casings. She also wanted to reinforce that she needed frequent patrols to keep her safe. The Sheriff had the manpower at that time to escort her to the grocery store.

She and Nathan got everything on his list. A Sheriff's deputy stood outside of the grocery store as Nathan pulled the car up. She got in the car while Nathan loaded the groceries. They thanked the deputy and were on their way back to her home. About three miles from her home, she again crouched underneath the dashboard with the blanket over her until Nathan pulled into her garage and closed the automatic door.

Just as she unloaded the groceries, Detective Carlson called her back. She relayed to the detective the activity of the last twenty-four hours, the cooperation of the Palisades Valley Sheriff's department, and the men on patrol at night from her security system company. Again, the detective reminded her to leave it in the hands of the SFPD. Jill remarked to the detective that the SFPD had been nowhere in sight when she'd been shot at the previous day.

Jill heard a long sigh on the other end of the phone.

"Yes, I understand that you have poor protection at your home and that you want to speed up the solving of this crime so that you no longer feel threatened."

"It's that I'm mad that someone nearly got away with murder, and I've always been a fighter for justice."

"Our disagreement about your involvement in this case is not why I called. I have new information from the San Juan Police Department. Mr. Gonzales has not been sighted on the island for the last day and a half. He failed to show up to work, and the address he listed for his employer was a fake. His scuba certification was also a fabrication. The police were attempting to decipher his fingerprints but everything that the employer had that Mr. Gonzales touched, was also touched by other people. The fingerprints lifted off the ointment tube were also contaminated by multiple fingers."

"That doesn't bode well for Gonzales."

"No, it doesn't. If I hear anything else, I'll contact you."

After hanging up, Jill thought the SFPD was a world-class organization, but it wasn't at all close to solving this crime.

CHAPTER 13

J ill needed another workout with Nathan. They couldn't use the barn that they had used the last time he taught her kickboxing. The barn where they had worked out was not on the alarm system, and she'd be vulnerable on the long walk across her property to that barn. They reviewed their options. They could drive over to Nathan's house, where he had a complete gym set up and work out there. They could clear space inside Jill's house and set it up as a gym. She chose the latter, as she was most safe when she was inside her own home. She had a relatively austere spare bedroom that would be easy to clear. Nathan went outside to get the exercise mats that they would need for padding.

Twenty minutes later they were ready for the workout. Like the last time, Jill was soon soaked to the bone with sweat. Nathan taught her a few new self-defense moves. She really liked this martial arts technique and thought she might want to pursue getting her own black belt in one of the arts. She was fortunate to be a student with Nathan as the teacher. With his third-degree black belt, he'd the qualifications to be a teacher. In fact, Jill could advance through the various levels to a black belt with only Nathan as her instructor if she chose Hapkido. She'd think about that after this case was over. An hour later with her muscles aching, Jill and Nathan hit the showers.

When she joined Nathan in her kitchen, she found him marinating some fresh fish that they had picked up at the market earlier. He'd let the fish marinate for two hours, and then they would cook dinner. But first, he would take Trixie to the dog park so she could burn off some of her excess energy.

Jill planned to hunker down and devote her brainpower to thoughts of who the killer was in this case. So far, she'd ruled out just two people, Emma, and the hotel concierge in San Juan. That left Graeme's family members, his law practice associates, his clients, or someone affiliated with the Silicon Valley start-up that he had invested in nearly a decade ago. She was not considering any random criminals. This was too deliberate and sophisticated of a murder for it to be the work of an average street thug. Jill had only reduced her list of suspects to roughly two hundred or so people. The greatest help she could be to her team and the closure of this case was to narrow that list.

She would start with Graeme's family, as that seemed an area of low probability. It was surprising that she would think that, given she'd yet to meet any members of the family, it just didn't feel like a good fit. She would use one of the online genealogy software programs to get to know Graeme's family.

Jill tracked one generation up from the great aunt who had given him three million dollars in her Will. She completed a family tree. He was an only child. His parents had seven siblings between the two of them. He had fourteen first cousins. In total, she'd about forty family members to review. She started by searching for any civil or criminal proceedings against any of the forty. None had minor traffic violations and that was a good sign. She'd been particularly interested in any bankruptcy filings, and again there were none.

Jill had a crime software program that used crude data

points to give her a probability that a certain person committed a particular crime. When she entered data on Emma, her software gave her less than a ten percent probability that she was the killer. So, she'd gone to work on Graeme's family, knowing that with the exception of his parents, no other family member was significantly mentioned in the Will. She did a little more research on his parents and found that they had made their own millions a decade before Graeme had. When she entered data about the remaining twenty-eight or so family members, she also tallied a probability of less than ten percent. For now, the four of them would not focus on his family. She flipped a coin to determine whether to focus on his partners or his clients in her next run. The coin flip pointed her to his partners first.

Nathan returned to the house with Trixie and went to work in the kitchen. Jill saved her data and joined him there. She stayed out of his way and poured him a glass of wine.

"I was really impressed with the workout for Hapkido. When I think of martial arts I think Judo, Karate, Kung Fu, and Tai Chi. How did you become interested in martial arts, and how did you pick Hapkido? Until I met you, I had never heard of the word."

"A few college mates and I attended a martial arts invitational. We entered the Sports Center thinking that we would see Bruce Lee in action.

"Instead, I became enthralled with the strength, beauty, and brutality of the various arts. My friends were bored within an hour and left to return to the university. I was hooked. I stayed the rest of the day and went back the next trying to decide what martial art I would study.

"You've only seen a small number of the moves and weapons used in Hapkido. It's a Korean martial art in which jumping kicks, joint locks, and throws are used. One also uses swords, ropes, canes, and sticks. From the time I watched the opponents at the invitational, I knew I wanted to learn bi-directional kicks as well as be proficient with the weapons used in the dojang. As a college student, I thought meditation was a waste of time. It took me two or three years of training before I began to appreciate the impact that meditation had on my mastery of the art. Now I also use meditation to help stay creative in the studio."

Nathan grilled a wonderful fish fillet. Jill always felt that no matter how she tried to cook fish it always came out tasting fishy. He paired the fish with jasmine rice and creamed asparagus. For dessert, he made Jill's favorite, Crème Brûlée with fresh berries. Wow, she would have considered the moment perfect if someone hadn't been trying to murder her.

After cleaning up the dishes and grabbing a second glass of wine, Jill settled down on the couch with her laptop. Nathan used his own laptop to complete some design work.

It was time to focus on the partners in Graeme's law firm. Checking California records, she pulled up the official data on the legal LLC. The firm had been around for some forty years. Graeme had joined the firm six years ago, becoming a partner in less than four years. The firm handled a wide range of legal transactions. Some partners were experts in employment law, others' estate law, some criminal law, and one was devoted to patents. The original two founding partners were retired. Between office staff, legal secretaries, and attorneys, the firm employed close to a hundred people. Thanks to the Internet she was able to bring up a picture of the office building housing the law firm. She would have to ask Emma why Graeme had chosen to join this law firm.

Jill reviewed cases that had been handled by the firm since Graeme had joined it. She started with culling the county judicial records sorting by the law firm's attorneys. She had nearly four hundred hits on that search. Marie was also focusing on the partners and might be doing some of the same searches as Jill. However, they were both looking at different perspectives on the law firm employees. Jill was trying to understand the legal nuances of the work the firm did, and Marie was following behavioral patterns. She couldn't think of a way to sort the data and therefore was stuck walking through some boring legalese.

She still felt as though her approach was not refined enough so she decided to try another data sort. She reviewed those cases that had at least one appeal or otherwise subsequent legal filing. Appeals would likely represent disgruntled parties in the legal action. That took her from four hundred to one hundred-seventy cases to explore. Then she decided to do another sort and reviewed those cases where there had been at least ten pleadings filed. She was now down to just ten cases. Graeme was the attorney of record on one of the ten. She sent Marie an email updating her with her strategy.

The one court case in which Graeme was the attorney of record had five people named in the pleadings for Jill to research. She spent the rest of the evening trying to digest this case.

Jill had not had any legal training outside of the standard preparation for providing testimony in court cases. It was painful sorting through the legal terms to understand the lawful basis for each case. She used her Internet search engines to look up many of the Latin words. If she ever had a case like this again, she would have to give thought to finding a legal consultant. She was simply too slow in putting together the legal terminology to understand the big picture.

The case in question had been an ongoing process for over two years. It seemed to be a combination of patent law and business law. Graeme had begun as the legal advisor for the start-up, which was devoted to genomic testing. The CEO of the start-up was a childhood friend, and they were almost as close as brothers, without the blood link, as they could be. Start-ups were a race to market with the next big idea. A new company had to get its idea developed, patented, and sold before someone else could beat them to it.

From the beginning of the company, Graeme had been busy with incorporation, then governance, and then employment law as others were hired by the start-up. Graeme had created very strict non-compete contracts as employees were hired. Corporate spying could sink a new company. After two years of lab work, additional angel investing flowed after the first patent was filed. Meanwhile, there were just enough rumors in the scientific community for the company to catch the attention of big pharma. As Graeme's childhood friend had predicted, a series of lawsuits ensued.

Based on what Jill read in the case proceedings, each of the lawsuits seemed to be mostly nuisance lawsuits meant to intimidate the start-up. It appeared Graeme had won all of the motions so far, not because he was a brilliant lawyer, but rather it seemed that the pleadings were without merit, an argument that could be won by a high school debate club member. Jill decided to cross the folks behind the pharmaceutical nuisance lawsuits off her list of suspects. It would seem that anybody involved in this case would do better to keep Graeme in court rather than see him dead. As the lawsuits were without merit, aggravation was the desired outcome by the pleadings against the company that Graeme represented.

Jill went back to the long list of cases to try to find her suspect. She decided that she would create an Excel file tabulating the kind of case it was when it was filed, and any dollar amount mentioned. She wasn't sure what this would do for her, rather she would have to see if the data directed her somewhere. After reviewing about forty cases, she found herself drifting off to sleep.

She shook herself awake, "I am heading for bed. Will you be up soon?"

He nodded absently. He was concentrating on a design. When he was in the creative zone, Jill knew not to interrupt him. He would catch up with her later.

After changing her clothes, she crawled into bed. She fell asleep thinking of how different this case was from anything else in her prior five years as a consultant and an additional fifteen years with the county crime lab. Despite the gruesomeness and immoral character of some of the suspects in the county cases, none had ever come after her personally. When Jill worked at the county crime lab, usually her work ended for her with the cause of death determination. Any further investigative work was performed by local law enforcement. She hoped that the trouble she'd had with this case was not a preview of what she might experience with future cases.

CHAPTER 14

$\mathcal{A}$s usual, Jill awoke before Nathan. Sipping her cup of coffee, she checked her email to see if any new information had come in while she was asleep. The only new piece of information was from her pathology associate Dr. Johnson. Dr. Johnson had been able to re-create the contents of the vial and the ointment tube contaminated with bacteria. As she represented an academic medical center, she was able to order a preparation of the same bacterial strain that had caused Graeme's infection from a laboratory supplier. She then explored the conditions required for the bacteria to grow in the same manner as it had with Graeme.

While the bacteria itself was hardy, the growth pattern was unstable inside the ointment and the vial. Dr. Johnson speculated that Graeme St. Louis would have easily recovered from the leg infection as the potency of the bacteria was much weaker inside the tainted ointment. It simply did not like to grow onto a petroleum-based product. There wasn't much to nourish its growth. The vial, on the other hand, was very potent with bacteria. It had been mixed in a sugar solution and maintained at an appropriate temperature, which would have maxi-

100

mized the bacteria's growth. An injection of the bacterial solution would give anyone a raging infection.

So now Jill knew technically how it could be done. Her associate had figured out how to turn bacteria into the murder weapon. She'd also clearly proven that whoever had created the solution was an expert in microbiology. A recipe was not readily available to download off the Internet. It required special skills and special equipment. So, had the person who had created the vial created it recently to kill Graeme, or had the technique been perfected several years ago and the person had just waited for the right target? Was it a hired killer? Since she still didn't know why Graeme was murdered, she could not speculate on the microbiology background of his killer. She forwarded Dr. Johnson's email to Detective Carlson and the San Francisco medical examiner for their records.

Jill had just started to work on the cases from last night when Nathan joined her.

"Would you like some coffee?"

"Yeah."

Jill had learned that he was a man of few words prior to that first cup of coffee. She grabbed a coffee cup filled it with coffee and cream and handed it to him.

"Would you like breakfast? Maybe some waffles?"

"Yeah, thanks."

Jill gathered the ingredients for the waffles and found the waffle maker. She was deliberately slow about making breakfast knowing that Nathan needed at least fifteen minutes to feel that first surge of caffeine in his system. It was not easy for a morning person like herself to stay quiet and calm until Nathan had reached her level of wakefulness. Forty-five minutes later, the caffeine and the sugar from the maple syrup had kicked in, and he was fully coherent. He walked to the sink, fencing her in for a good-morning kiss. He tasted like maple syrup. Given that he'd slept light enough to hear the intruder a few nights ago, she considered his morning grogginess a small price to pay.

"I planned to continue my research of Graeme's clients searching for possible motives. I went through about thirty cases last night and nothing popped. I'll be slogging away with my laptop all morning. How badly is staying here affecting your business? I know that this has been a huge disruption to be away from your studio."

"I'm doing okay with my business. I'm keeping up with my customers through email and my cell phone. I'm updating a label for a long-standing client. After I take Trixie out for some exercise, I'll keep you company by getting some of my own work done."

He didn't say that the attempts on her life were a far bigger distraction than having to relocate his studio to her house.

Jill felt like a prisoner in her own home. The only thing that kept her sane was the knowledge that this was a short-term change in her lifestyle. Once the killer was identified and arrested, she could go back to her former life. Jill settled into the sofa with her laptop and went to work on her list of clients. In the back of her mind, she suspected that this was a wild goose chase, but she really needed to eliminate some of the clients.

Nathan returned with Trixie and began to work on a design. His highly sensitive computer-aided design software gave him infinite variations on a theme. Intellectually he found that updating an existing label was more difficult than creating one from scratch. Depending on the winery, changing the label equaled changing the brand. Winery owners generally had a fair amount of trepidation when changing their branding.

They worked quietly on their respective projects for several hours. Jill's spreadsheet was taking shape, but nothing had leaped out at her of the—someone named in a legal case who was so mad that it would be worth murdering Graeme variety. Jill went to another room to conduct her scheduled phone call with Emma. The last thing she wanted to do was further disturb Nathan's ability to work at her house.

"Emma, do you know why Graeme chose the firm where he practiced?"

"We talked of many things, but I don't remember him ever mentioning why he chose that firm. It was close to his house, but he joined the firm before he bought the house."

"Overall, was he happy at work? Did he ever mention that he disagreed with a senior partner's decision-making?"

"He never really had a negative thing to say about work."

"What about his clients? Did he get along with all of them? Did he ever mention to you any problem that he had with a client? Did he have any kind of ethical concern or other unpleasantness with a client?"

Emma paused for a while on the telephone and thought back over the numerous conversations she'd had with Graeme. He very rarely spoke of his clients. Sure, he often read or did some paperwork at night, but it didn't consume his time outside of the office. He was also bound by the attorney/client privilege with all his clients.

"Jill, let me think about this some more, but off the top of my head I can't remember a client that significantly upset Graeme."

Jill went on to review Dr. Johnson's research into the micro-biology world and how the infection could have been spread to Graeme. Then she updated Emma on the work that she and her associates were doing. They scheduled the next call and said their goodbyes.

While she talked to Emma, Detective Carlson called Jill and left a voicemail.

After listening to the voicemail, Jill called the detective.

"I understand that you had some questions about Dr. Johnson's findings."

"Yeah, I did. I also wanted to update you on information I received from the San Juan police. It seems that hikers stumbled upon a body in the rain forest. Police identified the victim as Luis Gonzales. His throat had been slit and given that his body was in the rain forest, insects and other animals had gone to work on him. However, his fingerprints were intact, and that was how he was identified. A police artist reconstructed his facial profile from his remains. That sketch was shown to the scuba diving company, and a representative of the company positively confirmed that he was the gentleman that it had employed and who used the name, Luis Gonzales."

Jill asked, "So that was his real name?"

"Yes. When the San Juan police department ran a criminal check on Luis Gonzales, it found that he rarely used an alias. He'd been suspected of several crimes but had never been convicted. Interestingly, one of the other crimes that he was alleged to have committed early in his career was impersonating a scuba diving instructor and stealing the personal belongings of the divers aboard the boats he was working on."

Jill had not liked Gonzales, but she would not have wished that demise on him. It also increased her anxiety level, as there were now two murders associated with her current case. That, of course, was in addition to the two attempts on her life.

"Wow! From my perspective, that's very bad news. It means that whoever the killer is, in this case, is willing to shut down the case and anyone involved with it by any means. Detective, do you have a sense as to whether this is a single person, or do you think he or she hired someone to make the attempts on my life and to kill Gonzales?"

"As Gonzales is alleged to have been contracted to harm Graeme on board the scuba diving boat, I think it's safe to assume that the killer is more than willing to hire out his work. This is a very complex case between the science behind the murder and the fact that it is occurring in several jurisdictions. We may need to enlist the aid of the FBI. I'll be running that by my Lieutenant in an hour, and I suspect that he'll require that we bring the FBI into the case."

Just then, a window in the room where Jill was standing cracked. Her hair swayed from a bullet that passed far too close to her head and lodged in the opposite wall. Jill hit the floor, ducking any additional bullets.

"What the heck! Detective Carlson, call 911. I'm being shot at!"

Jill yelled down the hallway from her position on the floor, "Nathan, take cover. Someone is shooting at me."

She felt like a crazed woman at that moment. Seconds before she'd bent down to re-tie her shoelaces which she'd noticed when glancing down during her conversation with the detective, and that had saved her life. She wiggled out of the room on her belly, while Nathan crawled toward her when they both heard another window crack. Once they were in the hallway, they were out of the way of any more flying bullets. She heard Detective Carlson distantly on the phone and reached over and placed it to her ear.

"Jill, the Sheriff has an ETA of three minutes. Additional officers and the K-9 unit will be there in seven. What's your status?"

"I'm fine and Nathan is fine. The bullet missed. I bent over to re-tie my shoelaces just as a gun fired at me from outside."

Then she heard two sounds simultaneously. Just as she felt comfort in hearing the wail of a distant siren, she heard the crack of glass again in the room she'd just left. She peered around the corner of the doorway and saw that something burning had been tossed into the room.

"Nathan, I keep a fire extinguisher under the kitchen sink. Run and grab it!"

"Detective, please request a fire truck for this location. Something burning was just tossed into the house. Nathan's getting a fire extinguisher to put it out."

"Jill, stay out of the room and take cover, it may explode."

Jill looked behind her as Nathan returned with the fire extinguisher. She put her hand up, gesturing for him to halt. Just as he stopped, they heard an explosion in the room. The Sheriff had arrived in her driveway and grabbed two fire extinguishers from the trunk of the patrol car and ran into the house. Nathan sprayed the fire with Jill's small kitchen extinguisher. She ran into the guest bathroom, turned the trash can upside down dumped its contents on the floor, filled it with water, and ran back to the burning room. She and the others fought the fire with fire extinguishers and a few trash cans of water, and it was nearly extinguished as the fire truck arrived. She had long ago hung up on Detective Carlson.

CHAPTER 15

"I am so done with this homicidal maniac!" exclaimed Jill.

She sat there wondering what had happened to her quiet life of growing grapes, creating the perfect bottle of Moscato, and leisurely giving an occasional second opinion on a cause of death. She'd run her hands through her hair, but she couldn't remember any fashion magazine claim that charcoal and smoke were good for one's hair and skin. She was dying to take a shower, but that would have to wait. The Sheriff was in the house. Nathan, Trixie, and Arthur were safe. Detective Carlson, her superior, and the FBI were on their way and expected to arrive within the hour.

Both Jill and Nathan gave their statements about what had happened. They had repeated their story over the phone for an agent of the FBI. The Sheriff's K-9 unit was presently outside following the trail of the killer. The fire department had told her that she was lucky. The damage was contained to the original room into which the Molotov cocktail had been thrown. And yes, the incendiary device had been confirmed. She would need to replace the drywall, the carpet, the drapes, and the contents of the room. Thankfully, because of quick action, the fire had not spread.

Jill felt like she was on the verge of a complete meltdown. She needed to feel human again and that meant a shower and clean clothes. Unfortunately, her bedroom and bath had outside windows. She had Nathan do another belly-crawl to her dresser and her closet to get her some clean clothes. Then she used her guest bathroom to clean up with the Sheriff standing guard.

The last hour had been very action-packed. Fresh clothes and the shower made Jill feel like a new woman. It was past lunchtime, and suddenly she felt like could eat an entire chicken. The adrenaline rush had left her starving. She eyed Nathan to see how he was holding up. He appeared cool, calm, and collected. So, she asked him if he could cook for them and the contingent of law enforcement. He readily agreed and gathered the ingredients for a hearty meal.

Nathan had just put the finishing touches on spaghetti with meatballs, sourdough bread, and a tossed salad. Just as they sat down to eat, Detective Carlson, her Lieutenant and a member of the FBI arrived at Jill's house. As Jill was unwilling to be interviewed before consuming her lunch, the latest arrivals joined them at the table for Nathan's excellently prepared meal.

As they were finishing lunch, the officer returned with the K-9 dog.

"The same shell casings found are the same as the last time. The dog was able to track the shooter, and he parked in a different area than he did before. He brought a second Molotov cocktail that he left in the bushes."

The police officer would dust for fingerprints, but he doubted that it would be that easy. To launch the cocktail into the house, the killer had to get close. The dog was able to scent him within thirty feet of the house. Jill called her security company to come out to her house immediately since it appeared, her new system had failed to detect an intruder.

The Sheriff got ready to depart Jill's house. There was nothing more that he could do here, and he was looking forward to receiving direction from the FBI about how to handle the situation. Someone from the SFPD and the FBI sat down with Jill for a conversation concerning Graeme's death. Jill went over to her laptop and printed the report that she'd originally provided to the San Francisco medical examiner to convince him to change the cause of death to homicide.

Jill escorted the group out to her lab. With a little help from her analyzers, she provided a fascinating explanation of how she figured out that the bacteria had been injected into Graeme. Once everyone nodded that they understood her thought process, she moved on to the other incidents. With Nathan's help, she described the mess in the lab and what it had done to her testing process.

She moved on to the intruder in her house. Nathan described the car that had followed them to San Francisco. Jill spoke of the incident at the harbor in Puerto Rico. Next, she described the shooter that had aimed at her two days ago and finally today's shooting and incendiary device as they returned to her house. It had been a ghastly week when she connected all the happenings together. She shivered and thought she was lucky to be alive.

"What's next? How do I get additional security?"

Leticia Ortiz, agent in charge of the San Francisco office of the FBI, responded, "Ma'am, we'll keep you safe, don't you worry. What we really need to do is solve Graeme St. Louis's murder. Obviously, that's the best way to protect you. If you'll share with us what you and your friends have done to try to solve this murder, we'll take it from there."

"Excuse me?"

Agent Ortiz repeated her same inane statement about Jill's security.

Jill felt like the Molotov cocktail that had been tossed into her house. Nathan had been leaning against the kitchen counter watching Jill. He was looking forward to watching the fireworks when she exploded. He knew her well enough to know that she would have no time for Agent Ortiz's condescension about her case-solving skills. The agent had made it sound like some women's baking club was attempting to solve the murder.

"Protect me? Really, where have any of you been for the past week? Does one law enforcement agency not talk to another? Why should I trust you to guard me? I'm not some amateur Sherlock Holmes. I spent fifteen years at the county crime lab as a forensic pathologist. I have used those same skills as a private consultant to solve cases for the past five years. Have any of you bothered to fly to Puerto Rico? No! How much time have you put into investigating Luis Gonzales? Emma Spencer hired me, and she can cancel my contract at any time, as is her right. Even if she did cancel my contract, my team and I would continue with our investigation because of the personal turn it has taken. Is that clear? My team makes my personal safety its top priority. You buffoons needed a Molotov cocktail to get you to take notice of this case."

Jill really wanted these people out of her house. She was so mad! She felt she needed a Hapkido session with Nathan to let off her frustration and fear. And then, she wanted to get back to work on evaluating Graeme's legal cases. She knew she might be overreacting, but with an assassin on her trail, she thought she was entitled to a few tantrums. She met Nathan's eyes. He had quietly watched the interaction.

"Nathan, please show the agent out. I need to get back to work. I've got a case to solve."

Both Detective Carlson and Agent Ortiz tried to placate Jill.

"Dr. Quint, as you have so summarily stated, you need additional security. We can't leave at this point. Being bombed by a Molotov cocktail is a violation of federal law pertaining to attempted arson and possession of a destructive device. For that reason alone, we'll conduct an investigation," responded Agent Ortiz.

"We'll arrange for your protection. In the meantime, we need to interview you in detail about the research you have completed on this case, and we can't do that if you're dead. I don't think you're an idiot, and you're right that we have been slow to come onto this case. I apologize for the delay. We're involved now, and we plan to keep you safe. Let's start this relationship over and move on from here."

Since Jill was quite worried for her own safety and her temper had fizzled out, she was keen to have the protection.

"I have plans to live to be one hundred-three years old. I very much need someone's help at this time in order for me to make my hundredth birthday cruise. I'm game to start this relationship over if you are."

After a huge sigh, she put her hand out to Agent Ortiz.

"I am Dr. Jill Quint, and someone has been trying to kill me during the last week. This is my boyfriend Nathan and my dog Trixie. We would very much like to stay alive."

Agent Ortiz replied in kind, "Nice to meet you, Dr. Quint. I am Agent Ortiz. Let me introduce you to the other agents. This is Agent Ben Brown and Agent Kelly O'Sullivan. We are all based in the San Francisco field office"

The crisis passed, they regrouped to discuss theories about the death of Graeme St. Louis. Jill spoke at length regarding the scientific background necessary in the killer.

"To use bacteria as a weapon means that you have to have knowledge of certain things," Jill ticked them off on her fingers.

"Which bacteria to buy, how to incubate and keep it alive from a food and temperature perspective, how much bacteria it would take to harm someone, where to buy the supplies like the agars, the temperature-controlled environment, and the bacteria itself. One would have to know how to mix it in a vial and what amount to inject into Graeme. On a less technical side, he needed to know Graeme's location in the hospital, how to quietly enter his room, and where to inject the substance.

"My microbiology expert on this case, Dr. Johnson, took three days of experimenting to come up with a scenario of how it could be done. The killer had to experiment several times to make the weapon effective. He would have needed to try the substance on animals or humans to verify potency. The murderer was able to carry out a plan to murder Graeme while he was scuba diving with little advanced planning given when the scuba trip was reserved. These results also point to someone needing scientific knowledge and ready access to the bacteria, as a patient and organized murderer. Once the murder location was chosen, the bacterial weapon could have been prepared in under a week."

The officers and agents from both the SFPD and the FBI had rapidly taken notes on Jill's comments. They had legal power behind them that Jill lacked. They could request records of sales by legitimate microbiology supply companies worldwide. No legitimate supplier ever would want to see its shipment turned into a weapon. Garden variety bacteria were not viewed as a weapon. Rather when people thought of bio-terrorism, the Ebola virus or anthrax is what came to mind. In this case, the bio-terrorism source was actually the number one cause of sinus infections in the adult population.

Agent O'Sullivan called the home office, requesting information about the shipments of bacteria cultures.

Agent Ortiz turned to Detective Carlson and asked, "Did you contact the hospital to see if it had a camera turned on in the hallway outside of Graeme's room? Was the killer caught on tape entering Graeme's room?"

"Yes, I contacted the hospital. While it has many cameras on many hallways inside University Hospital, the corridor outside of Graeme's room was not a taped location. We have a six-to-eight-hour window of time when the injection could have occurred. We have a detective working with the hospital to see if there is anything unusual in any of the hallways or stairwells on the path to Graeme's room. As you know, it was a long period of time, and there was a lot of activity there. We are using facial recognition software to eliminate employees recorded on any of the cameras. There are more than fifty faces of non-employees. These faces could be visitors to other patients, contractors, or the killer."

"Adding to this complexity, some of the people on camera wore surgical masks. And, of course, the killer could have worn a disguise. It's too early to determine if we'll be able to identify a suspect recorded on one of the cameras.

"We've also surveyed the street where someone was alleged to have pulled a knife on Graeme. Sometimes we have traffic cameras on streets. Unfortunately, in this case, there was no camera trained on the street. It is the same situation with the building where the law office is. There is a camera on all entry or exit doors but not in any interior stairwells."

Jill had a thought about her own security system. She excused herself for a moment and left the room to call her security company. Bill Johnson, her security company employee, came on the line, and she identified herself, her location, and gave him her personal identification number. Her identity was verified.

"Regarding the system you installed on my property, are any of the cameras trained on the southwest hill?"

"Just a minute ma'am, while I review your camera locations. I am going to place you on hold for a few minutes while I check."

Jill heard the usual telephone hold music. He returned in less than sixty seconds.

"Dr. Quint, you do have a camera pointed at the southwest hill. In fact, you have 360-degree camera coverage."

"I'm just beginning to understand the features of my new

security system. Were you notified that I had a security breach today?"

"Yes, ma'am, we received that notification about half an hour ago of the breach. We are reviewing the specifics of your system to understand why no alarms were triggered. A technician should be arriving at your house within the next ten minutes to check the system."

"You may have some very valuable information at your disposal. I presently have agents from the FBI in my house, and I would like to include them in our conversation. Please hold on."

Jill returned to the other room. She explained to the group the features of her security system and the fact that the sniper should have been caught on camera. She asked the FBI agents to join her in the phone conversation with the security company. She returned to the room containing the landline phone with Agent Ortiz in tow.

"Bill, I have you on speakerphone. With me is Agent Ortiz of the San Francisco FBI office. You indicated that I have cameras trained upon the land surrounding my house. Can you recover images from two to three hours ago? Can you save those tapes, and can you send me a copy immediately so I can get a look at the shooter?"

"Bill, this is Agent Ortiz. I would like you to save whatever recordings you have for the past three days. Jill, you returned from Puerto Rico three days ago, right? We should look at all the recordings since you returned from San Juan."

"Bill, this is Jill again. Can you give me a call when you have all those recordings available for us to view?"

He agreed and they ended the call. Jill heard someone from the security company pull up in her driveway. It would be interesting to know why her alarm system had failed to sound when the shooter crossed onto her property. No security system was completely foolproof. As she had a mad scientist on her hands, perhaps he'd created some kind of jammer that confused her new system.

Law enforcement personnel had completed their questioning of Nathan. This latest case of Jill's had totally disrupted his work schedule. Nathan would have to start using his nights to catch up on his design work. Fortunately, his assistant would be competently handling the print side of his business.

From his perspective, the cops had completed about half of their interview of Jill. There had been so many happenings with her at the center. She understood the science of the weapon. She was leading a team doing research on the people in Graeme's life. He thought they needed another two to three hours of conversation, considering suspects, and planning the next steps.

He slowly moved toward Jill and murmured to her while the members of the SFPD and the FBI conversed. "Do you need me here?" she gave a shake of her head.

He peered at the group, "Guys, I am not of much use on this case at the moment. I'll be in the other room getting some work done. You know where to find me."

CHAPTER 16

*W*hile the person from the security company diagnosed her system failure and retrieved four days of video from her multiple cameras, she contemplated the next steps with members of law enforcement. Each of them had different perspectives. The SFPD needed to solve Graeme's murder. He'd been murdered in its jurisdiction. The FBI had a different focus. Agent Ortiz did not believe that she had a serial killer on her hands. The killer seemed to have one target and that was anyone with knowledge of the circumstances surrounding Graeme's murder. The role of the events and people in Puerto Rico had little connection yet. Jill's perspective was to fulfill her contract with Emma Spencer and still be alive in the decades to come.

"Any thoughts on why Emma Spencer has not been a target?" asked Jill.

"That's a good question for our criminal profilers. We'll be connecting with our profiler later this evening. We're waiting to see if the killer is on any of the camera recordings. His presence or lack thereof completely changes the profile."

"Agent Ortiz, do you mean that the killer has in-depth

knowledge of security systems or not based on his presence or absence on any of the camera recordings?" questioned Jill.

"Yes, knowledge of electronics changes the profile. Also watching the behavior of the shooter on the tapes may influence the profile."

With that remark by Agent Ortiz, Jill decided that it was time to move on to other parts of the case. Detective Carlson was up to speed on the avenues that Jill was exploring. Her Lieutenant and the FBI were only broadly aware of the path that Jill's group was taking to solve the case.

She started by giving all the detectives and agents a broad overview of her past work experience in the county crime lab and then moved on to the forty to fifty cases that she'd consulted on as a private pathologist. She followed that with the skills of Jo, Marie, and Angela.

While the FBI could outgun her with resources and computer systems, Jill was unwilling to relinquish the case into its very capable hands and sit tight waiting passively for the FBI to solve the crime. She felt a duty to Graeme and Emma. She had the added incentive of staying alive herself to motivate her to solve the case.

Jill shared her deductive-reasoning flowchart with the group to explain her approach. Angela had taken the lead in eliminating suspects in Puerto Rico. Detective Carlson also agreed with Jill that Emma could be eliminated as a suspect.

"I believe that the Bureau would agree with your conclusions at this point," stated Agent Ortiz.

"My associate, Jo, is reviewing the financial documents of the law firm. She has found nothing suspicious with the financial statements at this point. She's also evaluating Graeme's trust and the purchase of his house. Again, everything seems in order. Finally, she reviewed the SEC filings of the start-up company that Graeme was so heavily involved with getting off the ground. No discrepancies there, either."

"My associate, Marie, is conducting background searches on the law firm's partners. In her daytime job, she does national and international candidate sourcing and verification. She'll find any data on people, including criminal information, professional reputation, and what is being said on social media. With that kind of evaluation, she can put together a very accurate profile about someone.

"We need to get into Luis Gonzales's bank account, where perhaps we can trace who may have recently put money into his account for services rendered," Jill suggested to the group.

"Agent Brown will run down Gonzales' bank account. You're correct that this might be the easiest way to identify the killer. However, based on the science that it took to kill Graeme, I don't think we'll so easily solve this case."

Jill also doubted that it would be easy. So, she moved on to a discussion of where her research was focused.

"I reviewed Graeme's family next. Given that he did not make changes to the Will until after several attempts had been made on his life, it just doesn't seem to me that his family was involved. His parents were his original beneficiaries, but I couldn't find a motive there. They are wealthy. This is a very normal family with no criminal history, all of them with full-time jobs and no one in financial trouble. So, I crossed family members off my list of suspects.

"Next, I flipped a coin as to whether to explore his partners or his clients. The coin toss led me to his partners. Other than speeding tickets, DUIs, and college marijuana charges, nothing raised red flags for the firm\'s employees.

"Then I moved on to his client list. During his time with the legal firm, he was involved in approximately four-hundred cases. I eliminated all the cases that had no additional pleadings filed. I considered that without additional pleadings that the law cases were without conflict. That brought the number down to approximately one hundred-seventy.

"That sounds like you were looking for a needle in a haystack," exclaimed Agent Ortiz admiringly! "I like your line of reasoning about the cases. You're trying to find that one person who's mad enough about something to kill Graeme."

"Yes, that is exactly what I was searching for. I took the one hundred-seventy or so cases and searched amongst them for the ones that had ten or more pleadings filed. I figured these were the really mad people. There was just one case where Graeme was the lead attorney. In the other nine cases, a law firm partner was the lead and Graeme was in the second chair. That one case with all the pleadings filed concerned the start-up that he helped get off the ground almost a decade ago. The opposing party in the matter was big pharma, and the pleadings appeared to be in a nuisance lawsuit. Graeme easily defeated the plaintiff. Likely a high school debate team member could have defeated the plaintiff, the lawsuit was that lame."

"Nice approach to the analysis."

"Thanks, but I wasn't done with the client list. I didn't feel that I could dismiss all the cases just like that. So, I went back and created a spreadsheet of the cases. I defined the cases by the type of law or pleading involved, a dollar amount if mentioned, and the date of the suit. I thought the date might eliminate some of the cases or the dollar amount might highlight some of the cases. I had gotten through fifty cases before the interruption this morning. Nothing is grabbing my attention yet."

Just then, a knock sounded on Jill's front door. Someone from the security company wanted to update her on his findings. She was starting to go stir crazy stuck inside her house all day. She figured that with the happenings of the morning, the shooter was not in the neighborhood. She invited the personnel from the SFPD and the FBI out onto her veranda. They could form a human shield for her while she got some fresh air and listened to what the technician had to say. She hoped she would never take her freedom for granted ever again!

"Let me make introductions. Brett Thackeray of Secure One, meet Detective Carlson and Lieutenant Chang of the SFPD and Agents Ortiz, Brown, and O'Sullivan of the San Francisco field office of the FBI. Brett is here to tell me about the breakdown with the security system."

"Ma'am, we just did a complete diagnostic on your system. It uses ultrasonic frequency to determine movement. Using a wave imitator to exactly duplicate the waveform of your system, your visitor was able to enter your property. We detected this activity because you have a ten-second delay on the alarm. The delay is built into your system to stop it from going off whenever a bird, for example, crosses the perimeter. This is a standard feature of all systems, as you don't want to drive your neighbors nuts with frequent false alarms."

"Brett, tell me what you mean by imitator and how you could tell that my system had been hijacked," Jill asked the very questions that her law enforcement friends had been ready to ask.

"Your software showed where the alarm had been triggered but then re-set within that ten-second interval. I was also able to match that time with the approximate time of your 911 conversation. An imitator was designed by someone with engineering experience. To make this work, he or she would have needed to measure the wavelength frequency of your system and be able to dial it into a device that would emit the same wavelength frequency. This would signal to your system that the wavelength was intact and there were no intruders."

"I thought I had purchased a good system. Why wasn't I warned that it could be so easily tampered with? So, what is the solution? Should you reduce the alarm delay to four seconds?"

"Dr. Quint, I have worked for Secure One for twenty years. With thousands of customers over that time period, I've never seen the wavelength imitated like it was here. We read about imitator devices in the professional journal for security systems, but I've never seen one. Journal articles speculate about how such a device would be designed, but there's never been an acknowledgment that such devices exist in the real world. As to reducing the alarm delay, I can do that, but you'll have false-negative alarms in great number. I also don't know how many seconds your intruder took to measure the wavelength. I can't measure that with our current system. So, four seconds might still be too long, and you'd be back at the beginning with a lot of annoying alarms."

Jill asked the people from both the SFPD and the FBI if they had ever come across an imitator before. Lieutenant Chang could not recall any such device being used in a San Francisco breaking and entering case. Likewise, the FBI agents could not remember a case where such a device had been used, either. Like Brett indicated, they thought that such a device was more fantasy than fact since they read many of the same security news reports.

"I guess this again points to the fact that I have a scientist on my hands, one who can create bacterial weapons and security system imitators," Jill sighed. "Brett, what about the cameras? Was he caught on the camera anywhere? Have you spoken to anyone at your office to see if they have identified anybody on camera?"

"Someone at my office did find human movement on one of the cameras. That footage, including a date and time stamp, should have arrived in your email inbox."

Jill went inside the house to her laptop. As Brett had stated, an urgent email appearing to contain the footage sat in her inbox. Before opening the attachment, she forwarded the email to Detective Carlson and Agent Brown. She brought the footage up on the screen. A figure could be seen stealthily coming over the rise of the hillside that was her winery.

"Wow, this makes the hair on the back of my neck stand up. I see a figure moving across the screen moments before he tried to kill me," Jill remarked quietly.

Just then the screen went blank. They could tell that the camera was still recording by the time indicator on the screen, but there was nothing to view other than fuzzy white space. By this time, Brett and the agents were clustered around Jill.

Brett explained, "There will be another ninety minutes of blank screen if you let this attachment run, according to the person at my office. When I checked your system, the camera is recording white space even now. I'm running a diagnostic on the system. Let me go and check on it."

Jill went to the room where Nathan was working and asked him to see if he could help her with the video clip. Given his graphic design business, she figured that he was far more skilled than she in manipulating images. He returned to the room containing her laptop. He quickly located the frame with the best definition of the suspect. He then enlarged the headshot, and a collective gasp sounded in the room.

It was a woman.

Her hair was pulled back at the nape underneath a red ball cap. She wore an overcoat and carried something in her hands. Unfortunately, the flaps of the open coat covered her hands. Judging her height against that of her grapevine, they guessed her to be close to six feet tall. She was lean, with blonde hair, thirty to forty-five years old, and Caucasian. She appeared to have a bruise on her cheek.

Jill had a quick thought, "Nathan, do you think that she might be the intruder you fought with a few days ago? Do you think you might have hit her in the face?"

Nathan thought back to the encounter a week ago. It had been dark. He hadn't gotten close enough to know if he was fighting a man or a woman. He'd just assumed that it was a man, based on the height of the person. He remembered getting in a couple of kicks, one high and one low, and there had been grunts before the intruder exited.

"It could have been her that I fought, but I can't confirm that due to the darkness. Certainly, if she took a kick from my foot to her face, it might look like the bruise we see on the screen. I should add that she has some martial arts training as well, but I doubt that she got beyond the black belt level. She also seems like the driver in the silver sedan that followed us to San Francisco."

Staring at the screen, agent Ortiz stated, "We'll use facial-recognition software to try and identify her."

Brett came back into the room with two updates. "First, my colleague has located the film from the sniper incident a few days ago, and the same woman appeared on camera before it went to white noise. The camera went back to normal after ten minutes. This leads me to my second point. She had a device that interfered with your cameras, one that she could turn on and off. A few days ago, she had more time, so she hit some kind of resume button. This time she lacked the time to hit the resume button or lost the device somewhere in your vineyard. Perhaps the K-9 dog will locate it there."

"This woman was not one of the two people that confronted Angela and me at the harbor in San Juan. So, there are at least four people hired to harm or kill me: this woman, Mr. Gonzales, his accomplice, and the silver sedan driver. At this point, we don't know if the woman was hired to kill me or if she killed Graeme." Jill was so frustrated that she could have stamped her feet.

"Brett, couldn't someone at your security company explore the device used to block the camera in this situation? Since her device confused the security system, it would seem to be in your company's best interests to research the device and find a remedy. Personally, I think that the failure of your security system on my property is rather like driving a new car off the lot and having it stall at the first stoplight."

"I had already thought of that and called our national head-quarters office asking someone there to contact our local office immediately. We have some employees at our national office whose job description is to stay one step ahead of the creation of devices such as was used on your system. Obviously, in your case, we were one step behind, but I have to think that our staff has feelers out trying to find out what's new on the market for this sort of thing."

Jill nodded. "Let's summarize where we are now. My local Sheriff is running down the shell casings from the gun used to shoot at me. Agents from the FBI are using facial recognition software to try and identify the female shooter. They are also investigating Mr. Gonzales's bank accounts. Someone from the SFPD is researching whether it has camera footage from the street where someone pulled a knife on Graeme. It is also searching for the silver sedan and its driver. I'm evaluating the clients of the law firm, and my associate Marie is researching the employees."

"Jill, this brings us to your security," said Agent Ortiz.

"I'm going to assign Agents Brown and O'Sullivan to stay here and guard you. I'm going to bring additional agents in to be positioned around the perimeter of your property. You are going to be confined to your house. We are going to put black paper on the inside of all your windows so that you won't be a target as you move from room to room within your house. If there is another attempt on your life, I am going to move you to a safe house in San Francisco. I want to keep you safe, and I want my agents to have an opportunity to apprehend the sniper if she makes a move on your property. I would advise that Nathan return to his house with your dog. The less that both you and our agents have to worry about, the more effective we'll be guarding you."

"I agree with your recommendation that Nathan and Trixie go to his house."

Lieutenant Chang added, "I don't want to speak for the FBI, but I would guess that they'll join the SFPD in researching Graeme's partners and clients. As you know from your stint at the county crime lab, we have a few more computer systems that we can access as compared to you as a private citizen."

"As the Lieutenant suggested, the FBI will also review Graeme's clients and the employees of his firm. We'll also take a brief look at the family, but we agree with your assessment, Jill, that this is not someone from the family," Agent Ortiz said.

Nathan did not appear happy with their plan, but he understood their reasoning. He wanted to stay and protect Jill. He didn't own or know how to shoot a gun, which put him at a huge disadvantage with the female shooter. If only she'd come after Jill with a sword or cane, he would be very effective with Hapkido in taking her down.

It was getting late. The group thought that it would have new information by the morning. A conference call was set for the next morning to share any updates. Lieutenant Chang, Detective Carlson, and Agent Ortiz left Jill's house. A few minutes later, Nathan and an unhappy Trixie also departed. Nathan had boarded up the broken window in the burnt room. Rain was due overnight, and the last thing Jill needed was rainwater flowing into the already damaged room.

Jill set the two agents up in spare bedrooms. They set up eight-hour shifts between the two of them. Agent O'Sullivan liked to cook and offered to make the three of them dinner. Jill always took any opportunity to stay out of her own kitchen and gave free rein to the agent to cook for them any time she wanted.

With everyone settled in, Jill took her laptop and sat down to call her friends. This time she only reached Marie. Calls to both

Jo and Angela went to voicemail. She updated Marie on the events of the day.

"I have worked with you for what, four to five years? I have never seen your life put in danger like this before. Have you thought of retiring from this occupation at the end of this case? You know, just grow grapes and sell wine?" asked a thoughtful and anxious Marie.

"I've given retirement serious thought over the past couple of days. Retirement during this case won't help my situation now, though. The best thing we can all do is solve the murder. As to retiring after this case, I don't know. I've enjoyed the cases I've provided a second opinion on over the past five years. I feel like I've used my college training and brought real value to the family members of the deceased. I find this intellectually stimulating. However, if challenging my brain cuts my life short by fifty years, then I think my friends would call me stupid."

"Yeah, we would call you stupid. We would cry our hearts out at your funeral, but we'd still say you were stupid. So, what are your options? How do you continue the work you love but live long enough to join us on our hundredth birthdays' cruises?"

"I don't have an answer to that yet. I thought I'd wait till the end of the case. Talk to someone at the FBI and the SFPD and look up some data on the Internet. This may be a complete fluke, a once-in-a-lifetime bad case. Certainly, up to now I've never had problems. I thought I'd search for the statistics for private detectives, as that is what I actually am in this case."

"That response sounds like you. You don't want to change something that you're doing that you like without over-whelming data that it's the right thing to do. From this girl-friend's view, I can earn spare change some other way that doesn't put your life at risk. I've a few more minutes before I have to run. Let me update you on what I found," Marie added.

She'd run a search on every one of the law firm's employees.

No one was in huge debt, although a few employees were underwater with their mortgage, but that was to be expected in the poor housing market. No employees had been charged with or convicted of any crimes other than minor traffic violations. The small amount of employee turnover that the firm had experienced seemed legitimate. A few employees had stayed home after the birth of a child or had moved to another city with a spouse. She also hadn't found any inappropriate postings on any social networks. In total, she'd investigated thirty employees including the partners. It was a little unusual to find zero crime amongst those thirty, but then it was a law practice after all.

Jill had to agree with Marie's assessment of the research she'd completed. She had one more group of people that she wanted Marie to review. She found it interesting that the suspected murder attempts on Graeme had begun after he made the appointment to see the client in Puerto Rico. She didn't think it was coincidence.

"Marie, can you research one more group of people?"

"What do you mean by a group of people, Jill?"

"It seems to me that all the action began when the appointment was set up for Graeme to meet the client in Puerto Rico. I have the name of the client but let me talk to Emma to see what I can find out on the family. So, for now just research Jeffrey Lott while I try to locate the names of his family members. Angela interviewed Lott while she was in Puerto Rico with me and saw nothing out of order there. I'll drop an email to everyone to update them on the excitement here as well as ask a few questions about Lott."

CHAPTER 17

*A*fter a blissfully quiet night, Jill felt renewed the next morning. She went to the kitchen to make coffee. Agent Brown checked in with her as he made rounds. The agents had shared the shooter's picture with the local Sheriff. Deputy Davis had checked in with Agent Brown several times during the night.

Jill was anxious for the telephone conference this morning. She'd been thinking about the Puerto Rican client and was becoming more convinced that he was the origin of the problems for Graeme. She would check in with Emma to see if she remembered any offhand comment that her fiancé had made about the client.

"Emma, this is Jill. How are you doing today?"

With Graeme's estate to be settled and her own business to run, Emma had her hands full at the moment. The work was keeping her head above water, as she was immersed in grief. Talking to Jill gave her a few minutes free from the pain of Graeme's murder. She asked Jill for progress on the case, which was exactly the opening Jill needed to ask about the Puerto Rican client.

"Emma, can you remember anything that Graeme said about the attempts on his life prior to going to Puerto Rico? I'm wondering if the attacks started after he made the appointment with and travel arrangements to see the Puerto Rican client. A second follow-up question, do you remember any unease or misgivings that Graeme had regarding his client, Mr. Lott?"

"Graeme tried to describe the events in the hospital to tell me about the two attempts on his life prior to the trip to Puerto Rico. He rambled at that point, often not speaking in coherent sentences. I don't recall him saying that the knife incident or the shove down the stairs was a while ago. There was something in the way that he described the attacks that made me think that they had occurred the week before we left on the trip. I can't quote a specific statement he made. It was more an impression on my part," Emma replied, while pondering those last conversations with Graeme.

After a lengthy pause, Emma continued, "As to whether Graeme exhibited any uneasiness about Mr. Lott, let me think about that. He rarely spoke of his clients at home to me. He was in the habit of maintaining a client's confidentiality at all times. If we talked of work, we spoke about his partners or employees but never his clients. All I can say is that I saw him after he'd visited other clients both in the city and across the world, and his utter silence about this client was extreme. It was like he was trying to work through a problem either for this client or with this client in his head, and he couldn't clear his head until he came to a resolution of the problem."

"Did he indicate how long he had been serving this client or what kind of legal advice or paperwork he needed to provide to Mr. Lott?" Jill asked.

"When he mentioned that he wanted to go to Puerto Rico to meet with Mr. Lott, I asked him if the client had once lived in San Francisco but was now living in Puerto Rico. He gave me a vague 'yes,' and I let it go. It just wasn't important at the time.

Perhaps one of his partners can give us information as to how Graeme became his attorney. I'll contact one of the partners at his firm and see what information I can elicit. I hope that he'll give me some information about Mr. Lott and perhaps disregard the usual legal confidentiality afforded to clients. Let me go to work on that right away, and I'll email you later with any information that whoever I speak with gives me about him."

"Thanks, Emma; the people at the firm seem more willing to give you information. The one time I called, I got the usual litany on confidentiality.

They said their goodbyes and hung up. Jill thought with greater certainty that the Puerto Rican client was the one to focus on for the moment. Next, she contacted Angela to get her impressions, since she'd met the client in person. She got her on the first ring and updated her on the previous day's events. Angela had a photoshoot that she needed to leave for soon, so she could only give Jill a few minutes on the phone.

"I try to like everyone at an initial introduction. However, this man gave off a weird vibe, and I'm not sure I can tell you why. As you know, he said that Graeme had been in Puerto Rico to do a routine trust update based on new tax laws, and he seemed genuinely sad about Graeme's death. There was something else, though. I've been mulling it over since I met him but haven't come up with anything specific. Let me ruminate on it again while I'm setting up my photoshoot. I want to find the right words to describe his demeanor. I'll give you a call later when it comes to me."

Her friend wasn't trying to brush her off rather her day job took priority at this point. It was her art, her livelihood, and her joy. She would find the perfect words sometime in the next few hours to describe Mr. Lott.

Jill poured a second cup of coffee and settled in for her call with the people from the SFPD and the FBI. She was anxious to know if the facial recognition software had identified the shooter.

Agent O'Sullivan joined her for the call. Agent Brown was on post surveying the exterior of Jill's home. Jill had the security camera pointed at the hillside that the shooter liked to inhabit. She dialed the phone.

"Hi, any news of the shooter's identity? I may as well cut to the chase on what I really want to know," Jill said in a mild but determined tone.

"Jill, there is good news and bad news there. We were able to identify the woman caught on your surveillance. She is well known to Interpol. Her name is Aleksandra Gora from Albania. She is on Albania's most wanted list for crimes involving the use of explosives/weapons. She was arraigned in an Albanian court once but hasn't been captured in going on fifteen years. She is rumored to offer her services to anyone willing to pay an exorbitant fee. You have been very lucky to escape her attempts on your life. As a teenager in her native Albania, she trained to go to the Olympics as a shooter. Once the economy soured in that country, she began using her skills to support her family. For many years, she limited her activity to gun assassinations, but for the past three years, she's upped her game to include minor explosives.

"According to Interpol, you're the first target that she has missed in two attempts. Her previous kills are evidenced by a single bullet to the head. We don't believe that her skills have declined; rather you have extremely good luck in that you moved just as she fired the bullet. We don't want to depend on your luck the next time she gets close to you. She's rumored to sell her services for fifty thousand dollars a hit, so she has quite an incentive to come after you. She's not known to have any talent with knives, and therefore, we don't believe that she was the one who pulled the knife on Graeme. We've shared this information with your Sheriff's office in case she is sighted in your area."

Agent Ortiz continued, "This is her first known job in the United States. The central office of the FBI has put additional resources on this case given her status. Agents will be arriving in a few hours to both guard you and search the area for Aleksandra. Interpol thought she was connected to the Albanian mafia known for smuggling heroin and arms across Europe. However, recently the organization has concluded that she was strictly a hired gun. Besides being hunted by Interpol, the Italian Mafia is after her, as she is suspected of killing seven of its members, based on shell casings found at the scenes of those homicides. Her preferred weapon is the WKW sniper rifle made in Poland since 2001.

"She's unusual in her taste in that many of the world's snipers prefer the SSG 3000. Tracing shell casings left at murder sites to her is made easier by the rare rifle she chooses to use. Police psychologists speculate that she considers the casings her identifying mark, left at the scene so that she can continue to generate business as others note her past success. The question is, of course, who hired her?"

Jill felt like she'd been hit by a heavy linebacker from the NFL, flattened, lying on the ground, gasping for breath. She was in way over her head. Interpol? Albanian assassin? Sniper rifles? OMG! Was she starring in her own nightmare movie? She was a consummate professional when it came to autopsies. But seriously, she wanted to give her big-boy pants to someone else and curl up in her bed with her blanket over her head.

Instead, she went to her kitchen and retrieved a Belgian beer from her refrigerator that she knew to be sixteen percent alcohol by content, removed the cap, and took a giant swig at nine in the morning. Agent O'Sullivan observed her, alarm and concern warring with humor in her eyes. In the end, humor took over, and she lifted her cup of coffee to toast Jill's bottle of beer.

With a deep sigh, Jill re-joined the teleconference, "I checked in with my associates, and they haven't found a single issue with Graeme's partners. Angela was just heading out to work and lacked the time to give me extensive feedback on her conversation with Mr. Lott in San Juan. She is the only one of anyone involved in this case except Graeme who has met Mr. Lott. She wanted some time to give me a thoughtful summary of their meeting.

"With this new information on the shooter's origins, I'm going to have Jo examine Lott's financials, and Marie will search for information on all of her systems. Somehow, I think this case revolves around him. Something he told Graeme or requested him to do as his attorney. Graeme would be bound by attorney-client privilege yet still responsible to meet his client's needs. I asked Emma if she was aware if Graeme seemed troubled by Lott, but he rarely spoke of his work to her, and she had no new information."

Detective Carlson reported. "Overnight another body was located in a deserted area of the harbor. A San Juan policeman would like you to identify the gentleman. He suspects that he is Gonzales's accomplice in the encounter with you at the harbor. His murder was very similar to Gonzales's except that he wasn't left in the rain forest for animals and insects to feast upon."

Jill looked at the picture attached to the email from Detective Carlson.

"Yes, that looks like him, and I'll also check with Angela to confirm his identity. Do you know his name and what his relationship is to either Lott or Gonzales?"

"We asked the San Juan policeman the very same question, and he is investigating that answer. I hope to have an email from him before our phone call ends, and then we'll both know," Detective Carlson said.

"Let's move on and talk about the partners and employees of the law firm. By the way, Jill, we ran Graeme's family members through our computer systems, and nothing was highlighted as a problem. Likewise, we did the same with the partners and the employees of the law firm. There were a few speeding tickets and a couple of marijuana busts, which is about average for the size of that group so, at this point, we are focusing our attention on Graeme's clients. This is just a bureau confirmation of the work that you have already noted in your emails," Agent Ortiz commented.

"Let's spend some time talking about Lott. Jill, you mentioned in an email earlier this morning that you wanted to focus on him," stated Detective Carlson.

"Yes, I am shifting my focus to him. His is one of the four-hundred cases that have no appeals attached to it. Give me a moment, and I'll pull up the case document," Jill said, while she heard computer keys being tapped in the background.

Agent Ortiz broke into the conversation. "Jeffrey F. Lott, born in Pittsburgh, California, in 1950, retired to San Juan three years ago. Five-seven, two-hundred pounds, male pattern baldness with mostly a sunburned head. Glasses. Five marriages and four divorces. Married to current wife going on three years. Labeled a misogynist by the media. Tried but not convicted for lying to the public, and use of tax dollars to buy off the public, union bosses, and judges. He colluded with so many public officials and prominent citizens that no one could go after him without him bringing down the house. He is thought to have concealed some thirty-million dollars in the Cayman Islands from the northern California city he managed. Moved to Puerto Rico to be closer to the bank account in the Caymans and far away from the California Attorney General. And those were the nice comments about him.

"Basically, he was the smartest of a group of sleazy and corrupt public officials, so he escaped with the money and left the other officials to face the music. All these politicians related to Lott have since been voted out of office, and a few were convicted of some crimes. The community newspaper made sure that his reputation was so tarnished by the time he left town that he couldn't get a job elsewhere in the U.S."

"What kind of legal work did Graeme provide for Lott?" Detective Carlson asked.

"I am bringing up the case now," Jill replied, as she searched her notes. "It was a trust document. I wonder how Graeme got involved working on Lott's trust?"

"What are the dates on the document? Any sense of how long he worked with Lott? I remember the Lott scandal. It began about five years ago in a small city in the Bay Area. It played out in the newspaper for a good two years and then, as all the politicians were voted out of office, it died a quiet death. That must have been the time that Lott relocated to Puerto Rico," Detective Carlson mused.

"I'll explore whether Graeme's law firm had a role in Lott's dealings. As a new member of the firm six years ago, he might have been assigned to Lott by the partners. Perhaps he was trying to extricate himself from handling Lott's legal affairs. We have legal advisers at the FBI, and we'll have them review all the legal transactions handled by the firm for Lott. I hope to have an answer back about that this afternoon," Agent Ortiz said. "Let's schedule another call about mid-afternoon so we can all discuss any new information about Lott."

CHAPTER 18

*J*ill hung up the phone thinking of Lott. He sounded like a completely corrupt official. The opposite of what Graeme appeared to be. So, what was the connection? Corruption was one thing, but murder seemed like a whole other level of criminal behavior. It sounded like Lott had sufficient funds to hire an assassin to do his killing for him. He behaved more like an intellectual bully and white-collar criminal than a murderous one. She would see if Jo or Marie had any time to investigate him from a financial or personal perspective.

Just then an email arrived from Angela regarding Lott. In the rare instance that Angela had something negative to say regarding another person, her criticism was generally couched in the mildest adjectives possible. Jill kept that in mind when reading Angela's email.

'At the time I met Jeffrey Lott, I took him at face value, expecting him to express sadness over Graeme's death. He did express regret. But now that I think back to his actual words, I think he commented he regretted that we had to investigate his death, not the death itself...He tried to look down his nose at me despite the fact that I was three

inches taller than he was. Although I can't specifically tell you why I don't think he was telling the truth. Maybe there was a secondary meaning to all his words, I couldn't tell. I asked him for his impression of Graeme's frame of mind when they met, and he said "Graeme seemed preoccupied about something, and he assumed it was his upcoming wedding. He stated that with the faintest of smirks, which I hadn't thought about until you asked. I had my answers, and I didn't like the man, so I brought the conversation to an end.

'On a secondary note, he lived in a lavish colonial house with views of the Atlantic Ocean, a Puerto Rican version of the mansion that Graeme inhabited. As land was cheaper, the grounds were far more extravagant, and the interior had too much bling for my taste.

'If I think of anything more, I'll drop you another email. Got to run. Angela.'

Angela's email confirmed that Lott was worthy of further investigation. There was just something not right there. Jill did a search and located a picture of Lott. She decided to try a technique that she'd seen on television cop shows. As she was unable to visit her local office supply store with her shooter on the loose, she pulled out a box of freezer paper to create a sort of bulletin board on her office wall. She taped to the thick white freezer paper pictures of everyone involved in the case. She had a picture of Graeme St. Louis, Emma Spencer, Luis Gonzales, Jeffrey Lott, Aleksandra Gora, the as yet un-named man found dead in the harbor in San Juan, Angela, and herself. Then she rearranged the pictures to create a family tree, a visual of all the players.

It was late morning, and Jill had just gotten off the phone with Nathan and was starting to think of lunch. As she stood to go to the kitchen, the power went out. Oh, no. Aleksandra must be in the neighborhood. It was just too coincidental, and she hadn't heard from her in the last day.

Using her cell phone, she called Agent Brown, who was supposed to be outside on surveillance. There was no answer.

She ran up the stairs to wake up Agent O'Sullivan. Just as she reached the agent's bedroom door, she felt fresh air on her arms, indicating that the front door had been opened.

Jill slowly peered over the railing and caught a glimpse of Aleksandra. She was grateful for the carpet in her upstairs hallway that muffled the sound. She slid into the agent's bedroom and shook her awake.

She said softly "Aleksandra is in the house. Agent Brown is not answering his phone."

Agent O'Sullivan seized her gun, making sure it was cocked and loaded.

She tossed her cell phone to Jill, "Dial 911 and alert the Sheriff then phone Agent Ortiz and report the situation."

Agent O'Sullivan checked to make sure the bedroom door was locked and then looked out the bedroom window to see if they could escape. She pulled a rope from her bag of FBI supplies and tied it to the bed to brace Jill as she exited the window backward and she swiftly followed. It was awkward getting over the edge of the first story roofline, but Jill was glad for her arm and leg strength. The agent knew they couldn't stay there flattened against the house. She grasped the clutch piece strapped to her ankle, removed it from its holster, and gave it to Jill.

She then leaned in and said to Jill, "Do you know how to use it?"

At Jill's nod, she directed, "Jill, I want you to follow the house around until you reach the front. I'll be right on your heels but surveying the area for Aleksandra. When you reach the front, you'll have ten yards in the open before you reach the barn. Look up and see if you spot her. If not, sprint like it's the Olympics and take cover. Use the gun if you need to. Remember, she's an expert shot. If you meet up with her, shoot to kill because you won't get a second chance."

Jill swallowed hard and, following the agent's instructions, edged towards the front of the house. She heard sirens in the distance heading her way. She estimated that it would take one to two minutes for the squad car to arrive. She peered up and saw the edge of the barrel of a gun through the glass of the master bedroom window. Agent O'Sullivan also saw the gun and pulled Jill back from the corner of where the front met the sidewall of her house.

The agent contacted the 911 dispatcher to warn the approaching squad car of the shooter on the second story. The deputy turned off her siren, entered Jill's driveway, and parked the squad car behind one of the outbuildings. Jill saw from a distance that it was Deputy Davis. The deputy retrieved her bullet-proof riot-gear shield from her trunk and a rifle, in addition to having the gun at her waist.

Two additional sirens could be heard coming their way. Deputy Davis weaved her way around Jill's buildings carrying the clear plastic shield so that Jill could use it to defend herself from bullets. Yesterday, a Kevlar vest had been provided to her as soon as the agents began guarding her, but her head and neck were vulnerable.

They stayed flattened against the house, Agent O'Sullivan on one side and Deputy Davis on the other, sandwiching Jill in the middle with the shield mostly protecting all their heads from an overhead shot. They had slim cover from the narrow roof overhang above their heads. Aleksandra would have to lean far out the window to get a good shot.

A minute later, more cars arrived, two deputies from the Sheriff's department and the third an unmarked car carrying FBI agents that O'Sullivan recognized.

The moment the cars rolled to a stop, the officers exited the vehicles and ran to the house in an erratic manner in case the shooter was aiming at them. They entered the house and searched all the rooms.

Aleksandra had soundlessly vanished from the house. By the

time the house was cleared by the officers, she could have been in the next county. Jill's one thought was that she was glad that Trixie and Nathan were at his house while Aleksandra was in her house. She also knew that she would be moving to a safe house because Aleksandra was relentless.

Agent Brown had been located. He had a bleeding scalp and a concussion. He'd been tied up and gagged with duct tape, and he was unconscious from the hit he'd taken.

Why had Aleksandra cut the electricity again? It had given Jill the advance warning she needed to avoid the shooter. Jill called Nathan as soon as she finished giving her statement to the authorities.

"Aleksandra Gora just left my house."

"Are you hurt?"

"No, I was lucky. I'm trying to figure out why she cut the electricity again. That was the signal to me that she was in the area. Agent Brown was injured. She slugged him in the head, but otherwise, the cavalry rode to my rescue. I know that you were unhappy leaving me alone with the agents, but after the last thirty minutes, I am so happy that I didn't have to worry about you or try to get Trixie out the window and down the roof with Aleksandra roaming the house."

"What happens next? Jill, how are you going to stay safe?"

"Well, that is one of the reasons I'm calling you. Do you mind caring for Trixie a while longer? I'm being moved to an undisclosed location so that I am not such a sitting duck."

"Of course, I don't mind. I've been running with Trixie, and the pleasure of those runs seems to mitigate the presence of Arthur for her, though she still misses you. She's an easy dog to be around. Any thought on how long you'll have to stay in hiding?"

"I'm hoping for just a few days max. Now that Aleksandra has the FBI's attention as well as that of Interpol, there should be resources to apprehend her. Unfortunately, she has been successful in plying her trade as a sniper for years without being caught. She concerns me, but when the FBI takes her down, I bet that another hired gun will take her place."

"Another first! I have never dated a woman who had a contract on her head. Is this for real? Of course, it is for real, as the FBI is there, but the situation is so implausible."

"Imagine how I feel. If I told my story to a psychiatrist, I would likely get labeled as having delusions and being a danger to myself and others. Thanks for helping me find my sense of humor about this situation."

Nathan felt her smile across the phone lines. He felt better for cheering her up, and then he returned to the business at hand.

"I agree with you that another killer will be hired. It appears that the mastermind has hired three so far, the knife-wielder and stair-pusher in San Francisco, Gonzales, and now Aleksandra. If the trail goes back to Lott and he's got thirty million dollars to play with, then he can bankroll a few more hired killers. Will there be a way for me to talk with you by phone while you're in hiding?"

"Good question. I hadn't thought that far ahead. I'll need to find a way to keep communicating with you, my family, and friends that is not traceable to my physical location. My mother would be on a plane from Arizona if she knew half of what was going on. I've been entertaining her with stories of my quest for Moscato perfection. I haven't mentioned one word about this case to her. She's somewhat active on the Internet, and I'm hoping my name stays out of the press. I'll request the agents communicate with you if I can't do so myself. I miss you and can't wait for my life to get back to normal."

She packed a bag with a week's worth of essentials, her notes, her laptop, and a big tub of Red Vines candy. She needed comfort food in times like this.

She locked the house, set the alarm, and glanced one last

time at the vineyard. It would not need work for at least two weeks, and she very much hoped to be back by then. She got into the car with Agents Brown and O'Sullivan and departed for a safer location. She bet that the local Sheriff was cheering her departure, as her situation had required a lot of his resources and put the deputies at risk during the last week.

CHAPTER 19

*J*ill stared out the window as they drove toward San Francisco. She'd assumed that the safe house would be situated in the city closer to the FBI's office. It was housed inside an Internal Revenue Service building. American citizens had hated paying taxes back to revolutionary times and in the last century had taken to trying to harm the IRS. The building itself on any given day had a lot of security, which made it the perfect location to contain a safe house, or in this case, a safe apartment. She would have no access to fresh air. The unit contained two bedrooms, one for her and one for the agents to rotate sleep shifts. Another agent sat in the security room with building security, monitoring visitors. A fourth agent sat at the desk by which all pedestrian traffic had to pass.

As added security, Jill's bedroom had been outfitted as a safe room. She'd been instructed to go into the room whenever a visitor arrived at the apartment. Even if the visitor was an expected FBI agent, she had to stay in the safe room until she was notified that it was safe to come out. The FBI had taken her safety seriously. She'd been given a script to follow when talking to friends and family to make sure that she didn't accidentally disclose her location. Secure satellite phones were available for her to use. Calls made to her Palisades Valley winery would be forwarded to the FBI for screening. Jill could return any business or personal calls deemed important.

Jill phoned her mother and, following the script, told her how she could be reached, as she was having some work done on her landline wiring and the area had poor cellular reception. Since her mother was technologically challenged, she easily swallowed the deception. She also gave the information to Nathan. Nathan knew she couldn't be forthcoming about where she was, but he'd the means to reach her, and they could stay in touch. She was free to email as long as she made no reference to her physical location. Her calls to Emma had been reduced to every few days, so she could put off an explanation to her.

It was time to get back to the case. The apartment had secure Wi-Fi, so Jill planted herself on the sofa with her laptop and got to work. She'd lost two-thirds of her day to Aleksandra and her subsequent relocation to San Francisco. She had emails waiting from Jo, Marie, and Angela. There was another email from Detective Carlson.

Jo had written I have been reviewing the financial affairs of Lott. *Wow, what a mess. I think I could waste a lot of time trying to track the money trail for his years in office. But all of that is well known and in the public record. I thought instead that I would examine his finances starting with his move to San Juan. He has regular payments hitting his bank account titled trust fund interest. Those funds are a quarter of a million dollars every month, which adds up to over three million on an annual basis. No legitimate investment in the world gives a person that kind of return. Need some more time to run this down. Got to run, Jo*

It was great that Jo had a full-time day job, but for the first time, she wished that she'd Jo's full-time attention. She felt like she'd been left with a cliffhanger. Jill sent back an email thanking her for her work. She gave her a breezy update of her encounters with Aleksandra and added her request that Jo urgently work on the case. She truly wished that she could employ her friends full-time, but she'd never planned her second opinion on the cause of death business to be a full-time job. Right now, it was a race for information on who could find it first, the SFPD, the FBI, or Jill and her team.

Next, she opened an email from Angela. *She had one more thought regarding her interaction with Lott and had reviewed her notes. He said that he met with Graeme for a routine update of the trust. He said the trust rather than my trust. Which may be kind of odd? I'll keep thinking about my meeting with Lott, but I think I've emailed you all the relevant nuances.*

Jill had to agree with Angela that it was an unusual statement. She'd have to go back to the law firm and inquire as to whether there was more than one trust associated with Mr. Lott. Next, she opened the email from Marie. Her sources at times seemed equal to those of homeland security or at least what she thought homeland security might collect on a person.

Marie had sent a long email about Lott. She'd verified his impressive education. *His undergraduate major was biology. He served as a research assistant while at the university. He took a year off and served in the Peace Corps in Macedonia in 1980. He had planned to go to medical school but couldn't pass the admission interview. So, he was re-directed to law school instead. He then held a series of political aide positions. None of these positions paid particularly well. By the time the political aide positions ended so had marriage number two. Marriage number one had ended during his last year of law school.*

Lott then held two positions to which he was appointed. He'd been appointed by his local city council to advisory committee roles. He then ran for a board role with the local public utility. He moved on to run for the city council and was elected to serve four years but was not re-elected. About a year later, his ex-city council members appointed him as the city manager, a position he held for ten years (through two more marriages). It was during these ten years that he seemed to bully, bribe, or threaten nearly every public official with something. He knew their secrets and used those secrets to extort money or power and then do it all over again because he'd been successful the first time. With full city council approval, his salary was increased to nearly one million dollars a year. Likewise, his pension matched his highest year of income.

He set up a trust called the Ttolyerffej in the Caymans. According to newspaper accounts, he routed the money from the city to Albania. A city clerk had thought it a misspelling for the nearby city of Albany. The money moved from Albania to Iceland to the Caymans. With the collapse of the Icelandic banking system beginning in 2008, valuable paperwork was lost and the critical link between bank accounts disap-peared. The Iceland meltdown (no pun intended) allowed him to escape prosecution at that time.

Three years ago, a complete turnover of the city council occurred, and Lott was fired. The Attorney General worked out a deal for him to leave the country with all the money if he sold out the two most corrupt politicians. He quickly did so and moved to San Juan. Everyone cheered his departure, thinking that their secrets would be buried out of the country. He built a house and found a new wife. I don't have his most recent tax returns yet, but I expect to have them by tomorrow. My advice as a human resources expert is—don't hire him! Have fun with this, Marie.

"Fun?" doubted Jill.

The two agents stared at her and said in unison, "What?"

Jill peered up and said to them, "My friend Marie gave me the complicated history of Lott. Her parting message was to have fun with the information. Yeah, I'm having fun all right. I miss my man and his cooking. I miss my dog. I'm being shot at by an Albanian sniper. Yep, that is in Webster's dictionary for the definition of fun."

One agent, all business, ignored her meltdown and asked, "What's the complicated history of Lott?"

"Did you know that Macedonia shares a border with Albania? Our Mr. Lott served in the Peace Corps in Macedonia. Makes me think it's not a coincidence that the sniper is from the neighboring country. What are the odds that these two have a connection somehow? Give me a minute, and I'm going to insert this data into my software program and see what probability comes up for Lott being our crook."

Jill entered the data that Marie had given her into her software program, and the algorithm gave her a seventy-two percent chance that Lott and Aleksandra knew each other. It gave her a sixty-one percent probability that Lott was her criminal. She would concentrate all her efforts and those of her team on Lott. Lott was undoubtedly an unscrupulous character, easily sliding into white-collar crime at times. So, the big question was what information Graeme had on Lott that was worth killing for.

Jill provided an email summation of her findings so far to Detective Carlson and Agent Ortiz. Unfortunately, they were not as forthcoming with Jill as she was with them. She knew she couldn't complain given the level of protection around her at the moment. She could not have organized or afforded it on her own.

She did have an email from Agent Ortiz.

The legal experts in the FBI are still wading through the huge amount of information regarding the Lott case. The one comment made by one of our attorneys was that while Lott was still employed, he sought counsel with Graeme's law firm. Graeme is not listed as the attorney of record for that advice.

Jill entered this one new piece of information about Lott's relationship with the law firm into the software program. The probability that Lott was the culprit climbed to eighty-one percent. Now that was a statistic guaranteed to catch Jill's attention. She shared this probability with everyone involved in the case in hopes of generating a renewed sense of urgency and purpose to center on Lott. Both the SFPD and the FBI used criminal behavior analysis to help direct investigative work, but that was different than her software. She would ask what probabilities they were getting on Lott.

Jill made a list of the things she wanted to know about Lott to help her focus her research. She wanted to find the source of the quarter-million-dollar deposit made to his bank account each month. She wanted a list of all the work the law firm had done or would be doing for Lott. Included in that would be the names of the partners and employees that did work for the client. She wanted to track the relationship between Alexandra Gora and Lott. She needed to know if there was more than one trust. She also wanted to know if as a research assistant Lott had ever ordered bacterial cultures for the university. Finally, she wanted to know how he occupied his days in San Juan.

She thought that if she had the answers to all her questions, she might know why Graeme was dead. She shared her thoughts with members of her group, knowing that they were all at work and unable to provide her with any useful information until later this evening. She really needed Jo's financial expertise to track the money. She decided that she would ask Marie to research the relationship between Gora and Lott. She would take her final two questions and see what she could do with them.

Jill called the university where Lott had been a research assistant. "Hello, this is Dr. Jill Quint, and I would like to be transferred to one of your biology labs. I'm a forensic pathologist with a question for a research assistant."

Jill thought she was a lousy actor, so she tried to go with the truth whenever possible. It seemed to work in this situation.

"Yes, may I help you?" a male voice sounded in Jill's ear.

"Hello, this is Dr. Jill Quint. To whom am I speaking?"

"This is Joe Chan. You were transferred to the molecular biology lab."

"Are you a research assistant?"

"Yes, ma'am, I am."

"Thank you for taking my call. I am a forensic pathologist, and I have a question for you. Does your lab purchase bacteria colonies or agars in either the student classrooms or in the research lab? Do you order agars with specific bacteria for use in the lab?"

"Yes, ma'am, a part of my duties is to keep supplies on hand for teaching and research purposes."

"What company supplies your agars? Is there anything special in the order and delivery process because they're dealing with live bacterial cultures?"

"The university has used the same supplier for thirty or forty years."

"Really? That is unusual."

"I was given a history of the supplier when I first started as a research assistant because I was told that it was the only company, we have a contract with. We do so because the lab supply business originated with this university. Fifty years ago, we needed agars for much the same purpose as we do today. We were having problems consistently supplying our classrooms, which interfered with the teaching process. Two biology fellows at the time developed their own process for creating clean, ready-for-sale bacterial agars. They moved the business off-campus to a warehouse located in Albany about thirty years ago when the business became too big for the university to handle. The original fellows became the CEO and COO of the company and have passed it down to their respective families."

"And the delivery process, anything special about that?"

"Special how?"

"Do the cultures need to be refrigerated? Do they come by a special delivery truck, or do they come through a standard shipper? Is a signature required for delivery?"

"These are unusual questions, Dr. Quint. The agars are stored at room temperature. They're not supposed to be exposed to extreme heat or cold or bright sunlight. The company sends them via UPS. A signature is required to accept delivery. A copy of that signature is submitted with the bill for our agars to our billing department. Does that answer your questions?"

"Yes, you have been very helpful. One final question, when an order is submitted for an agar, are you required to prove that it is to be used at the university?"

"No, ma'am, we have been doing business with the company for fifty years."

"Thank you again for your help. I may have a few more questions for you in the future if you don't mind." Jill ended the call.

So, Lott would have ordered agars in his work as a research assistant for the university when he was a student there decades ago. Now the question was, had he stolen agars from the university supply room, or had he been able to convince the supplier of his university relationship? Who was the source of the agars needed by Lott, if indeed it was Lott? Was he even the manufacturer of this bacterial weapon? Had he done the work himself or hired someone else to experiment?

She would ask Agent Ortiz to investigate if Lott had left Puerto Rico in the last 90 days. Surely, she had a way to trace that. Next, she would try placing an online order with the supplier to see how strong its controls were. It was getting close to dinner time. Jill took a break and explored the kitchen. She hoped that it was stocked with wine. She could use a large glass after her adventurous day. The refrigerator had the basics: milk, butter, eggs, cheese, condiments, salad dressing, and a few bags of ready-made salads. The freezer was a single person's paradise, filled with frozen dinners, frozen pizzas, frozen soups, frozen bread, and frozen vegetables.

"Agents, what's the protocol for meals? Do we dine together?"

"Jill, you are on your own. We have scheduled shifts and time off and will take care of our own meals during that time. We have both been in this safe house before, so we are aware of the provisions."

"Is there any wine?"

"Yes, have you ever had two-buck Chuck from Trader Joe's? We stock all five varieties here. All the comforts of home. They are in the cabinet under the sink," Agent O'Sullivan said, with a huge smile.

"As I haven't produced my first wines yet, I can't afford to be a snob about the Charles Shaw winery. He's sold a few million bottles of wine. After I sell my first hundred-thousand bottles, perhaps I'll consider myself to be more his equal with commercial success. Until then, I'll gratefully drink a glass of two-buck Chuck."

Jill grabbed a bottle of Merlot and removed the cork. She poured a glass and allowed it to breathe. She went back to the freezer to study her choices. She selected a pepperoni pizza, knowing that it was a good complement to the Merlot. The pizza and wine fortified her for more research. She didn't think that Aleksandra had given up on her. Jill figured that she would make her next attempt tomorrow.

She'd asked her FBI guards about Aleksandra wearing a disguise to get into the building, and they had assured her that the facial recognition software would still sort through a disguise. Jill would look up what info Interpol had on Aleksandra. Perhaps she would be able to anticipate the sniper's next move. She was happy to be sleeping in the safe room as she thought she would rest better. She doubted that Aleksandra would be able to cut the electricity of this building.

She spent the next hour studying the crimes Interpol credited to Aleksandra. Damn, she was accurate. It was Interpol's guess that she averaged one hit every three months for ten years. She'd been less productive at the beginning of her career. She concentrated her work in Europe, Africa, and Asia. She avoided Australia, North and South America, and the Middle East. She liked to shoot victims in their homes and often cut the power. Interpol speculated that this was to reduce her victims' access to telephones, elevators, alarm systems, and security cameras. She had likely cut Jill's power from habit, a big mistake on her part.

Jill asked Agent Brown, who sat on the other couch, "Can you find out more about Aleksandra's hits from Interpol? I feel like I'm stuck with one-sentence summaries rather than the full details of her hits. Surely sometime in her career, she had a hit in a high-rise like this building. How did she arrange the hit?"

"Jill, keeping you safe is the sworn duty of the FBI. You don't need to worry about her next move. You're safe here," Agent Brown said reassuringly.

"So, Agent Brown, were you prepared to have Aleksandra knock you out and tie you up this morning? Since it worked, I would like to think that you didn't know of her style in advance. From the sketchy detail I can read in these cases, she usually takes out bodyguards in this very same manner. She never kills anyone except the person she's paid to hit. She seems to be an ethical sniper. Did any of your briefings tell you that?"

Agent Brown looked at her with chagrin, "Actually, I did know of her record of not shooting bodyguards, but I did not know that she typically strikes the guards from the back. Sad to say I know now."

"What else do you know about the way she operates?"

"Probably not much more than you do. I don't have the

answer on high-rises. Let me see what I can find on the Interpol computers," he said making a few computer keystrokes.

Fifteen minutes later, he sent her an Excel file that contained information about all of Aleksandra's hits. The list was full of data like time of day, day of the week, weapon, and bullet placement. They both studied the data looking for clues as to how she would strike next. She thought the FBI had a profiler, but this was different. Her only target was Jill, and the timing was as soon as possible.

Simple. Find the victim. Kill the victim. Collect your fee. Aleksandra seemed to disappear until her next job. Maybe she used her hit fee to remodel her kitchen. Bought a new rifle scope, got a face job to hide her identity. She'd avoided the police for over a decade. That suggested that she was as skilled at hiding in plain sight as she was at shooting.

Jill examined the hits by location. About ten percent were window-to-window. Aleksandra got across from the victim's window on approximately the same level and aimed and fired. She looked up at the windows in this apartment. The view was San Francisco Bay, so there were no buildings directly in front of her windows. Jill looked at Agent Brown.

"About ten percent of her hits are through windows in high-rises. I can see that we have a view of the bay. Can you get close to the window here and in my bedroom and see if she could get a shot angled from another building into these windows?"

The agent got up and followed Jill's request. The building directly in front of the IRS building in which they were housed was approximately seven stories shorter as was the headquarters of the San Francisco FBI. Agent Brown planned to ask their firearms expert if the marksman could hit the safe house windows. The agent had the requisite shooting certificates, but the physics of bullet trajectories was beyond his ballistics knowledge. It was a question of the bullet's distance, the wind, and angles. He sent a text to the ballistics division asking someone there to confirm that the roof would not make a great sniper's perch to hit residents in the safe house.

"Jill, the only building potentially within rifle range of these windows is the headquarters of the FBI across the street. It's shorter than this building, but I'll affirm that a hit can't be made from the roof across the street. I think you're safe for now. Aleksandra must find you first, and then she would have to make it through the highly secure FBI building to gain access to the roof. I'm expecting an answer from our ballistics expert early tomorrow morning."

"Thanks, Agent Brown. I'll move on to her other methods of gaining access to high-rise buildings."

Jill resumed her examination of the spreadsheet. Another tactic Aleksandra had tried quite successfully in about forty percent of her targets was to trip the fire alarms and in the ensuing chaos gain access to her victim's home. She had also completed two of her hits in the stairwell as the victim evacuated. With these hits, she didn't use a rifle, as it was too difficult to hide with so many people around. Jill thought that Aleksandra would try the fire alarm tactic in her present building.

The final half of hits came from her impersonating a delivery person. Her favorite delivery was flowers, followed by milk which Jill found strange as no one had milk delivered in the U.S. When the mark opened the door to her, she shot them with a gun with a silencer attached just inside the doorway. She made sure that the body was inside, left the delivery in the home, and then quietly exited the area.

Jill thought that this last method showed how relaxed and unsuspecting her marks could be. No wonder she was mad with Jill as the mark. There had been three failed attempts so far unheard of given her past record. She composed an email to Agent Ortiz copying Agents O'Sullivan and Brown with her thoughts regarding Aleksandra's probable behavior.

Jill's only unknown now was how long would it take Aleksandra to find her location? How did one go about finding an FBI safe house? She thought it would be next to impossible unless Aleksandra had planted a GPS tracker on her, or someone had followed the car containing the agents from Palisades Valley. Since she was now officially paranoid, she decided to go through her possessions to see if she could find anything.

CHAPTER 20

*A*leksandra had indeed planted a GPS signal device on the agent's car as it sat parked in Jill's driveway before she entered the house searching for Jill. She believed in covering her bases in case she was unsuccessful at this latest attempt on Jill's life. Surely the FBI would move her. It would be incompetent to leave her in her own home.

She picked up the GPS sensor and followed the car at some distance to San Francisco. She tailed the car as it exited the freeway. She wanted to make sure she didn't lose sight if it turned into an underground garage, and she lost the signal. She suspected that they intended to travel to FBI headquarters and was slightly surprised when the agent turned into the government building across the street. After the car with the agents and Jill turned, she continued straight and pulled into a parking garage four blocks away.

She thought that law enforcement might have her picture posted from video cameras at Jill's house which she was sure her face had been caught on. The city was windy, so she could legitimately tie a scarf around her face. She also put on a wig that made her a brunette with her hair pulled back in a ponytail. She applied an instant bronzer to her face and hands and completed the look with a pair of large, nerdy-looking glasses. She walked back to the building to scan the security.

America had added a lot of security around their federal buildings after the 9-11 terrorist attacks. Cement barricades prevented trucks with explosives from getting too close to a building. There was one pedestrian entrance with a metal detector and two security guards. She counted four cameras around and inside the entrance. She kept on walking past the building. She walked another two blocks and found a stone wall to sit on. She pulled her iPad out of her purse and connected it to the Internet. She pulled up the schematics on what she saw to be the IRS building and thought about her strategy to kill Dr. Jill Quint.

First, she needed to figure out where in the IRS building Jill was located. She looked at the FBI building and knew that she could hit her from directly across if she was on a low enough floor. Of course, that would mean that she would have to break into the FBI building, but she thought she was up to that challenge. Studying the schematics, she discounted the first fifteen floors solely devoted to government offices filled with cubicles. So, it was unlikely that she could use the FBI building to get off a shot.

There were two floors near the top of the building that looked to be more divided into small businesses or apartments. She eliminated the divided spaces that had no windows. If the people protecting Jill were keeping someone here for several weeks, the person would need a window. Through a process of elimination, she narrowed her choices down to three spaces on the twenty-fourth floor. She then reverted to thinking of her two favorite methods to get into the building, pull the fire alarm or make a delivery.

She was going to make a disturbance with the fire alarm. She studied the schematics again to decide how to make the maximum disturbance. Should she go into the building during the day when there would be more pedestrians to create confusion, or should she go at night when resources were reduced?

She decided that she would strike the next day close to nine in the morning when employees were arriving to work, and the public was lining up to visit the IRS. She picked the three places where she planned to set off an alarm. She would have to set off the first alarm before she hit the security checkpoint; otherwise, there was no way she'd get her gun into the building. She needed the fire alarm shrieking to cover up the metal alarm alert when she walked through.

Aleksandra contemplated how to get upstairs. This might be one of those buildings where the elevators were brought to the ground floor and placed out of order once the alarm activated. She hated to climb twenty-six flights of stairs, not because she was out of shape, rather it was the time she would lose time climbing the stairs and steadying her breath before she would have good aim at the target. No shooter could pant and have good aim. One always needed slow breath and a slow heart rate. Once there, she would have to go through each apartment searching for Jill. She could waste further time if she happened to be in the last apartment.

She pulled up information about the elevators from the planning department in the city, and according to the documents, she should be able to ride the elevator to the twenty-sixth floor. She memorized all locations of elevators and stairwells and their proximity to the three apartments. She had a variety of master pass keys, electronic credit card keys, and an excellent pick-lock kit. One of those three things had always gotten her into an apartment. Once she had her game plan ready, she packed up her purse and returned to take one more pass at the building in which she intended to kill Jill Quint the next morning.

Meanwhile, FBI agents were developing a plan to implement in case the fire alarm was activated any time in the next week.

CHAPTER 21

*J*ill was leaving nothing to chance. She sent an email to Agent Ortiz outlining Alexandra's modus operandi with a specific request that she be told how the agents would respond in the event of any of the three scenarios that Aleksandra typically used in her hits.

Agent Ortiz responded back, *Jill, our ballistics experts have determined that no shot can come from a sniper on the roof of the FBI building, so you can delete scenario one. A delivery to the building will never make it past security. The lobby guard, with the help of the FBI agent stationed there, has orders to immediately detain and hold any delivery person for questioning in your second scenario.*

In response to the third scenario of a staged fire alarm, I'll be arriving at your apartment in thirty minutes to discuss everyone's roles.

Jill felt comforted by the email. They were taking her analysis seriously. She looked forward to the agent's arrival.

Thirty minutes later she stepped into her safe room, while Agent Brown opened the door to Agent Ortiz. A minute later she was given the all-clear to unlock her bedroom door and come into the living room.

"Hi, Jill. How are you settling into the apartment?"

"Well, I would rather not be here with a trained killer on my trail, but the bedroom is fine, the refrigerator is well stocked, and there's wine on hand. So, I have no complaints with the lodging."

"Great. Let's discuss your email about Aleksandra. We agree with your analysis, as she seems to be a habitual person. Everything she has done so far fits her pattern of operation. I don't know when she'll locate this building and figure out which apartment is your temporary home. It could be that she knows now and has scoped out the building already. Let's plan on that. So, this building's evacuation plan is approved by the San Francisco Fire Department, a requirement of all high-rises.

"We can't just ignore an alarm and assume that Aleksandra is in the building. We could be wrong with a deadly outcome. She has to get a gun into the building through the metal detector or find a way in through a delivery area. We're locking down the delivery doors. They had good security already, but I made a small change to improve them further.

"I think our biggest vulnerability is that front lobby, especially during shift change. The guards will have to stand away from the metal detector so as not to block the exit if the fire alarm is activated. The sound is loud and will mask the metal detector alarm if someone walks through with metal on them. We expect those evacuating the building will have metal on them and thus set off the metal detector. I can't predict how vigilant the guards will be at securing the entrance. I've got one plain-clothes guard in the lobby now, and I'm thinking of putting a second guard in plain clothes back by the elevators. Depending upon the number of people in the area, two may be plenty or not enough."

"Given that you're on the twenty-sixth floor and she can't afford the time to walk up all those flights of stairs, we think she'll try for the elevators. We know that the elevators will be working even as the fire alarm is sounding. We'll make every attempt to grab her in the lobby. She rarely wears a disguise, but I think she'll this time. We provided our agents with her picture and some mockups of her appearance wearing a disguise. They're under orders to shoot her if she fails to yield to their command to stop.

"If she makes it up to this floor, we don't know if she knows which apartment you're in. She may have to search the other two first. If the alarm goes off downstairs, you'll be notified in this apartment. One agent will assist you into the bedroom to make sure you engage the locks. That agent will stand in front of the door. The second agent will stand behind the front door waiting for her to try to enter. The three of you'll remain in those positions until one of the lobby agents comes to your door to give the all-clear."

"And if there is a real fire?" questioned Jill.

"You all will still assume the same positions. We'll work with the fire department to find out if it is a real fire and to determine if that real fire is limited in scope and does not require evacuation. If evacuation is required, we'll try the stairwell on the west side of the building, as that stairwell is inaccessible by the main lobby without passing all of the guards."

Agent Ortiz looked at the three of them and asked, "Is the plan clear, and have I left anything out?"

"I hope to God, you get her in the lobby," Jill said.

"So do I, and I hope we capture her alive. I'd like to know who hired her."

Agent Ortiz wrapped up the conversation and got ready to leave. Jill was exhausted. The adrenaline rush of the morning had long ago disappeared. She washed her face, brushed her teeth, and dropped off to sleep twenty minutes later, secure behind the locked door of her safe room.

Early the next morning, she showered and dressed. There was coffee in a pot in the kitchen, and she reached for a cup.

Searching the refrigerator for breakfast choices, she selected a cheese and bacon quiche. She finished breakfast, cleaned up the dishes, and settled on the sofa with her laptop. She felt confident that she had Aleksandra as completely understood as was possible from the data collected by Interpol over the years. It was time to again focus her attention on Lott. Agent O'Sullivan sat on the opposite sofa also doing some work on a laptop.

Jill looked at the clock as it chimed eight. Shift change, a potential opportunity for the fire alarm to be triggered. Had Aleksandra found her this soon? She listened intently for about ten minutes but heard nothing, so she relaxed and went back to work researching Lott. She was intent on understanding the plea deal that he'd worked out. She couldn't figure out why he had been able to keep thirty million in taxpayer dollars.

Just then the fire alarm sounded. Strobe lights inside the apartment flashed. Jill started, picked up her laptop to return to her bedroom, and locked herself inside the safe room. Agent O'Sullivan assumed the position in front of her bedroom door. Agent Brown, who had been asleep in the guest bedroom, hurried out with his bulletproof vest and gun in one hand and zipped up his pants with his other hand while he got into position behind the front door.

In the lobby, chaos ensued. Aleksandra had played one more trick. She'd dropped a smoke bomb in a trash container. This gave the sense of a real fire and reduced visibility in the lobby. She held a shoebox labeled 2012 Tax Year so that she would look like the average citizen trying to visit the IRS. She'd put foil around the gun to make its shape less obvious on the scanner.

Throngs of people exited through the metal detector area. The alarm shrilled, and the metal detector was alarming as people exited with purses, lunch boxes, and briefcases in their possession. Perfect, thought Aleksandra, just the chaos she'd sought. She reached up to make sure that her wig and nerd glasses were in place. The guards were distracted by people chatting at them on their way out of the building. She supposed she could've heard the fire trucks except that the noise was so loud inside the lobby that it was difficult for people to be heard by the guards.

She easily slipped through the metal detector and walked toward the elevator bank. The doors opened, and people exited the elevator car. She set one foot in the car before she felt a hand on her elbow. She looked over her shoulder, prepared to say something, when her arm was pulled behind her. She felt handcuffs being slapped onto first one wrist and then the second. The shoebox fell to the floor, and the gun spilled out. The appearance of the gun caused a fresh commotion in the lobby. She attempted a sidekick to the groin of the man who had placed her in handcuffs. He turned at the last moment but took a hard hit in his thigh and went down.

Aleksandra, hands behind her back, took off running but found herself tackled a few steps later. She took a hard fall without her hands to brace her, wrenching her shoulder and splitting her lip, momentarily winded. She struggled to get loose, but too many people held her. She felt the wig pulled off of her head.

The man who had originally handcuffed her said, "Aleksandra Gora, you are under arrest for the attempted murder of Jill Quint."

He followed with her Miranda rights, and she was soon surrounded by at least five officers.

She knew that this was the end of the line for her. She should have known better than to do a favor for an ex-lover. She knew she was on Interpol's most-wanted list and that she wouldn't make it out of an American jail.

She had no intention of going to prison and had for years carried a lethal capsule of cyanide to take at the appropriate time. All she needed was to have her hands cuffed in front of her to carry out that final task.

She was searched for weapons and then walked across the street to an interrogation room inside the FBI building. Once inside that room, she was shown to a chair, and her hands were moved from the back to the front and she was re-cuffed with a chain to a hitch cemented into the floor.

Aleksandra asked for a glass of water. Agent Ortiz left the room to get the water. Assuming that she was being observed through a two-way mirror, she very subtly grabbed the tiny capsule from her front pocket. She habitually carried three capsules on her person to make sure that she could reach one of them when the time came. Just as the glass was put on the table in front of her, she moved her head to her hands, popped the capsule into her mouth, swallowed, and made a grab for the drink to make sure it ended up in her stomach. It would be all over in less than five minutes. No oxygen was being carried to her brain; her nervous system seized as she slid to the floor. Paramedics were unable to revive her.

Agent Ortiz was disgusted with herself and her team. They had searched her for weapons but not cyanide pills. They had subsequently found two additional pills on her person. Aleksandra would not be a source of information about Lott.

Back in the apartment, Jill had been released from her bedroom. Agents Brown and O'Sullivan were still with her. She knew that Aleksandra had been captured and was now across the street in an FBI interrogation room. She hoped that the FBI would learn something about Lott from the woman. The agents heard a knock on the door an hour later and opened it to Agent Ortiz.

"Unfortunately, Aleksandra committed suicide with a cyanide capsule a short time ago. We got nothing out of her before her demise. This was a failure on my part to instruct my team to search her for more than weapons. We wonder how she found this apartment so quickly. First we scanned your possessions for GPS trackers and found nothing. Then we tried the agent's car and found the tracker she'd placed just behind the front grill. We've notified Interpol and the Albanian embassy in Washington DC."

"Well, the world just got safer, given her success rate for killing people," Agent O'Sullivan stated.

"It's too bad that she died before the FBI could question her. I'm not sure of my next step. Do I assume that Lott will hire another killer to immediately go after me and therefore it's not safe to go home?" Jill asked.

"I've been thinking the same thing myself, and frankly, I don't have an answer. Since I don't have an answer, I believe it would be best for you to stay in the safe house while we resolve that question. Certainly, Lott could afford to hire additional assassins. I think we need to find the other people who tried to end Graeme's life and put all efforts toward understanding Lott better."

"If there's a new assassin after you, we won't know his or her style. The contingency plans we put in place to protect you from Aleksandra will continue until further notice," Agent Ortiz added.

Jill was willing to stay in hiding a while longer, but for her own sanity, she couldn't give it more than a few days. They would all re-double their efforts to find out the secrets of Lott. To take her mind off her troubles, she decided that she would create a table about what she knew and what remained unknown on Lott. Getting to the heart of his evilness was the secret to her freedom.

Jill emailed Jo, Marie, and Angela on the death of Aleksandra. She phoned Nathan but reached his voicemail. She left him a message about Aleksandra's capture this morning. She then called Jo, who was her key to understanding Lott's finances. Fortunately, Jo had sensed Jill's panic and had been able to arrange to take some time off work to focus on examining Lott's finances. She thought she might have an answer tonight.

Jo thought she could see a pattern to Lott's financial records, and with the additional analysis she would be able to confirm it and explain it to Jill.

Jill sent Detective Carlson an email asking if the second murder victim in Puerto Rico had been identified. Seconds later she received a response.

'His name was Luke Perez. He was twenty-eight years old and had had several brushes with the law. He was convicted of driving under the influence and suspected of selling illegal substances, suspected of petty theft with Gonzales while on scuba diving expeditions. So we know they had a prior history. We suspect that Lott hired Gonzales and Gonzales hired Perez. There are no unusual deposits to either of their bank accounts. Likely they would only have been paid if they had succeeded with their mission. We've come to a dead-end, no pun intended, with these two. I'm not expecting any further information,' Detective Carlson.

Another piece of missing information was the original legal action about which Lott had contacted Graeme's firm for representation. She asked Agent O'Sullivan if she'd seen a brief from the FBI's legal experts on the firm's work for Lott.

"I just got an email from our legal division. Let me see what it says," the agent proceeded to read aloud the lengthy message.

"It seems that the law firm has had a relationship with Lott dating back fifteen to twenty years. It handled two of his divorces, one DUI, two trusts, and the majority of the firm's work went for his defense for the extortion and racketeering charges by the Attorney General. The original relationship with this firm dates back to when Lott was in law school. Lott's classmate, Mark Lucas, became his attorney shortly after graduation. When the classmate died five years ago, the firm transferred the account to Graeme," Agent O'Sullivan read.

"What did the classmate die from?" Jill asked.

"It doesn't say in the email, it's just a notation as the cause of the attorney change."

"I'll do an Internet search about his death. I would like to make sure that he wasn't murdered."

Jill started the search on one Mark Lucas, attorney at law, deceased five or six years ago. She waited for the search engine to do its thing, clicked on an article, and started reading. He'd been found at the base of the cliff in Pacifica where he was known to like to run the trail in the early dawn. It was assumed that he lost his footing in the partial light and fell over the cliff to the rocks below. It was a foggy day, and the time of death was estimated to be just ten minutes past sunrise.

Well, Mark might just be another victim of Lott's, or it could have been an accident. Certainly, Graeme's death had looked like an accident. Mark Lucas's body would appear in the same condition whether he tripped and fell himself or was shoved over the cliff. She would have to accept his death as ruled, accidental.

"How long had Graeme been employed when Lott was transferred to him?" Jill asked.

"It looks like Lott was the first client assigned to Graeme. It makes you wonder if he was hired to be the fall guy for the law firm. By the date of Mark's death, there would have been plenty of time for questionable things to happen at the law firm. If he was reaching the end of his comfort zone in handling transactions for Lott, that might have caused him to miss his step on the cliff's edge a few weeks later."

"Would the FBI have reasonable cause to question a senior partner in Graeme's firm at this point?" Jill asked.

"I'll put that question to our legal advisors. Given the track record for attorneys with knowledge on Lott's dealings dying in seemingly unfortunate accidents, our legal advisor may be able to apply some pressure to the law firm to cooperate with us."

"Did Graeme defend Lott for the extortion and racketeering charges? Was he considered to have expertise in this area of the law?"

"Good questions, I'll forward them to Janet. She's the FBI agent who's been doing the legal review on this case," Agent O'Sullivan advised.

Jill obtained a copy of the case briefings for Lott's extortion and racketeering case. She had a sixth sense that this was where Lott's secret could be found. She would spend the rest of the afternoon reading and re-reading the case to decipher the legal language. She hoped that while she read, someone at the FBI would get back to her with some information about Graeme's law firm.

CHAPTER 22

$\mathcal{I}$t was getting into the evening hour, and she felt like she was brain dead. She was tired of thinking about this case, trying to understand the legal words and the source of Lott's behavior. She hadn't had a normal life since the day she'd met Emma Spencer at her home outside of San Francisco. She would have loved to settle into a pity party, but that would not help.

Likely her biggest problem was lack of exercise. There was nothing like the agony of exercise to shut down her mind and give it a rest. Maybe the agents could arrange for her to visit a treadmill somewhere. She would bet that the FBI building had a fitness center, and she would be safe there, right?

Thirty minutes later, dressed in exercise clothes and under armed escort from Agents Brown and O'Sullivan, Jill left her apartment for the walk across the street to the FBI building. During the walk to the fitness center, they encountered no danger. Ninety minutes later the Agents had to drag her back to the apartment. She had needed that workout. Her brain felt completely re-energized. She would shower, fix something for dinner, and then review all the data that she'd collected through the day. She hoped to receive an email from Jo in the next few hours.

Jill settled on the couch with a glass of wine and a beef burrito and watched Jeopardy while she dined. She loved the show and had wanted to be a contestant but had not passed the test. She was not well-rounded in her knowledge. She could blow away any contestant when it came to biology, but she was an absolute dunce for the music categories. She took her empty plate and glass into the kitchen and rinsed them out. The two-hour break from the case had done her a world of good.

In her inbox was the email from Jo. As usual, her research was lengthy, and her conclusions were brilliant. Janet, the FBI legal expert, had also emailed and a complete picture was formed. She now understood the source of Lott's wealth, the corrupt decisions, and why perhaps in his mind that knowledge was worth murdering for.

So, it seems that Lott's empire evolved from a single badly negotiated contract. The first contract that amounted to more than a hundred million dollars was a private-sector labor contract for emergency responders, the police force, and fire-fighters. He personally negotiated the contract, accompanied by his city's head of personnel. On the opposite side of the table was alleged to be the head of a for-profit security corporation. It is alleged because there is no record of who he actually negoti-ated with for the contract.

The emergency services contract had ballooned out of control. This small city in the Bay Area had the highest-paid police and firefighters of anywhere in the United States. It was also an unusual city in that the vast majority of cities employed police and firefighters as their own workforce. They did not enter into contracts with for-profit security companies for their police and fire services.

As a council member he had boasted to his fellow city council members that he was an accomplished contract negotiator. He was an attorney after all and excellent at skilled negotiation. The other Council members in some cases had not been to college and were intimidated by his level of education. As the employed officer of the city, the council members were happy to wash their hands of the situation, and as these police and firefighters were not city employees there was no impact on the voting public. Council members had no need to get involved, as it did not influence their public approval ratings with their voters.

Mr. Lott, in his infinite wisdom, made calculations in his head on the cost of the contract. There was no spreadsheet analyzing the costs of the contract. A letter addressed to the council describing the contract's services and its proposed financial impact was provided to the council, but the accuracy of that financial impact was not discovered for three years by the council. The security firm's provision of services as described in the contract was accurate. However, the number of people it took to deliver those services in the actual contract did not match those in the summation letter, a large miscalculation of cost for the city. The cost of the security firm's police and firefighters missed the estimated cost listed in the council letter by more than fifty percent. The hundred-million-dollar contract was spending at a rate that compounded itself to nearly a two-hundred-million-dollar contract. It was speculated that Lott knew of his miscalculation four months into the contract. While it was a mistake that should have cost Lott his job and likely his employability in the future, by letting it go undetected, he created a situation that appeared that he'd colluded with his city council overseers.

The city council members became aware of the problem just as they were running for re-election. It was a complete non-starter for anyone trying to get elected. To have so bungled the city's finances and not checked the work of the city executive was an appalling oversight. With three years of experience on that contract, they'd had plenty of time to note the problem and re-negotiate the contract. The city executive made a pact with the city council members since it was in both of their interests not to confess to the error. The private company involved in the contract was thrilled with the miscalculation and determined to let it ride as long as possible. It was the taxpayers that were wronged by Mr. Lott and his associates on the city council.

The council, Lott, and the security company needed a method to get it by the city's outside auditors. Lott approached his personal attorney from his collegiate days and bound him by the attorney-client privilege. He set up a dummy account under a trust in the Caymans a year into the bad contract. In return for keeping the contract in place, the city made a payment to that account in the Caymans, which Lott forwarded on to the security company minus a processing fee. He amassed three million dollars per year due to that fee.

Lott was brilliant in getting this by the auditors. An abandoned oil refinery sat within the city's limits. Significant lead and other harmful by-products of petroleum existed in the soil. He created a fake document from the EPA that stated the city had to set aside a certain amount each year for the Superfund cleanup of the refinery site. Coincidentally, the contract overages equaled the allocation recommended by the EPA for that site cleanup.

About eight years into this illegal situation, Lott was still in his job, the city councilmen had all been re-elected twice, and the security company continued to be pleased with the overages in its contract. The citizens thought they had excellent management of their city police and fire services of their property. This might have continued for several more years, but then the housing market and local economy crashed, and the city found itself trying to cope with a lack of sales and property tax revenue.

The city was pushed to bankruptcy and had its books examined by a different group of outside auditors when it failed to make mandated payments to the state-managed pension fund. One of the auditors was struck by the oddity of the city having to pay for the refinery's misdeeds regarding pollution. When the auditor pursued it, the whole scheme fell apart.

The Attorney General believed that Lott was the master-mind, but she ran into problems proving it. None of the city councilmen would provide any information about the case and they were protected by their own city attorneys hired by Lott. Furthermore, since the money trail died with the Icelandic bank crisis, there was no paper trail. Lott was believed to have tied up the local judges in the same manner. The Attorney General subpoenaed Mark Lucas after tracing some dealings back to the law firm. Unfortunately, he slipped off the cliff before he could testify, and that left the key piece of evidence, that original letter from the EPA, without explanation.

When someone inquired of the EPA about that letter, it replied to the city asking about the location of the bank account into which the city had been sending payments. That question started off a new round of forensic accounting by the state which spent two years of searching but was unable to identify where the money had disappeared to. Finally, the Attorney General sat down with Lott, and a deal was cut.

She told Lott that she could continue to examine and take legal action for the next decade. It was, however, in the city's best interests that he leaves the state. Rightfully, the community was the victim, and therefore, all the council members were recalled and removed from office. Lott's newly elected bosses planned to cancel his contract with the city. He was so corrupt, with so many connections, that it was generally believed that he could still manipulate city contracts. So, she'd offered him a deal to renounce his California residency and move to Mexico. They settled on Puerto Rico as a compromise. She also issued a restraining order that he not step foot in his former city nor contact any elected official.

It was a sweet deal for Lott. He was able to keep funds that he'd siphoned from his city for over a decade. It would stop the active legal prosecution of his case. Unless new evidence came to light, no further legal action would take place. Estimates were that he kept at least thirty million dollars. His life seemed the only one not wrecked by the circumstances.

It was a very long and detailed report from Jo, and it gave Jill plenty to consider. So, what if Graeme had come across proof that attorney Mark Lucas had created the original EPA letter at Lott's direction? He just had not been wise enough to see that he needed personal protection after confronting Lott. What a naïve guy. Jill thought under the circumstances that that would fall under the definition of new evidence. If convicted, Lott would lose all his money and spend the rest of his life in jail especially if a murder charge could be proved. This seemed like a good motive for homicide, as his entire empire and lifestyle could come crashing down. Now all Jill needed to do was prove it. Given the trail of people wronged by Lott, she thought she might get some help in her quest for evidence.

She wanted to examine two aspects of this case. First, she wanted some help locating whatever evidence Graeme had come across in dealing with Lott. If Graeme had discovered it, then the secret hadn't gone off the cliff with Mark Lucas. Second, she bet that some crack forensic accountants could follow the money trail beginning eight or nine years ago. The order had been restored to Iceland's banking industry, and new information might be available. The moment she could find whatever document Graeme had in his possession; she would be free of needing this safe house.

Jill had a brainstorm that Graeme might have left something in his residence relating to this case. She'd forged a pretty good relationship with Emma, and Jill wondered if she would allow her to go through Graeme's home office. She would see if she could set up an appointment with Emma in the morning and take with her someone with some computer knowledge from either the SFPD or the FBI.

Jill closed her laptop having arranged with Emma to meet for ten the next morning. The FBI had agreed to supply Jill with assistance for the search. The FBI had no warrant and therefore needed Emma's approval to search the residence. Emma was cooperating fully, and the FBI wanted to make sure that it stayed that way.

It had been a long day and her muscles were starting to ache from the workout earlier. She hoped she would find that piece of evidence in the morning and be home in the Palisades Valley by afternoon. After the excessive excitement of the past week, she thought she'd be happy to sit on the soil in the middle of her vineyard and watch her grapes grow.

CHAPTER 23

*J*ill entered the kitchen the next morning searching for coffee and a bagel with cream cheese. She prepared her interim statement for payment for Emma and emailed it to her earlier this morning. She'd been informed by Agent Ortiz that Agents Brown and O'Sullivan would escort her to Emma's house. Agent Brown was the local computer geek and would assist in examining any computer records. Emma had agreed to a full search of the house. She saw the law firm as complicit in Graeme's death by assigning Lott as a client to him.

Jill and the agents arrived at the mansion shared by Emma and Graeme. Emma gave them a tour and showed them Graeme's home office that included a file cabinet, a beautiful old-fashioned desk, and a computer. In addition, Emma provided the briefcase that Graeme had used to transport work between office and home. She mentioned that he took it with him to Puerto Rico. She also gave the agents permission to look through luggage, sock and underwear drawers, car trunks, and essentially any space that she could remember Graeme using. Jill hoped they would find something.

Emma and Jill retreated to an enclosed pool area to stay out of the way of the agents and have some privacy for their conversation. Emma had a check waiting for Jill as payment for her services. It was the most that Jill had ever billed a client, but it was also the most hours she'd ever put into solving a case. Jo, Marie, and Angela would be glad to see the increase in cash for their vacation accounts.

"Emma, how are you doing? I imagine a lot of your time has been taken up dealing with Graeme's estate. Have you returned to work?" Jill asked.

"I'm really heartbroken. I feel as though someone at Graeme's law firm knowingly assigned an unsavory and unethical client to him. Whether someone ever suspected that Mark Lucas' death might be suspicious and might be related to Lott, I'll probably never know unless this case goes to trial. I don't trust the firm and I have fired it in the probate of Graeme's estate. I did an interior office design for a different law firm in the city, and I feel that that they have more ethics and honesty than Graeme's firm exhibited.

"I went back to work this week. I had clients' interior spaces under contract to renovate. All my clients graciously granted me these few weeks to deal with Graeme's death and his estate. Now I need the creativity of design to move on. If the agents find evidence, then Graeme's murder will linger on for several years in the legal process. While that's a painful future, I can only hope that justice will be served in the end," Emma said.

Jill moved the conversation on to interior design. She thought in three to five years she might want a tasting room for her winery and shared that thought with Emma. So, she picked Emma's brain about tasting room interiors. Fortunately, Emma had been to several wineries in the Napa Valley and thought that she could improve upon the interior of ninety percent of them. Jill wrote ideas down and Emma volunteered to give her a gratis plan when she was ready to build. Jill had to bottle, sell, and have success with her wine before she set up the tasting room, however. It was something to look forward to in the future. She was glad that she'd had the creative discussion with Emma. It would give her time to consider what she wanted in a tasting room.

Jill thought the search through the house would take several hours, and she didn't want to monopolize Emma's time, especially since she was trying to play catch up with her design business. Jill had her laptop with her, and the entire house was wired for Wi-Fi. She offered to occupy herself with her own work if Emma wanted to return to her design studio. Thanks to Nathan's occupation, she was used to an artist needing studio time. Just as Emma got up to leave, they heard an explosion in another part of the house.

"Emma, take cover!" Jill yelled as she flattened herself to the pool area deck.

Another explosion rocked the house. They quickly determined that the pool area was not under attack. Jill wanted to check on the agents, and Emma was frozen in place.

Jill went to Emma and commanded, "I'm going to make my way to Graeme's office. I need to check on the agents. They saved my life several times in the last week. It's the least I can do in return. You stay here. Stay flat on the ground unless you see an explosion in this room, then run for your life. Call 911. Here's my cell phone."

Jill waited for her to nod that she understood, and Emma dialed 911 as she left the room.

The pool area was at the far opposite end of the house from Graeme's office. Jill eased open the door that connected the pool area with the main house. She slowly stuck her head into the corridor, ready to close the door if someone was there. She could see smoke and flames from the other end of the hallway, a long corridor stretching the whole length of the house. She heard no shouts or other human conversation coming from that end of the house.

Jill inched down the hallway, ducking into each doorway, and running across to the next. She'd worn a decorative scarf that morning, and she pulled it up over her nose and mouth to filter her from the smoke. As she got close to Graeme's study, she crouched low, first on her hands and knees, and then dropped flat to the floor, letting the smoke roll over her head. The air still felt pretty good six inches above the ground. She rounded the corner and glanced into the study. The house had a fire alarm and sprinkler systems that were both noisy and effective as the fire did not seem to be spreading. She thought she might have heard sirens in the distance, but the sound could have just been ringing in her ears from the explosion and the alarm.

Agents Brown and O'Sullivan were face down on the study floor. She could see no intruders in the study. Neither agent moved. At best they were dead weight. At worst they were dead. She eyed a small Persian rug that she could use to drag each agent out of the room. She pulled Agent Brown first, as he was closest to the door. She dumped him off the rug and into the main corridor and went back in for Agent O'Sullivan. She rolled the agent onto the rug and pulled her out close to Agent Brown. She checked for a pulse and found one in Agent Brown. When she couldn't detect one in Agent O'Sullivan, she rolled her over and started CPR. She glanced up to see Emma coming down the corridor.

"Emma, see if you can help Agent Brown. He hasn't moved since I pulled him out of the study, but he has a pulse," Jill directed while performing CPR on Agent O'Sullivan.

She thought she felt Agent O'Sullivan attempting to cough. She stopped CPR and checked again for a pulse. It was faint, so Jill continued CPR. She looked at Emma and Agent Brown and he seemed to be rousing. She sent Emma outside to bring paramedics in when sirens heralded their arrival. Just as they ran in to assist Agent O'Sullivan, she choked. Jill had spent fifteen years doing autopsies on the dead. This might be the first human she'd saved since medical school.

Paramedics had oxygen on Agent O'Sullivan and were starting an IV. Agent Brown also had oxygen on, and his eyes were open, but he was too dazed from the explosion to say anything just yet. Likely his hearing was impaired from the blast as well. She advised paramedics that they both might have sustained neck injuries because of being thrown by an explosion.

Agent O'Sullivan was stabilized and loaded into the ambulance within ten minutes. Agent Brown was coming around. The fire department confirmed that sprinklers had extinguished the fire in the office. The sprinkler head had been damaged by the explosion but still managed to throw enough water out to stop the fire from spreading. Emma spoke with the Fire Chief, and he had a piece of a bottle in his hand.

"Chief, you'll want to talk with the fire department in Palisades Valley. Last week, two Molotov cocktails were tossed into my house. A hired assassin was the source of that crime and she committed suicide in FBI custody yesterday, but I recognize the glass," she pointed to the man on the floor and offered introductions. "Chief this is Agent Brown from the FBI. Agent Ortiz is the person in charge of the San Francisco FBI and is aware of this case. You'll want to contact her. I'm Dr. Jill Quint, a forensic pathologist."

Emma was just barely holding it together. Jill had never seen someone who so appeared to need a hug as Emma did. Jill was not the touchy-feely type, but she put her arm around Emma's shoulders. She thought with some direction that she could get Emma over her shock and move her on to deal with the situation. When she was done talking to the Fire Chief, Jill suggested that Emma phone her insurance company and her alarm company to see if someone could help her with the cleanup. She also queried Emma about who she could contact to help her. An assistant? A sister? Emma took Jill's advice and made the calls.

Jill turned her attention back to Agent Brown. The paramedics were getting ready to transport him to the hospital. He seemed to be back with the living, but they would check him over for smoke inhalation and a concussion. She had a few minutes to get details from him on what had happened before they loaded him up. Again, she hated to be insensitive, but she wanted to know if the agents had found any useful information in the study. Agent Brown was hoarse from the smoke, and his hearing was improving but nodded that they had found something.

In a thin, wispy voice he stated "We found an email from nine years ago from Mark Lucas to Lott that contained the draft of the EPA letter. In the email, it is clear from the tone that Mark wrote it according to Lott's specifications. I had just copied that email onto a flash drive and printed out a copy when the Molotov cocktail was thrown into the room. If the printer didn't burn up, the copy should be in the paper tray. The flash drive should still be in the USB port of the office computer. We'll want to save everything in that office. Do not let any cleanup crew throw anything out," he lapsed into coughing as paramedics took him away.

Jill watched the paramedics roll Agent Brown to the ambulance. Both agents were lucky to be alive. She would go to the hospital to check on them just as soon as she retrieved the flash drive, the paper, and everything else in the office. She felt like she needed to guard the evidence with her body until the police arrived. The Fire Chief allowed her into the office, and a search turned up a wet piece of paper and the flash drive. She put the flash drive in her pocket and moved the paper to the pool area to dry. Then she moved the computer to the dry hallway. If by some chance it still worked, she did not want any more water getting into the device.

Just then Agent Ortiz arrived with Detective Carlson and Lieutenant Chang a few steps behind. She was very grateful to see law enforcement arrive. The SFPD had a crime scene to rope off once the fire department cleared the area. The fire marshal had preliminarily determined the Molotov cocktail as the source of the fire.

Jill looked at Emma and was glad to see that she'd found her composure. Jill had always been good in an emergency, and after the past weeks' shootings and other attempts on her life, nothing was shaking her resolve. She handed the evidence over to Agent Ortiz.

The security company had arrived and would coordinate protection of the property until the repairs could be made. Emma resolved to stay at the house, as the master bedroom was untouched. She would have a security guard outside, and her sister would stay with her overnight. She understood that the agents had found evidence before the explosion that would implicate Graeme's killer. Although this was the first step in a long legal process, Emma felt better knowing that the case was working toward being solved.

Agent Ortiz had checked with the hospital, and both agents were doing well. The doctor was keeping Agent O'Sullivan overnight since she'd required CPR at the scene. Agent Ortiz and Jill were headed over to the hospital now to interview the two agents and to take Agent Brown with them back to the safe apartment. The FBI deferred the crime scene to the SFPD, who would need to interview agents Brown and O'Sullivan later. Being close to Silicon Valley, it had experts that would squeeze any useful information out of the computer.

CHAPTER 24

*J*ill and Agent Ortiz arrived at the hospital. She was thrilled to see Agent Brown sitting in a chair at Agent O'Sullivan's bedside. Both agents were talking as they entered the room. She'd secretly been worried that Agent O'Sullivan would suffer brain damage since she'd had to do CPR on her. It was very gratifying to see that, at least on the surface, Agent O'Sullivan had not sustained any long-term injuries because of Jill's CPR. The agents looked up as Jill and Agent Ortiz entered the room.

"Jill, thanks for saving my life today! It's so strange that I would say that to a medical examiner."

"You're welcome. You're the first person I've saved since medical school. It was my privilege to use my CPR training for the first time in nearly twenty years to save someone," Jill said, humbled.

Agent Ortiz smiled and said, "Jill, the FBI is so grateful for your service. We were supposed to be guarding you and, in the end, you saved one of our agents."

"Okay, enough thanks. Let's move on before I am massively embarrassed," Jill said blushing.

"Guys, I retrieved the flash drive and a printed copy of the email and placed it in the hands of the SFPD for evidence," Jill commented as she took a chair in the room.

Agent Ortiz added, "The SFPD has taken the computer with them to their computer lab to see what else they can find that might be incriminating evidence against Lott."

Agent Brown reflected, "I'm rather amazed that the computer with evidence on it has had been untouched for all of this time. If Graeme indicated to Lott in Puerto Rico that he was uncomfortable with what had been done in the past, you would have thought at that point that Lott would have destroyed the computer in Graeme's house."

"I think this attempt to destroy evidence points to Lott's arrogance in thinking that he can't be touched. He must have been very sure that Graeme's death was well hidden in the necrotizing fasciitis diagnosis," added Jill.

"I'm interested in everything that is on that computer. I would like to put a warrant out for Lott's arrest as soon as possible. I think that as soon as we publicly discuss the recent evidence we collected at Graeme's house, it will become safe for you to go home Jill," Agent Ortiz stated.

"Obviously going home and being safe while at home is at the top of my mind."

"I wanted to check on my agents in the hospital and transport Agent Brown and you over to the safe house. Our legal team is meeting with the San Francisco District Attorney and the SFPD as we speak. As you can imagine, the Attorney General is keenly interested in this case. While they don't want to spook Lott before they have adequate evidence, we also have a strong reason to suspect that he has been on quite a killing spree. Whoever just tried to kill my agents at Graeme's house is still on the loose. The SFPD will have a guard posted outside of Agent O'Sullivan's hospital room until she goes home tomorrow. Its forensic team is looking for evidence.

"Agents, someone will want to question you, as do I. Tell me about your search of the house," Agent Ortiz said.

Agent Brown described the events, "It's a big house and we had a lot to search. In fact, someone needs to complete that search. I would estimate that we were twenty percent complete. We had not searched papers in his desk, or his file cabinet, nor the remainder of the office. We had not searched his briefcase, his car, or his suitcase. The file I printed was one of about thirty in a directory labeled ML archive. I had not had time to review all the files in that directory nor to view other directories on the computer.

"I was sitting at the desk directly in front of the monitor. The desk faced the opposite wall and if I looked to my left, I could look out the window. I wasn't admiring the gardens out the window because I was looking at the computer screen. Agent O'Sullivan stood to my left going through the drawers on the left side of the desk. I think that's why she took a harder hit from the explosion. She concentrated on her work, and I viewed the screen. Suddenly, the window shattered, and seconds later we heard an explosion. That's the last thing I remember until I saw Jill in the hallway."

Agent Brown looked at Agent O'Sullivan and queried, "Can you think of anything to add?"

"I remember browsing through the desk. There were four drawers on the left side, and I had gotten through the bottom two. I was just closing drawer number two from the bottom and was about to open drawer number three when the window shattered. The next thing I remember was waking up in the ambulance on the way to the hospital. I don't recall anything of importance in those two drawers. The bottom one was filled with manuals that came with electronic gadgets, and the one above had pictures in it that were labeled and had been taken at different scuba diving spots around the world."

Agent Ortiz thanked the agents for their description of the

explosion as well as what they had seen on the search. Agent O'Sullivan appeared ready to go asleep. Agent Ortiz motioned to Agent Brown that she was ready to leave. The three of them left the hospital room passing the SFPD guard as they exited. As they reached the parking lot, Jill looked at Agent Ortiz's car and had an attack of paranoia.

She said to the Agent as they approached her car, "You know your car has sat unattended in this lot for the hour we were inside the hospital. Is it possible to have it checked for a bomb before we get into the car? Perhaps I'm paranoid, but it wouldn't have been difficult to follow the car here."

Agent Ortiz sighed, "I hadn't thought of that possibility until you questioned the car's safety. Given all that has happened in the past week, it's reasonable to worry about if the car is safe. Why don't I quietly get the bomb-sniffing dog from the airport to go over the car? Meanwhile, I'll request that someone in my office transport you back to the safe house and join you there later once the car is cleared."

They returned to the hospital lobby to await the arrival of transportation for Jill and Agent Brown. Until Lott and his latest hired gun were in police custody, Jill felt unsafe out in open public spaces. She hoped the District Attorney would agree that there was enough evidence later today to take Lott into custody.

Their car arrived at the hospital. Jill got into the backseat and lay flat on the seat with her coat over her head. The ride to the safe house was undisturbed. Jill's adrenaline rush was really starting to dissipate. She felt a headache and extreme tiredness overwhelming her. She excused herself and returned to the bedroom for what she hoped would be a thirty-minute nap.

Agent Somerset had replaced Agent O'Sullivan which gave Agent Brown some much-needed downtime to collect his thoughts and check in with his family, something he'd felt he needed after this near-death experience.

An hour later Jill returned to the living room feeling a bit more human. She checked in with Emma and was glad to hear that she was doing okay. Agent Brown likewise had appeared to have fully returned to the land of the living. Agent Ortiz was en route to the apartment, the car having been cleared by the dog. Jill was pleased to hear that the unknown offender had not thought to go after Agent Ortiz's car. She subtracted a few IQ points from her offender for missing that opportunity.

A conference call was scheduled within the hour between the FBI, the SFPD, and the District Attorney. Jill hoped it would bring good news.

Sitting on her sofa with her laptop, she dropped an email to her friends informing them of the deposit to their vacation accounts and Emma's pleasure with their work. She also updated them on the morning's events and her hopes that the DA would find enough evidence to arrest Lott. She'd talked to Nathan earlier and shared with him that she hoped to return to Palisades Valley the next day.

Agent Ortiz joined Jill and the agents, and they set up a speakerphone for the teleconference. After everyone identified themselves, the discussion began with the SFPD findings from Graeme's computer. In addition to the letter that Agent Brown had saved onto the flash drive, an officer had found several other pieces of incriminating evidence, including multiple drafts of the EPA letter with Lott's revisions to it and threatening letters to Mark Lucas and a variety of other people if information concerning Lott's activities ever came to light. There was no murder threat, just a reminder that they would go down as accessories if they leaked any information on the fake EPA-required cleanup. Better still, a paper trail existed describing the bank accounts in Albania, Iceland, and the Caymans.

"We have hit a jackpot of evidence as to how Lott's corrupt empire was constructed. As the Attorney General was originally involved in the case, we have invited her into the discussion. While the San Francisco DA will take the lead on the Graeme St. Louis homicide, the state will handle the charges regarding the financial fraud against the city. The San Juan police will pursue charges for the Gonzales and Perez homicides. Finally, the FBI will direct the investigation for the attempted homicides of Jill Quint, Agent Brown, and Agent O'Sullivan, as well as for overall coordination between all law enforcement agencies.

"Judge Kamiguchi has issued a warrant for Lott's arrest that the San Juan police are executing as we speak. As soon as he is in custody, a press release will be issued jointly by all agencies discussing the arrest. Each of our public relations people is working on the draft.

"Jill, you and your team have found the evidence to crack this case. It all started with your accuracy and curiosity related to an autopsy. Today, you saved two agents' lives. You are a hero within our agencies and keeping you alive is more than a job. It's an opportunity to show a small amount of appreciation for all that you have done in this case. It is our promise and our mission. We need to keep you safe in this apartment until we can be assured that the person hired by Lott is captured," said Agent Ortiz.

Mostly, Jill was embarrassed by this speech. She hadn't set out to be a hero and felt that she had just done what any decent human being would have done. In a very private place inside she felt like her card had been punched for a free ticket to heaven if such a thing existed. That was all the satisfaction and recognition she needed.

She also wanted to give credit to her group. They had each brought different skills to an inquiry, and they had unearthed critical information on the case. Her life had been at risk, and the separation from Nathan and Trixie had been hard. Otherwise, she'd enjoyed the challenge of discovering what had led to Graeme's death. As a medical examiner, the dead had always talked to her. Not literally, but by the clues that they left for her to discover during an autopsy.

"Thanks, Agent Ortiz, but really I just used my skills while reacting to the situation. I would rather give thanks to the members of my team, who helped decipher Lott's financial, political, and personal connections. I would also like to thank members of law enforcement, as they have certainly saved me over the past weeks. Can we end the mutual admiration? I'm uncomfortable with that kind of thing."

The speakerphone buzzed in a new caller. It was Captain Rivera of the San Juan police department. Introductions were made so he would know who was in the room.

"As requested by the San Francisco Police Department, we arrived at Señor Lott's house in Humacao to enforce the warrant for his arrest. It is outside of our jurisdiction in San Juan, but the municipal police force was happy for us to coordinate his arrest. We knocked on his door, and a housekeeper answered. She led us to Señora Lott, who indicated that Señor Lott was not on the premises. We conducted a full search of the property and did not locate him. The maid indicated outside of the hearing of Señora Lott that he had packed a bag and left three days ago. We have no record of his exit through the San Juan International Airport. We contacted the Humacao airstrip, which flies charter jets, and he traveled under the name of Mark Lucas to Hermosillo, Mexico, and perhaps crossed into the United States at Nogales, Arizona. We lost track of him after he left our airspace.

"We are on our way back to his house to question Señora Lott, and we have frozen his bank accounts in Puerto Rico. We will see if Señora Lott has knowledge of Señors Gonzales or Perez. What can you tell us regarding the case there in San Francisco?" Captain Rivera asked.

Agent Ortiz replied with an update. While they spoke, Agent Brown ran a customs search on Lott and Lucas. It seemed that

Lott had stolen not only Lucas's life but his identity too. The SFPD and FBI would have to look in other places, such as the bank accounts, for the name Mark Lucas, as it seemed to be a current stolen identity favorite of Lott's. A moment later Agent Brown's search results came back.

"This is Agent Brown of the FBI. U.S. Customs shows him crossing the border at Nogales, Arizona, three days ago by car. I'm running a search on rental cars assuming that he ditched the car he took from Mexico. No record of him anywhere in Arizona. I'll check Amtrak and major airlines. Please wait a minute while the computer searches."

There was silence in the room as they all waited for the computer to arrive at an answer.

"Here it is. He boarded a train in Tucson and reached Los Angeles the next day. I'm checking car rental companies, planes, and trains. Riding a bus doesn't require an ID. It's about a six-hour drive from Los Angeles to the Bay Area. We lost him after LA. LAPD has facial recognition software embedded in its streetlight cameras, as does the SFPD. The problem is that it doesn't collect one hundred percent of images. It usually only collects pictures when there has been a violation, and it is only at busy or high-security sections of the city."

"This is Lieutenant Chang of the SFPD. We'll program our cameras to search for his image throughout the city. It'll take ten minutes for our system to start searching for his image. Please keep us informed of any relevant information from Mrs. Lott and let us know what evidence you collect on the Gonzales/Perez homicides. With so many serious crimes in so many jurisdictions, we'll need the courts to sort out where we prosecute him once we locate him."

The call continued, and elsewhere in the city. . . .

CHAPTER 25

*J*effrey Lott was a misunderstood guy. He'd loved each of his wives. They had each stopped loving him. He would still have been married to Susan, his first wife, if she hadn't freaked out so completely when he'd provided inaccurate income data and then forged her name on a loan application. The money had been for a good cause. He'd used it as a down payment for their first house.

She had said that she loved him enough not to want him to go to jail, but she couldn't trust him anymore. He still didn't understand what she was so upset about. Everyone lied on their loan applications, and furthermore, the loan officers knew this and expected some false information on an application, after all. Oh well, it was a shame that she'd died so long ago. He bet she would have been impressed with what he had now and the house in San Juan.

He supposed he could try finding his second wife, Rebecca. He'd searched briefly for her two months after their divorce, but it was as if she had vanished. The job, the apartment and even her name had vanished when he'd tried to find her all those years ago. That was before the Internet. Maybe with some effort, he could find her now. He made a note on his iPhone to Google her once he finished his business in San Francisco. He was a lucky guy. He wasn't paying alimony to any of his previous four wives, as two were dead and the other two he'd been unable to find since shortly after they divorced him.

So far, he'd contracted with a bunch of incompetents. He couldn't believe how many times they had missed trying to kill that she-devil, Dr. Jill Quint. Even Aleksandra had let him down. He had hired her a few times over the years since they had met and had a brief liaison back in his college years. She'd gotten rid of his third wife, Stacey, while on a safari in Africa a few months after she'd divorced him. Aleksandra was a brilliant shot and had evaded Interpol for over two decades. He was fond of her, and she mostly viewed the world the way he did. He was annoyed that she'd been increasing her rates with each job. After all, he was a friend and former lover.

She'd had the nerve to say that she was going to have a face-lift with the fee from this last job and retire from the business. He liked her face, but she was tired of evading Interpol. Every city was getting so wired with cameras that it would only get harder to stay free. She had more money than she thought she could spend in a lifetime. So, she was going to take up a new hobby, like running a pheasant hunting camp. She had plenty of guns and thought she would enjoy instructing everyday hunters on how to be a better shot.

The guy that he'd hired initially in San Francisco to get rid of Graeme had lost his nerve after two failed attempts. Lott included him with Aleksandra's contract to kill Jill. He'd been so easy to dispose of off the end of the ferry traveling from San Francisco to Sausalito using the silencer. Really, how hard could it be to kill one attorney?

Aleksandra had been unwilling to come to Puerto Rico, so he'd had to hire locals, and they were incompetent also. He should have known better. Gonzales was all talk and no action, and Perez's elevator didn't go to the top floor. Gonzales uttered lots of big words but had no idea what the big words meant. Lott hated to spend much time with such stupid people, but he'd thought he needed them for the job. They screwed that up, and he'd had to fly to San Francisco to finish off Graeme. He'd met each of them separately to pay for their services and had instead slit their throats. He hadn't even felt bad leaving Gonzales to be eaten in the rain forest, while Perez had been shoved into the harbor water to choke on the water and his own blood. Gonzales was a man with a small brain who had gotten eaten by a bunch of insects with smaller brains. Lott chuckled at that thought.

He was in San Francisco for the second time in a month. It was so easy to take a private charter plane to Mexico where a sufficient bribe to Mexican officials kept his travels off the radar of those in the United States. He knew the well-traveled route from Hermosillo to Nogales and enjoyed the nostalgic train ride on a sleeper car into Los Angeles. He always brought lots of cash with him, and he'd kept an open account in his first wife's name all these years so he would always have cash in the U.S. He liked to use the cash to buy guns and cars. When he was finished with both, he wiped the items clean and left the guns in the cars with the keys in a very poor neighborhood so they would be easily stolen. It was his version of recycling.

It was also helpful that he'd kept some of Mark Lucas's identity before he had that accidental fall off the cliff in Pacifica. He had kept his identity alive all these years and had even filed tax returns under Mark's name. He often spent up to an hour laughing each year before he mailed the tax return. The joke was on the IRS.

Just as soon as he took care of this problem in San Francisco, he thought he might never again return to the United States, and then he could safely end Mark's life for a second time. He had thought of going so far as to try and obtain social security disability payments under Mark's name but had decided that the payback was too small on that one. So, he'd just left Mark unemployed with no income year after year. He even had a laugh about that.

His college friend had thought himself so successful having joined the firm upon graduation when Lott couldn't find a job with a law firm. He'd gone on dozens of interviews, but no one had any openings. His friend had been reported as an unemployed bum for ten years on Mark's fake tax returns.

Lott knew himself to be a very smart man. He wouldn't even break a sweat evading police. It was child's play. In addition to his law degree, he'd been smart enough to tell a few small lies and amass a fortune over the years. He'd designed the perfect way to kill Graeme. His experience as a student running a lab at the university had come in handy. He knew how to kill with bacteria and had used it on Stacey in the bush of Africa. She'd been too far away from a major city hospital to be saved in time from the overwhelming infection. Aleksandra had booked the safari that Stacey reserved and had followed Lott's instructions and put the bacteria in her water, her food, and on a cut just like he had Gonzales try with Graeme. It had been her only non-gun assassination.

He'd also taken a chemistry class at the university as an undergraduate. He'd never forgotten the thrill of the chemical reaction that resulted when making Molotov cocktails. He had used that knowledge while serving in the Peace Corps to be a worker by day and a terrorist at night, blowing people up for the sheer fun of it.

He'd continued to use that knowledge over the years. When he'd served on that stupid city council and the other members had all wanted to come clean on the error in the contract for protective services, he'd had to bomb one of the councilmen's properties to demonstrate that he meant business when he needed the councilmen to stay quiet about what they knew.

After the demonstration, no one broke ranks to give evidence to that idiot Attorney General. Maybe when he was done in San Francisco, he would drive north to Sacramento and see if he could arrange a convenient accident for the Attorney General.

He'd used that same knowledge to bomb Graeme's house. He had seen a man and a woman in the study and assumed that the woman was Jill Quint. He'd learned on the news that he'd injured Agent O'Sullivan rather than the good doctor. Then Jill was being portrayed as a local hero, and he really hated that. How dare she be honored for saving the lives of the agents? She'd just been lucky to be there when he decided to bomb Graeme's home office to make sure that Graeme hadn't left any evidence behind on his computer. The news said the office was destroyed so he was sure it had done the job. He couldn't stick around to confirm that the job was complete.

He was sure that every rich person had a few skeletons in the closet. Literally. Didn't everyone have to kill a few people who were in their way to get ahead? He'd asked himself this question on many an occasion.

Jill Quint wasn't smarter than he was. She had been to medical school, and he hadn't. She just had luck. He was still smarter than she was, and he would get her in the end. Without her test results and testimony, the police had no case against him. He would return to the high life with Cecilia in San Juan. They had plenty of money, a beautiful house, friends at the local resort and country club, and if the sex ever got boring, he could find a new wife.

Lott had spoken with Aleksandra before she died, and he knew where Jill was staying. He surveyed the building now. She'd returned about two hours ago. He wanted to watch the building a while longer, study the traffic. He watched for another hour and then he figured he how he would go through the security screening to reach the upper floors.

He'd never shot someone, so he didn't carry a gun. He had a

ceramic knife that he planned to use. It was sharp enough to cause her to bleed to death, but it contained no metal in it, the metal detector stayed silent when Lott passed through with the weapon on his person. He also carried an empty pizza box that he had dug out of a dumpster, although he exceeded the age of the average pizza delivery boy. He assumed that Jill was in the same apartment as she had been for Aleksandra's visit with two new agents. The agents who had been guarding her were staying in the hospital at least overnight according to the news.

What he didn't know was that while he'd been sitting in the front of the building, his face had been recognized by the facial recognition software in a camera across the street. Police had been watching him for nearly three hours. SFPD and FBI officers in plainclothes had gradually replaced nearly all of the pedestrians in the area as well as the guards at the metal detector. They had an operation going in and around Lott. They wanted him to make another attempt on Jill's life to make sure that they had enough to hold him for a very long time while unraveling his actions over the past twenty years.

While he went through the metal detector without setting off the alarm, he didn't seem to realize that his ceramic knife could be seen quite well by the CT scanner, which had been put in two years ago after someone had tried to get this same type of knife into the IRS to hurt someone.

He took the elevator up to Jill's floor. Law enforcement personnel were in all three apartments posing as occupants. The officers had a much-rehearsed plan to welcome him in and give him enough rope to hang himself.

He approached the people in the first two apartments in the same manner. He stated he was meeting a friend who lived on that floor, and that they were going to have pizza. He said that he knew the floor but not the apartment number.

Each apartment door was opened by a disguised SFPD officer, the first a Goth woman in full make-up and clothing. Her aggressive stance and conversation put him off his stride. So, he moved on to the second apartment, which was opened by a thirty-five-year-old detective posing as an eighty-year-old gentleman who was hard of hearing and who yelled in a loud voice, making Lott repeat his question. It wasn't easy to appear to be stooped when you wore a bulletproof vest. Both officers had perfected their characters over five years of running ops and were generally considered hits at Halloween parties as well.

If Lott had stopped to wonder what these people were doing in an IRS building, he might have been more suspicious. They were likely not the profile of someone renting or owning an apartment in a government building. It was the best that law enforcement could do on short notice. Lieutenant Chang knew his officers well and didn't hesitate to pull them into the Op on extremely short notice. They had just had time to run home and retrieve their costumes.

Lott didn't stop to think of the unusual characters that had opened the first two doors, as he was so intent on finding Jill Quint. Instead, he had prided himself on how soon he'd identified that the apartments were not occupied by Jill.

He moved on to the third apartment. The lobby law enforcement personnel had provided a description of the knife that Lott carried. Based on his history, he would try to slit Jill's throat, as he was unable to kill her by infection or pushing her to fall off a cliff, two of his favorite methods of killing someone.

A makeup artist from the San Francisco Opera occasionally provided services for the SFPD, and an example of her best work was found in the final apartment. She'd used all of her stage props to make a detective from the narcotics look like Jill. The alterations to Detective Branson had Jill herself taking a second glance. Better still, Detective Branson taught hand-to-hand combat at the academy and was one of the detectives best suited to evading a knife.

Due to the lack of time, Jill was still in the apartment but locked within the safe room with Agent Brown for protection. Detective Branson was in the living room with Agent Somerset. Two more agents and two other SFPD officers were in the second bedroom. Cameras and microphones recorded all angles of the apartment and hallway. Detective Branson, imitating Jill, sat on the sofa with a laptop.

A knock on the door announced Lott's presence.

Agent Somerset headed to the door and asked, "Who is it?"

Lott answered, "This is Main Street Pizza with a delivery for Jill."

"We didn't order a pizza."

"Can you just sign a slip of paper for my records? My manager requires that for me to get paid for the delivery," Lott asked.

The officers gave him kudos for offering a decent reason as to why they should open the door.

"Okay, just a minute. Let me unlock the door," Agent Somerset said as she unlocked the door.

As she started to open the door, Lott charged through it and at Detective Branson. He slammed the door into Agent Somerset and threw the pizza box at her. Although he hardly touched her, she feinted like she'd taken a strong hit. Playing her role as Jill, the detective stood, dropping the laptop to the floor.

She exclaimed, "Who are you? And how dare you rush in here!"

Lott had wasted no time pulling out his knife and going right for pseudo-Jill's throat.

Detective Branson timed it just right, and as he got close enough, she kicked the knife out of his hand, spun him around, and knocked him to the ground. She slapped the cuffs on him before he could answer her original question. Agent Somerset joined her in restraining Lott as the officers from the second bedroom entered the living room.

She read him his Miranda rights as he fought, shouting a

variety of obscenities at her. He kept saying over and over that he was smarter; he was smarter than she was. She read him his rights a second time, but she couldn't quiet his litany of vulgarities. Until she could get him to say that he understood his Miranda rights, they couldn't question him.

Jill had reached the end of her rope with the case and Mr. Lott. She could hear his rantings from her bedroom. As the officer was reading him his rights, she knew he had to be in handcuffs. She exited the bedroom, and walked over to him and stood next to Detective Branson, and asked, "Which Jill are you talking to?"

Her appearance had silenced him. He stared at the two of them, and something must have broken through in his brain. After a long silence, he muttered "I have nothing to say."

CHAPTER 26

*A*n officer from the SFPD hauled him away in handcuffs with all but Agent Brown in tow. With Lott captured, Jill was free to go. It was early evening, but she still wanted to go home. Agent Brown was assigned to drive her the ninety minutes to her home. She knew the agent was tired from his close encounter with death earlier in the day. She checked with Nathan, and he and Trixie would meet them at the rest stop in an hour close to the halfway point of the drive home. That would reduce the driving for Agent Brown. As a physician, Jill believed that he needed more time to recover, but she was too anxious to wait until tomorrow to get back home. She hadn't wanted to stay in the safe house a moment longer than she had to.

She packed her bag and joined Agent Brown in the car. She was glad the case was at an end for her. With Lott in police custody, she would sleep well tonight in her own bed. She wondered what the police would find out once he was questioned. She'd thought him mentally ill with his 'I'm smarter than you' rant, but perhaps he was not, as he had clammed up right after his rights were read to him.

All that mattered was that the case was over, the check from Emma was in the bank, and she and her friends could plan their next vacation. She wished that it would start tomorrow, but she knew that they could not rearrange their schedules for at least three months to go on vacation.

It was dark when they reached the rest area. She pointed Agent Brown towards Nathan's car. As they pulled in, Nathan got out of the car and put her bag in his trunk. He then gave her a long hug and kiss. Trixie's head hung out the window and her tail wagged in ecstasy. Jill gave Agent Brown a hug, checking his pupils as she did. She wanted him to be healthy and safe on his drive back to San Francisco. On a close-up inspection, he looked fine, so Jill felt secure in watching him leave the rest stop.

She shared another short kiss with Nathan before Trixie broke it up. Dog slobber on the face caused an end to any romantic moment. On the drive home, Jill gave Nathan all the details she hadn't been able to provide about the last few days.

Nathan, as an artist, had not seen the violent world that she had as a medical examiner. He'd never been a victim of a crime. He was sort of awed and offended by Lott's evilness. He was mystified by Jill's reaction to it. She was clearly done thinking and worrying about it. He thought that he might be scarred for life if he had lived through what she had during the past few weeks.

None of Nathan's clients even had lives like Jill's. He hoped that this was a one-off case. He wasn't sure how he felt knowing that she was putting herself at risk in her pursuit of the truth of death as she liked to call it. He guessed that he would hang in there once she took her next case and would wait and see how he felt at that time.

Meanwhile, he was privately committed to seeing her pursue a black belt in one of the martial arts. There was a martial arts exhibition coming up in two weeks at the fairgrounds in Sacramento. There would be thirty different arts to choose from, and he would take her to see if he could interest her in any of them. He would enjoy teaching her his art or joining with her to learn a new martial art.

Jill heaved a mighty sigh as they turned into her driveway. Nathan had wisely ordered a take-out pizza on the drive home. The smell had been driving Trixie nuts even though the pizza was in the trunk. It was too dark to see the repairs that Nathan had orchestrated for her house to repair the damage done by the Molotov cocktail.

She got out of the car and despite having sniffed pepperoni for the last ten minutes; she could smell the sweet grapes coming from her vineyard. She couldn't wait to survey the vines tomorrow. She found it very soothing to trim each vine to make sure that each bunch of grapes got enough sun to manufacture the sugar she needed to create a delicious Moscato. She and Trixie would also go for a run tomorrow. For now, she intended to gorge herself on pizza and red wine.

Nathan caught her up on his life and local gossip. He also had some amusing camera shots of Arthur and Trixie. After eating, he took her on a tour of the repaired bedroom.

She sat down on her sofa feeling good about the end of this day. She had saved someone today. She had assisted law enforcement with arresting someone who appeared to be a sociopath with a violent criminal history. She checked her email for an update from anyone in San Francisco, but there were no messages. She guessed that everyone had their hands full interviewing Lott for various crimes. She would wait until the end of the day tomorrow for an update, and then she would seek one out if it had not been provided for her.

One moment she was glancing at her inbox and the next Nathan nudged her awake to get her to walk upstairs to her bedroom. She didn't budge when he slid into bed a few hours later.

She was out of bed at her usual obscenely early hour the next day, leaving Nathan asleep. She made herself a cup of coffee and cooked breakfast. While she'd only been at the safe house for a few days, she had hated not being in her own home. She and Trixie ambled through the vineyard searching for small cuts she needed to make or grape bunches that needed support while they grew.

They returned to the house two hours later just as Nathan got up. They cycled through his normal thirty-minute wakeup period, and after a little conversation and a few kisses, he left for an appointment at his own studio. Jill couldn't thank him enough for caring for Trixie over the past week. He mentioned the martial arts expo that he wanted to take her to in a few weeks as he left.

He'd a very busy day in front of him with several new clients to meet. In addition, one of his clients that he'd had a relationship with for more than twenty years was expecting him to fly to Seattle to discuss his labels later that afternoon. He would be gone for three days, and Arthur would be content on his own with enough food and water. His printing assistant would check on him daily as well. He hadn't been sure he would make the trip, as he had felt both helpless and yet unable to leave Jill by herself, although he hadn't told her that. With Lott, the sociopath, locked up, he could safely depart the Palisades Valley.

Jill enjoyed the quiet after what seemed like days of noise. She changed clothes to take Trixie on one of those hated runs. She hadn't run outside in nearly three weeks. She wondered how out of shape she would be. She would probably psych herself out on the small hills. Oh well, the only way to get back into shape was to face the devil of the two to three-mile run. She thought about Nathan's request that she learn a martial art at the expo in a few weeks. She would do her best to find one that suited her.

After the run, she did some yoga from a tape she had as a

means of stretching her leg muscles. She had a feeling she would be in pain the next day if she didn't spend a few minutes working on her flexibility.

After showering, she went back to her email. Again, no email from anyone in San Francisco; although the Chronicle contained a story about Lott. There was, however, a message from Jo and one from Marie that she had missed last night in her tiredness.

She opened the two emails. Oh, no! I thought I was finished with this case. She picked up the phone to call Detective Carlson. She got her voicemail, so she tried Agent Ortiz and got voicemail again. Wow, out of sight, out of mind. She tried Agent Brown and planned to quit just as she got Lieutenant Chang on the phone. Finally, someone she could talk to in person.

CHAPTER 27

"$\mathcal{L}$ ieutenant Chang, there's someone else involved in the case! Two of my friends sent me emails late last night, but I didn't open them until now. Lott isn't the only person involved. I think he committed the murders, but I believe that he was just the puppet in the theft of the city funds."

"Jill, we are on a break now from questioning Lott. Detective Carlson is in my office along with Agent Ortiz. I'm going to put you on speakerphone so you can explain to all of us at once."

"Thanks, and hi to the others present. As you all know, I think the world of the members of my team. Their curiosity keeps them going on cases even after payment stops sometimes. So Marie, who is my expert at finding personal details about someone, did more work on this case even after I considered it closed. She discovered a relationship between Mark Lucas and the CEO of that original private company that provided fire and police services to the city that Lott managed. I think the reason it remained hidden before was that Mark Lucas was already dead by the time the contract became controversial.

"So, the name of the CEO of the company is Lark Sumac. She is Mark Lucas' older sister. The siblings decided on anagrammed names when they Americanized their names. Both children dropped their last names legally when they reached eighteen. Their parents were politicians in the communist government of Albania. After a government-backed scheme bilked just over a billion dollars out of investors, a rebellion started, the country fell into anarchy, and more than two-thousand people were killed. Lark's and Mark's parents were two of them. Both children were outside of the country at boarding schools when the riots occurred.

"The parents had set up education accounts for them outside the country, which allowed them to complete their educations, and then the money ran out. The Americanization of their names made it more difficult for Albanians and others in the world to associate them with their parents. Lott came into contact with Aleksandra, Mark, and Lark during his service in the Peace Corps.

"Lark was older than the other three by almost ten years and was a beautiful woman. She married an older American by the name of David Schmidt who served in the military in both Vietnam and Lebanon. After he left the military, he owned a successful security company in the 1980s that specialized in training people in security and black ops. Mr. Schmidt suddenly died two years into the marriage, leaving Lark as the owner of the company. Schmidt Industries' success continued under her leadership.

"Lark paid for Mark's law school tuition and provided him with an allowance. It's rumored that she assisted him with getting the job at the law firm. All during this time, Lott socialized with Mark and his sister. It was ten years later that the security contract came up for the city that Lott managed. There were some rumors at the time that Lott supplied the security company with the scoring detail that the city would use to evaluate the bid, but this was before the era of mass electronic business interactions, so the bid process was handled through mail and courier. At least we know why the contractor stayed quiet concerning the errors in the transmittal to the councilmen on its costs. We can speculate why Lark was so willing to pay into Lott's account."

"Why did she stay friends with Lott after he murdered her brother?"

"Well, it seems as though there was no honor among thieves. Additional income was more important than her brother's life. She is one cold woman. While I continue with my explanation, can someone on your end trace where Lark is now?" Jill asked.

"We have been tracing her since you mentioned her name in conjunction with this case. She is presently purported to be at her company's headquarters in Virginia. We will put her face into facial recognition software. Just let me bring up her picture. Crap!"

Dead silence came across the phone lines.

"What's wrong?" asked Jill.

"She is the woman who just showed up claiming to be Lott's attorney. Jill, we'll have to reconnect with you later. We need to make sure that Lott is still alive!"

Jill heard the phone disconnect after that. She debated what to do next. She decided that there was no safe place for her at the moment. Lark operated a black ops company. If Lark wanted to go after her, she was dead meat. She decided to jump in her car with Trixie and drive to her local Sheriff's station. She figured that in the Palisades Valley, the one safe place for her now was jail.

She watched the road, sped, and tried to keep Trixie down on the seat all while looking frequently in her rearview mirror. She made it to the jail without incident. She heaved a sigh of relief as she and Trixie entered the ugly concrete Sheriff's station. She asked for Deputy Davis and was relieved to find her there.

Jill gave Deputy Davis a condensed version of what had

taken place during the last few days and the discovery today about Lark Sumac. Deputy Davis thought that Jill Quint was a smart, intuitive woman. She had seen the damage done to her home and thought Jill wise to come to the Sheriff's office.

They went down the hall to a conference room where Deputy Davis left Jill with Trixie. She wanted to update the Sheriff and get some water for the dog. She returned a few minutes later with the Sheriff in tow and the bowl of water, and re-introductions were made. The Sheriff secretly hoped that this was a one-off case for Dr. Quint after the explosion at her house. He hated to see his resources being utilized to protect her from the next group of bad people who wanted her dead.

The Sheriff called the SFPD to get a status report on the location of Lark Sumac. There was bad news out of San Francisco.

Lieutenant Chang stated, "Lott was found unconscious and with a weak pulse in the jail holding area about ten minutes after Lark Sumac was recorded leaving her client. Rather than the fast-acting poison that killed Aleksandra, Lark gave Lott a nutritional supplement bar that contained a lethal amount of potassium, which slowed rather than stopped his heart. As the emergency response personnel were unaware of the potassium concentration, they didn't administer the antidote until after CPR had been performed for over thirty minutes, which, by then, his heart was unable to come back, according to the physicians who worked on him.

"Our cameras show Lark leaving the building and getting into a black SUV driven by a male. She runs a black ops organization, so by the time we caught up to the first SUV, we estimate that she may have transferred several times into different vehicles and in disguise. She has vanished from San Francisco. The driver who picked her up originally is in our custody, but he's giving us no information, and there are no hairs or fingerprints to prove that she was ever in the car. We only have what was on tape. Her employee will probably be a dead-end, but we are remanding him into custody regardless. By the way, he's also an Albanian citizen with a legitimate work visa."

"Sheriff Arstand, this is Agent Ortiz, we met at Dr. Quint's house a week ago. Our guess is that she's heading to Palisades Valley. There's no reason to go after Jill since the case has completely broken open. We don't need her testimony about anything. Her company will be going down as will Lark herself, thanks to your input on this case. We're reviewing all of the cameras around the city at the moment, but so far, we haven't found her. We also have been unable to track her cell phone. Her company uses satellite phones, disposable phones, and international cell phones, which are very hard to trace.

"She also has helicopters and lots of guns at her disposal. We have called in the California Highway Patrol and FBI air resources, which are heading your way as we speak. Sheriff Arstand, what resources do you have at your building? People, equipment, and the like?" asked Agent Ortiz.

"We have a SWAT team organized for this region, but so far I'm not sure what or if there is anything that needs tactical support. Beyond that, we have more weapons than people. I've a total of six deputies on shift now and another three that could be here within thirty minutes."

"Sheriff, we're mobilizing resources from our end, and I feel much better knowing that Jill is inside your station rather than alone at home. I would advise you to question your deputies if any helicopters are sighted in the area as a start. Our own helicopters transporting ten agents should arrive in twenty-five minutes."

The Sheriff replied, "Well, that sounds like pretty solid suspicion that she's coming our way. Give me a few minutes to mobilize here, and we'll set up communications lines with you." He hung up the phone and issued orders.

Jill and Trixie were to stay in the conference room. All officers were ordered to return to the station and were advised to be careful in their approach. The Sheriff had his clerk and two deputies with him there. He would have liked to move Jill's car to a vacant lot, but he was afraid to risk an officer doing that.

Officer Davis returned with rifles, ammunition magazines, bulletproof vests, smoke bomb grenades, helmets, and riot shields. She wrapped a spare vest around Trixie. Doors were locked, and a third deputy returned inside the building with the news that a helicopter could be seen in the distance.

Jill's job was to maintain the connection with Agent Ortiz in San Francisco and report in. In twenty minutes, the friendly helicopters should arrive. Sheriff Arstand hadn't wanted to call for help from outlying cities for fear that he would put their officers in harm's way, and he thought it would take them forty minutes to mobilize and arrive at the station. The incoming force from the FBI should be enough manpower and it would arrive sooner. Each officer had a window to gaze out of, and there were cameras on the outside of the building.

Time was now nineteen minutes to the arrival of the CHP and FBI helicopters.

A single black helicopter approached the Palisades Valley looking for a place to land having spotted Jill's car. Aleksandra must have reported a description of her vehicle at some point to Lott or Lark. The copter set down in a vacant field about three blocks from the Sheriff's station. Time was now seventeen minutes. Three people got out of the copter. The three appeared to be heavily armed, dressed in all black, wearing body armor. The pilot stayed inside. It was unknown if any additional personnel were on board as they couldn't be seen through the tinted windows of the helicopter. Jill indicated to San Francisco that Lark's helicopter had arrived and the three people that exited looked ready to wage war, couldn't the FBI and CHP fly faster!

Agent Ortiz responded, "Good news was the FBI copter had been able to speed up, and the ETA was now fourteen minutes."

The Sheriff relayed through Jill where they could put the copter down close to the building. One copter would put down immediately, and the other planned to disable Lark's copter from the air before landing. She used radio and the intercom to keep everyone inside the building informed and the four deputies relayed information back to her to transmit to Agent Ortiz in San Francisco and then on to the incoming copters.

The Sheriff used a megaphone to speak to the approaching group of people. "You are under arrest. Throw down your weapons and lay face down on the pavement."

No one listened to him.

Meanwhile, Jill stated over the intercom, "Helicopter ETA twelve minutes"

Deputy Davis, a supreme markswoman, studied the approaching group and determined which hand was their primary hand for shooting a gun. She took aim and shot two of the approaching team in their shooting hands and followed that with a shot to their ankles. The two dropped their guns, but their boots had protected their ankles. The third person responded by spraying bullets at the station. Jill heard glass breaking and bullets pinging inside the building. The shots had slowed down the men and forced them to use their non-dominant hand for firing. Davis hadn't been able to get a decent shot at the third person.

Jill announced, "Helicopter ETA nine minutes."

Another Deputy hurled a smoke bomb through the broken window at the two men. They changed course and avoided that approach to the building. The original three had separated, and one person went along the side of the building, avoiding the smoke.

"Helicopter ETA eight minutes," said Jill.

In the far distance, the approaching helicopters could see the smoke coming from one side of the building.

The Sheriff announced the now-visible approach of the copters and spoke to Lark and her accomplices. "Throw down your weapons and lie face down on the sidewalk."

Again, they ignored him.

Jill's voice droned on over the intercom. "Helicopter ETA seven minutes."

Deputy Davis had swapped positions with another deputy and was well-positioned to take aim at Lark. She hit her in the hand on the gun's trigger, which caused her to drop her weapon. The two remaining deputies, who had been unable to return to the station before Lark's copter arrived, took aim at her copter. A bullet pierced the gas tank, causing gas to leak out.

Jill continued the countdown. "Helicopter ETA six minutes."

With five minutes remaining, Lark and her cohorts made a run for their copter. Shots rang out at them until they were out of range of the Sheriff's station. The other two deputies remained behind the cover of the building, well aware that they were outmanned and outgunned. The deputies had observed on Lark's employees the grenades, smoke bombs, the numerous ammo clips on their belts, and what appeared to be semi-automatic assault weapons. The helicopter blades whirred, and it prepared to lift off with the fuel tank dripping gasoline.

Lark's helicopter rose in the air as the helicopters from the FBI and the California Highway Patrol approached the Palisades Valley. The FBI copter gave chase while the CHP's copter landed. Jill heaved a sigh of relief that she and the deputies would make it to the evening. Agent Ortiz in San Francisco was relieved that re-enforcements had arrived in time to save the Palisades Valley Sheriff station and all its occupants. The clock had been running out. Thank God for the quick actions and precise marksmanship of one deputy.

CHAPTER 28

The FBI copter gave chase to Lark's company copter. The pilot had to know that gas leaked out of his copter at an alarming rate. One of the occupants aimed a rocket-propelled grenade launcher and fired at the FBI copter. It took evasive action, and the missile missed. A self-timer in the missile exploded it harmlessly a few seconds later. Lark's copter started to lose altitude, but it was still a controlled descent to the ground. It got about a hundred feet from the ground, lost power then nose-dived to the ground, landing in a cornfield.

The FBI copter prepared to set down at the edge of the field, not wanting to get too close to Lark and her rocket launcher. Unfortunately, the copter burst into flames after the hard landing. The agents waited to see if anyone exited from the explosion. The last thing they wanted to do was walk into gunfire. No one appeared to be moving, and they cautiously approached the blaze. It was too hot to get closer than about six car lengths. Jet fuel burned at a very high temperature.

Firetruck sirens could be heard, and the agents tried to put out the flames with the fire extinguishers that they carried on board the FBI copter, to no avail. The farmer who owned the land approached the agents on his tractor. The Agents explained the situation and suggested he tell his insurance company to seek reimbursement from Lark's company. The farmer had his San Francisco Giants cap off and stared in amazement at the burning copter.

During this conversation, the fire truck arrived, and the fire was extinguished. Four corpses had nearly been cremated by the heat. An FBI agent arranged for a cleanup crew to clear the mess in the field. The agents returned to their copter, landed close to the CHP's copter, and exited to join the others at the Sheriff's station.

Inside the station was one very relieved Jill. She thought to herself that she was proving hard to kill and that was good. She took Trixie outside for a quick nature break and then returned inside. She wondered if she had a house to return to or if Lark and company had destroyed her home. She asked if anyone in the group knew. Everyone shook their heads responding that they hadn't gotten close to her home in the previous hour. She couldn't ask Nathan since he was en route to Seattle. Thankfully he hadn't been around for this latest crisis of Jill's. She thought that he might dump her, tired of the drama defining her life now.

They all sat in a large conference room and were joined by members of police forces from surrounding municipalities. Once the station was secure, Sheriff Arstand notified those police forces of what had happened and the scheduled debrief. The Sheriff felt it was important to learn from any situation and he wanted an objective review of his decision not to request aid from those police forces. Someone at the SFPD and Agent Ortiz had initially been connected by telephone, but given the size of the group, the conversation volume was too hard to maintain, so Lieutenant Chang and Agent Ortiz would debrief later when they arrived in the Palisades Valley in another hour. In the end, the Sheriff had so many people needing to participate that he moved the meeting across the street to the city council chambers.

The media was also on the Sheriff's doorstep given the savage shootout. The Sheriff's station had the appearance of a building in a war zone in Baghdad. Fortunately, one of the FBI agents took the media lead, as the Sheriff doubled as the department's media representative. The mayor and other city heads were also at the debriefing. At the very least, significant repairs were required to the Station, and the jail itself was out of commission until repairs were made. The neighboring town had a mutual aid agreement with the Palisades Valley for exactly this kind of disruption to the jail. That town would handle any custody needs until the repairs could be made. First, the Sheriff, the FBI, and the CHP needed to have a large but private debriefing about the events of the day before anyone spoke to the media.

The Sheriff started by requesting Jill introduce herself and tell her story.

With the faithful Trixie sitting at her side, she spoke. "I'm Dr. Jill Quint and the cause of all this mess at the Palisades Valley Sheriff's station. I spent fifteen years in the county crime lab as a forensic pathologist. Now I'm growing grapes and consulting with families who wish to have a second opinion on the cause of death of a loved one. I never had any kind of criminal go after me until this case.

"I retired to quietly grow grapes here five years ago but kept my hand in my old profession by doing consulting work. Family members hire me to confirm a cause of death as determined by their local medical examiner or physician. I work on cases across the nation. I also work with three other women who provide investigative research into the deceased's life, and they turn up some interesting details.

"As you can imagine, I usually must rush to a new job, as I need to evaluate the deceased before the burial process begins.

So, my work is unpredictable, and in fact, I hope I don't catch another case before repairs are complete at the Sheriff's station.

"Before I tell you about this case, I would like to thank the Palisades Valley Sheriff, as well as the California Highway Patrol and the FBI. Trixie and I are alive and well thanks to their collective skill. I watched the Sheriff mobilize resources in a very short time and Deputy Davis is the most amazing markswoman."

Jill turned and applauded the Sheriff and the team that rescued her. The whole assembly joined in with her embarrassing the humble Sheriff. Once the applause died down, she began her story.

"A few weeks ago, I was hired by a client from the San Francisco suburb of Woodport to investigate the death of her fiancé, Graeme St. Louis, a young attorney, shortly after a scuba diving misadventure in Puerto Rico. He seemingly died of septic shock caused by necrotizing fasciitis."

She took a minute to explain the disease in layman's terms to the assembled group.

"Through microbiology studies of his body and the amputated leg, I was able to convince the San Francisco medical examiner to revise the cause of death to homicide by infection, and the SFPD opened the case, as the death was in its jurisdiction. The original killer, in this case, was Jeffery Lott, who had been a research assistant in college and knew how to obtain and cultivate the bacteria that caused the infection. You may recognize that name from about four years ago when a Bay Area city he managed was investigated by the Attorney General for extortion and racketeering and misuse of taxpayer funds.

"He hired someone in Puerto Rico to pose as a fake divemaster. That divemaster first made an attempt to send the victim into the water with a tank that appeared full but was probably close to empty. When that failed, he shoved the victim into the coral, thus causing a wound that required antibiotic ointment from a first aid kit aboard the dive boat. That ointment was intentionally inoculated with bacteria. The victim cut short his trip to Puerto Rico because his leg was red and swollen. He went right from the airport to University Hospital in San Francisco. He had turned the corner and was improving when, in the middle of the night before he was due to be discharged, we believe Mr. Lott entered his room and injected him with another dose of the bacteria. I identified this by the biomarker of the bacteria. This could not have been an accident or a case of unwashed hands on the part of hospital personnel. The bacterial DNA and growth pattern could only point to something intentional like homicide.

"While I could prove that this was a homicide, I didn't know who or why. So my team and I went to work and investigated the deceased's law practice, his family, his friends, his whole life. Our investigation eventually led us to one of his clients, Jeffery Lott. One of my team members is an amazing whiz with finances and another is brilliant at locating personal information about anyone. Meanwhile, in San Juan, two people connected to this case turned up dead. That was followed by a series of sniper attempts at my home, including one from an Albanian sniper from whom Deputy Davis was able to protect me. The FBI entered the case based on the wide geographies in which connected crimes were being committed as well as the federal law violations.

"For my own safety, I was relocated to a safe house with FBI guards in San Francisco. The Albanian sniper was apprehended but committed suicide while in FBI custody. Lott himself came after me at the safe house as well and was arrested by the SFPD. He was poisoned soon after he arrived in jail by his fake attorney, who arrived to represent him. Lott's fake attorney happened to be the CEO of a security and black ops training company named Lark Sumac. After she finished off Lott, she and her associates were suspected to have taken off in a helicopter for the Palisades Valley to end my life. When I heard that Lott had been murdered at the jail, I knew that my own safety was at risk. So, I got in my car with my dog and drove to the Sheriff's station.

"The FBI and the California Highway Patrol put helicopters in the air to chase the black ops helicopter they believed to be heading in this direction. We had somewhere between ten and fifteen minutes to survive an assault by the black ops team. Those were the longest minutes of my life. We barricaded ourselves in the station. The Sheriff was able to call two deputies in from the field before the copter arrived. We suffered a barrage of bullets to the station. Deputy Davis accurately shot all three assailants in their dominant hands. These actions held them off long enough for the re-enforcements, in the form of two helicopters, to arrive. The company helicopter took off, and the FBI followed it while the California Highway Patrol assisted us inside the Sheriff's station.

"There are more details about the suspects in this case, but I think those are the highlights. I would again like to thank Sheriff Arstand, Deputy Davis, and indeed everyone in this room for helping me stay alive long enough to watch the sunset tonight."

Jill was finally overcome by emotion and had to kneel and hug Trixie while she regained her composure. Agent Ortiz, Lieutenant Chang, and Detective Carlson arrived just as she finished her story. Now it was time for Sheriff Arstand to discuss what could have gone better today and what could be done in the future. In the back of his mind, a small voice told him that Jill Quint might require the same level of protection sometime in the future. Although he had just met her, he much appreciated her passion for the truth and the justice system.

Jill sat down with Trixie in the back of the council chambers. A headache burned in the back of her eyes, and surprisingly she was hungry. She looked around the council chambers and decided that there were forty to fifty people there. She knew the owner of the bakery down the street. She hurried to the bakery and asked the woman behind the counter what could be delivered for fifty people. After negotiating the price, she expected a quick delivery of cookies, muffins, bread, cold cuts, cheese, and cold drinks. The bakery would close for the day after she bought it out.

She returned to the chambers and the discussion centered on the Sheriff's decision not to request the help of other local law enforcement agencies. In the end, members of those agencies agreed that small contingents of officers would have resulted in additional injuries. If the copters hadn't been so close to arrival, then a different strategy would have been required. The assembled group moved on to a discussion of defending the station.

Just then the food was delivered, and a quick break was taken before the debriefing continued. With food onboard, she felt her brain cells returning and tuned back into the discussion. She hoped that she would never need the Sheriff to perfect this operation, but she somehow thought that the publicity would bring new cases and new maniacs into her realm.

She concluded that her presence was no longer required. She would make sure she took plenty of opportunities in public to thank her local Sheriff and his staff. She whispered to Agent Ortiz that she was leaving to go check on her home.

CHAPTER 29

$\mathcal{S}$he went outside to discover that her beloved '56
Thunderbird had suffered from the flying bullets. Just
as Lark and her men had fired many shots at the station, her car
had also got caught in the crossfire. She could have cried at her
beautiful car looking so damaged. All the windows were shattered, the convertible roof had holes in it, and the paint was
chipped. But the tires were still good.

She got on her cell phone and arranged to have a rental car
delivered to her at the Sheriff's station, then phoned her
mechanic in town to explain the situation. Her insurance would
cover the damage, or perhaps a crime victim fund would, but
first, she wanted the car protected while her insurance worked
on getting the repairs authorized. Her mechanic would collect
the car and store it for her until she could move ahead with
repairs. He loved the car nearly as much as she did.

While she waited for a loaner car, she called her mother in
Arizona to tell her the story. She needed to hear that her
daughter was safe before hearing of the incident in the media.
At first, her mother hadn't believed her because the story was so
strange. However, the story had come on her mother's local

news station, and she wanted to listen to the TV. Assured that her daughter was fine, and they ended the call with a plan to talk later that evening.

With the old car towed away and the loaner car delivered, Trixie and Jill were set to make the drive home. Jill was very apprehensive about what she would find. At worse, her house would be burned to the ground. Possibly it would have bullet holes in the windows and perhaps a rocket launched at it. The best-case scenario was that it was fully intact with no apparent change. As she drove, she saw a call come in from Nathan. She had left him a voicemail to contact her upon landing, hoping he wouldn't hear of her shootout on an airport TV.

As he was up to speed on the case, she only needed to update him about Lark and the episode at the Sheriff's station. This time she didn't hold back in her description of events, as she knew that he would see the story on the news. She reached her driveway as she was three-quarters of the way through the story. She paused in her conversation as she turned through her gates and approached the house. She had gratefully seen the house from the road. Now she could see that it was unharmed. Lark's copter must have landed, discovered her absence, and then took off searching for her car on nearby roads or in town.

She exited the car and settled on her front stoop. Trixie made a run around the property checking the smells out. She finished telling Nathan the story as well as commented that her property was unharmed. There was dead silence on his end for a minute.

Finally, he formed words. "Wow, just when I have heard the peak of your crazy story with this case, you find a weirder angle still to add. I've known Sheriff Arstand for at least ten years, and the next time I see him I'll thank him for saving your life. I must tell you that I'm having a hard time comprehending how crazy your life got during the past four hours. Frankly, if I had been unaware of the whole strange story, I would not believe your description of what just happened. I'd be getting you help from mental health experts for your hallucinations. I'm frustrated that I'm two-thousand miles away in Seattle and not there to help you. I have a second car. It's not the best, but you can borrow it to get rid of that rental car.

"I was planning on returning home in two more days, but I feel that I need to come back this evening. I care deeply for you, and I feel bad that I haven't been with you when you needed help the most over these past several days."

Jill was stunned at this revelation.

"Nathan, wow! I'm relieved to hear you say all that. I was afraid you were going to dump me as your girlfriend after I told you about this latest incident. I'm sort of scary girlfriend material these days."

"Jill, I realize that your work giving others a second opinion is intellectually important to your soul, and I respect that. While I don't like all the dangerous situations you have been in during the last couple of weeks, they're not situations of your making. You're the victim here. Besides, since we've been dating, you had ten other cases in which no one tried to kill you. So, let's hope that your caseload goes back to normal," Nathan said with a laugh.

"I'm back at home now, and from what I can see on the outside, Lark and company did not damage my house. However, I'm taking a walk-through now just to make sure. Certainly, in the distance, the vineyard appears untouched. I'll go over to the wine cellar and my lab to make sure everything is in working order. Why don't you give me a call later tonight after you have reached your destination and had a relaxing meal with your client? I think you should stay in Washington, I'm fine here. I need to go inside and make some coffee. The adrenaline rush of two hours ago is dying a very quick death inside me," Jill ended the conversation.

Jill saw nothing disturbed in the house. She wondered if the helicopter had even been to her home. As she looked around the land, there were not many options for a flat and clear landing area. She didn't see dust stirred up anywhere like there had been copter blades close to the ground. So, had they spotted her car from the air? Perhaps she'd carried some kind of tracking device on her so Lark knew immediately where she was. She thought back to what she'd taken to the Sheriff station: her purse, a lightweight jacket, and Trixie's leash. She did not know what a tracking device looked like, so she simply looked through her stuff to see if anything was out of order. If it was on the car, then in the immediate future, it wouldn't be serving as a GPS.

Jill completed the search of the vineyard, her wine cellar, and her lab. Everything looked undisturbed. Next, she went through her purse and her cell phone and couldn't find anything she thought might look like a tracking device.

She wanted to bring closure to the case. Using her forms, she completed and filed the paperwork. Then she did a summation of everything and emailed it to Emma, Jo, Marie, Angela, the detectives, and agents in San Francisco. The case was now closed.

She would call her insurance company tomorrow and go through the steps of filing a claim for her car. She would need to get the police report from the Sheriff and the insurance company could take it from there.

The Schmidt Industries helicopter encounter at the Sheriff's station played out on the national news, and she wondered how many more minutes of free time she had before the media caught up with her. She spent a few minutes weighing her options in her approach to the media. The media could be a hassle, so instead, she gave thought as to what it could do for her business.

It was too bad that she didn't have signage up advertising the winery's first production run. It would be great free publicity.

Jill could say no comment. Or, at the opposite extreme, she could be a good sport and describe her story to every media outlet. Neither of the extremes sounded good to her.

She needed to talk to Jo, Marie, and Angela to get their feedback as to whether their names should be mentioned to any media. She sent a text message to see if they were available to chat. Luck was with her. They were all at Jo's house prior to going out for dinner. She gave them a few minutes to read the case summary and then called them in Wisconsin.

"Hey, how's it going? I'm lucky to catch all of you together."

"First, we're happy that you're safe, and second, we're happy that we don't live your life. You may have great weather in California, but we don't have helicopters chasing us in Wisconsin," Jo commented with a laugh.

"Yeah, I could do with some snow and a boring life right about now. I hit rock bottom an hour ago after the most amazing adrenaline rush in my life dissipated. I had a big cup of coffee and sort of rebounded back to normal. So, I was watching the nightly news, and the story is playing out on television. I figure that sooner or later some reporter is going to contact me about this case. So, my question to the three of you is, do you want me to mention you by name?"

"At the moment we say no but let us talk it over during dinner and drinks to see if we change our minds," Marie said.

"I wish I was there dining with you. I thought you would say no but let me know if you change your minds over dinner."

They spoke for a few more minutes then Jill ended the call. While she had been on her cell phone with them, her house phone had rung three separate times and she had voicemails waiting for her. She walked to her phone just as it rang again. She decided then that she would screen all her callers. Thankfully, her cell phone was blissfully silent. She listened to the messages. She thought about her property and went outside. Normally she kept the gates open to her driveway. She shut and latched the gates. She hoped that would keep people off her property. She left Trixie outside to sound the alarm.

She went back inside and decided to call the FBI spokesperson that she'd met at the debriefing to discuss what information to release. She didn't think that there were any secrets except perhaps the location of the safe house. Really, though, if Aleksandra had found it, was it really a secret? The spokesperson was busy giving interviews. No surprise there. So, Jill decided that she would go at it her own way. Rather than speak to each news agency separately, she would appear outside her gates at the stated time. That would give the media a chance to arrive if they were interested in her version of the incident, and give her a chance to prepare a statement, which she would begin by reading. She would then answer questions and was prepared to withhold all the names that she could.

Now the question was how to get the word out. She didn't want to email or call members of the media, as then they would have her private information. So instead, she simply posted a sign on her gates with the announcement of the press conference. She would see how well the old-fashioned way of communicating worked. She put the notice in large font on a letter-sized piece of paper and with tape in hand walked out to her gates. At the gate, she knew that her system would work because there were already media vans in the vicinity.

They rushed her with microphones and cameras in hand. She ignored them, taped up the sign, and walked back to her house to work on her statement. It took her twenty minutes to describe the entire case and give lots of kudos to all the members of law enforcement who had kept her alive. Her goals were to tell her story just once, compliment law enforcement, and get the word out just a bit about her business of giving second opinions. Finally, the FBI's public spokesperson returned her call and gave her a few pointers, but basically, she was on her own.

At the appointed time, she went outside and slipped through her gates leaving Trixie behind. She wanted to avoid having her driveway and house as the background while she spoke. She walked to the other side of the road and turned around, ready to face the cameras. She looked briefly around her and counted at least twenty crews. Where had they come from? Palisades Valley did not have its own network affiliate, so everyone at the press conference had to have come from a distance of at least seventy to one hundred miles. Wow.

She didn't own a podium, which became immediately apparent as multiple microphones were stuck in her line of vision. She couldn't concentrate and speak with the distraction of people holding microphones. This was creating a problem, as the news teams had nowhere to place their microphones. In the end, she moved back to her side of the road. The media people duct-taped their microphones to her fence, which worked well, and the nearby trees hid her property and vineyard.

She read her statement, which took all of five minutes. The media wanted a copy of it, but she decided not to release her statement. She took a few questions and then announced that she was done and would have no further comment ever on the case. Any additional questions should be referred to law enforcement. She was relieved to return to her house and relax. She was finished with the case of Graeme St. Louis.

Jill and Nathan spoke later that night. He had seen her on the local news in Washington. It was a sensational story that had captured the imagination of the national media. He thought she'd handled the situation well. Give the facts once, answer a few questions, and promise to never again speak about the case. Like her, he was optimistic that the media would go away and stay away.

"How was dinner with your client?" asked Jill.

She was secretly happy to talk about his work. It felt so normal after several tense weeks.

"It was great. Your involvement in this national case increased my prestige since you're my girlfriend," Nathan said, tongue in cheek.

"That sounds like a typical dumb guy remark. You know that if I was standing there next to you in Seattle, you would have just felt a blow to your solar plexus."

"As you know, I've known this client for years, since before either of us made a name for ourselves in the wine world. So, we catch up on our lives, gossip about the industry, and talk football. He is a Seahawks fan, and I'm a Packers fan, so we have to talk trash on that bad ref call early in the 2012-13 season."

"Sounds like a great time. Have you discussed his new label yet?"

"Not really, we had so many other things to discuss. He has an impressive restaurant attached to his winery, and I was too busy eating some amazing dishes. He had melt-in-your-mouth steak. Everything was excellent, and the dessert was a chocolate pastry paired with cognac. I couldn't have a serious conversation after all that gourmet delight. I feel like I've just eaten Thanksgiving dinner and all I want to do is go to bed and sleep."

"That is my idea of a great evening. I am not a fan of chocolate, but everything else sounds great. I think you should find another glass of cognac and head off to dreamland. Things are calm here finally, and I'm looking forward to working on the vineyard tomorrow. I also researched that martial arts show you wanted to go to, and I have it on my calendar."

"Great! I am looking forward to watching the exhibition and watching you watch the various martial arts. I think you'll like learning one of the arts, and certainly, you'll be better able to defend yourself if you should ever need to in the future."

"Well, sweet dreams, and I'll talk to you tomorrow. Love you, Nathan," Jill said ending the call.

Jill walked to her kitchen to cook dinner. It had been such a dramatic day that she felt like she could eat an entire pizza by herself. Instead, she had the ingredients for a chicken quesadilla to be paired with a couple of glasses of her Moscato. Trixie was sniffing for some treats as well. So, Jill would take care of her first.

They ate in harmony, listening to some pop music. Jill then spent some time on the Internet catching up on news and wine-growing discussions. It was such a relaxing way to spend the evening, and she had felt out of touch for the last few weeks, as her world had narrowed to solving the case. After a couple of hours, she felt sleepy and retired to bed.

CHAPTER 30

*J*ill awoke to a day that promised to be sunny and warm. Since she had run the previous day, she would get her exercise working in her vineyard. She had a great cup of coffee with breakfast and then went outside to work.

She was armed with different types of pruning shears, gloves, a special nutrient that she had created to strengthen the vines, and a wheelbarrow to take away her trimmings. She often listened to music when she worked outside, but today she was content to soak in the sun and listen to the birds chirp.

She worked all morning until it was time to break for lunch. She spoke with her mother just after breakfast and Nathan mid-morning. He had no ill effects from the cognac indulgence the night before, which was good. Trixie had intermittently played fetch with a ball all morning.

As she started to make a turkey and cheese sandwich, her cell phone rang, and she could see that it was Agent Ortiz. She supposed that she was calling to wrap up the case on her end. She hoped that her press conference hadn't upset anyone in law enforcement.

"Hello."

"Jill, how are you this morning?"

"Fabulous, I just spent the morning out among my grapevines. It was the first day in several weeks that I wasn't worried or thinking of the case. How are you doing? How is Agent O'Sullivan?"

"I am afraid I am calling with bad news. We just got the preliminary crime scene information report. There was no female DNA in the four bodies recovered from the crash site of Lark's company helicopter. Seems that sometime after the Sheriff's deputy shot her and when everyone jumped aboard the copter, Lark vanished into the town."

"Oh, no! Just when I thought my life was back to normal."

"I contacted the Sheriff's office prior to calling you, and he has a deputy on his way to pick you up and keep you safe until Agents Brown and O'Sullivan arrive to take over that duty. We are going to need to take you back to the safe house."

"Oh no! I'll have to bring my dog as well. Nathan's out of town, and I would think that Trixie would be her own target."

While she talked to Agent Ortiz, she paced around her house looking out the windows. She saw the Sheriff's car enter her driveway. She had kept the driveway closed overnight but had re-opened the gates this morning. She would have hated to have to go out there now and unlock the gate.

"The Sheriff's car just pulled into my driveway. Yeah! How far away are your agents?"

"At least another seventy minutes."

"Let me pack a bag for Trixie and me. I'll lock up and see if the Sheriff can drive me toward the agents. I'll call you after I speak with the deputy."

Jill hung up her phone and checked Trixie's whereabouts. She did not want to waste any time hunting down the dog. She was happy to see that it was Deputy Davis who had come to escort her into the FBI's capable hands. She loved that the deputy was such a fabulous markswoman. In less than five minutes, she had her bag packed and had Trixie's leash and treats, and they were out the door heading for the patrol car.

She hadn't had time to set her alarm, so she would call the alarm company from the road and request someone there to reset it. Both she and Trixie sat in the backseat behind the custody bars of the police car. She was glad that she was riding in the car for protection rather than because she was on her way to jail.

Jill said to the deputy in the front seat, "I was so glad to see you driving this car when it pulled into my driveway. You're such an excellent shot that I know I'm well protected."

Deputy Davis looked into her rearview mirror. "Jill, these bad people who are after you have brought more excitement to the small town of Palisades Valley than at any time in its history. I'm both honored and nervous about driving you to meet the FBI agents. I hope to make it to the meeting place without having to use my shooting skills."

They were four miles from the Interstate. Deputy Davis would heave a sigh of relief once she hit the Interstate and could go faster. If another Lark copter reached them before she passed Jill off to the FBI, it would be quite the fight: Sheriff's car versus a helicopter. The deputy had thought about the route for the next hour. She planned in her head where they could take cover if Lark sent another helicopter after Jill. She was glad that she'd had Jill and the dog put bulletproof vests on, and Jill wore a riot helmet as well. In the end, she decided that they were better off if she shared her game plan with Jill.

"Jill, I have been planning for the worst, anticipating a sneak attack by Lark. I spoke with Sheriff Arstand on the way over to your house. Lark's mad and probably mentally unstable. Her company has significant resources as far as copters, surveillance equipment, light planes, and weapons. As CEO, she can commandeer any of those resources for her personal use. The fact that she didn't attack immediately last night is probably an indication that she needed time to recover from her wound and to get resources to the Palisades Valley."

"The Sheriff has put a request into the FAA to see if someone can determine if there are any copters in this area that can be spotted on radar. It can be a slow process, as any private, legitimate copters in this area must be considered. We, of course, have an all-points bulletin out for her, but she could be coming at us from any angle. The good news is that her shooting arm is injured. I made sure that my aim would make it hard for her to squeeze her trigger hand.

"I think we have to assume that she'll have at least one accomplice. At the very least the person who flies the helicopter to her if, indeed, that is how she's going to pursue you. The next question is how will she find you? Have you gone through all your belongings from the past few days and looked for GPS trackers? She found you quickly yesterday at the Sheriff's station. I hope that was because your distinctive car was parked in front of the building. We know that GPS trackers were placed on the FBI agent's car, so it's a tactic that has worked for this group in the past. Why don't you start going through all of your belongings as well as the dog's stuff to see if you notice anything."

"I searched my belongings yesterday, and I didn't find anything that looked like a tracker but let me check again."

Jill searched her belongings as well as Trixie's and could not find any sort of a tracking device. Deputy Davis now approached the on-ramp to the Interstate. They'd discussed the need for lights and a siren but thought that was more likely to bring attention to the car. The deputy put the car on cruise control at seventy-five miles per hour. Trixie was being a good dog by lying in the footwell of the backseat. Jill slouched in her seat, keeping an eye out for what she thought to be suspicious behavior by any of the vehicles around them. She soon found that the passengers of nearly every car were curious as to who was in the backseat of a cop car. She was amazed at the number of disapproving looks she received from people thinking that she was being driven to jail. More than one set of parents pointed to her while talking to their children. Whatever happened to innocent until proven guilty?

Given the freak of curiosity that she was in the backseat, Jill decided that she should just look out the window to see if anyone or anything was approaching their car. Jill relaxed when nothing happened after five minutes. She and the deputy returned to their conversation regarding the strategy to fight Lark and her toys.

"If we should see the helicopter, I think we need to take cover as soon as possible. None of these overpasses look big enough to protect the car. What we need to do is pull the car into one of these orchards, as the trees would give us some cover against a copter. If we're lucky, we might find a multi-level parking structure that would give us good cover. The downside of this idea is that we would potentially risk other lives."

They were both secretly worried about rocket-propelled grenades. They knew from the FBI debriefing that the previous helicopter had that weapon on board and had fired at the FBI. Tree coverage would not do much for protection. What they really needed was a redwood forest in which to take cover. Of course, the real question was would they see the copter soon enough to take evasive action?

While they drove, someone at the Sheriff's office relayed information to them as to whether there were any copter sightings. They were lucky in that it was late morning, so there was no traffic to slow them down or box them in. Word came over the radio that the FBI's helicopter was on its way east to meet the agents and the deputy's car. Initially, it had been tied up in a hostage situation somewhere in the San Francisco Bay Area.

Apparently, that situation had ended, and now the copter was heading their way following the Interstate route.

Jill heaved a sigh of relief that they might get equal firepower before the battle raged. She didn't even know if Lark was after her now or whether she was hiding while her hand healed. They continued the drive for another half an hour. Jill was getting exhausted scanning the sky for a helicopter that might or might not be there. Jill appreciated law enforcement's ability to shelter her.

Deputy Davis and Jill completed their journey by meeting the agents at a freeway rest stop. In the distance, Jill saw a helicopter approaching the rest area. She and Trixie made a dash for the woman's restroom, thinking it would be the safest and closest place to hide.

Agent Brown stopped her. "Jill, that's the FBI helicopter. You don't have to run for cover."

Jill turned around, planning on returning to the cars. She could hear the helicopter landing in the now-empty pet walking area at the back of the rest stop.

"Oh, crap! Jill, take cover it's not the FBI copter!" yelled Agent O'Sullivan.

Jill wanted to return to the safety of the vehicles, but they were too far away. Her options included getting closer to the copter by trying to hide behind the building, or she could choose a picnic table, a tree, or a cement trash can. She should have made her choice five seconds before, but she was sluggish.

The rest stop was relatively light with travelers. Deputy Davis used her car PA system to advise the seven visitors to take cover and return to their cars if possible. So far Lark and her crew had not injured any bystanders. She only hoped it would stay that way.

Members of law enforcement had a better view of the situation than did Jill. With hand signals taught her by the FBI agents while she had been in the safe house, the agents guided her

ALEC PECHE

movement. Jill, with a tight hold on Trixie, managed to get within ten feet of the vehicles when she got the signal to halt. Deputy Davis created a shooting diversion to help Jill cover the final ten feet and get into the shield of the agents and their vehicles.

It appeared there were a total of three passengers on the copter with Lark being one of them. One of the three was the pilot who stayed inside the copter, and the other two were on the ground making their way toward Jill. She thought that the woman had really lost her mind. Killing her would not change the evidence in the case. There was no logical reason to still be pursuing her.

"I have been using my binoculars to determine what weapons the two helicopter passengers have. It appears that they have many weapons and that there may be more under their clothing. They have a few grenades, magazine clips, Glock pistols inside holsters, and they are carrying semi-automatics. I can see that Lark's hand is wrapped up. It looks like they have some sort of protective vests and helmets on," said Deputy Davis.

"The FBI helicopter has an ETA of four minutes, and the pilot knows that we are about to be engaged in a gunfight. As they don't seem to have respirators, I think we should launch smoke bombs at the two of them to slow them down," said Agent O'Sullivan.

Jill had no experience with knives or guns. In college, she had played NCAA women's baseball, and she thought that her contribution could be the accurate placement of the smoke bomb. She informed the agents of this.

"Well, give it a try. What you want to do is create a line in the sand metaphorically with the smoke bombs to make it hard for Lark and company to breathe and see us. Rapid placement of two bombs in front of each of them should be effective. As soon as you pull the pin, the bomb will start smoking, so you want to throw them quickly and in fast succession, so they don't have the opportunity to move around the bombs. Remember, the bombs will bounce, so factor that in your placement. Judging by the way the flag is blowing atop the restroom, the wind is blowing into them," Deputy Davis said as she handed Jill the grenades.

The trick for Jill was to reduce her accuracy by using a base-ball overhand pitch, which was how she warmed up for the underhanded softball pitch. By throwing overhand she could keep more of her body hidden longer by the vehicles. Fortunately, she had maintained her skill over the years by pitching balls to Trixie. It wasn't a foreign movement long forgotten.

Jill took a moment to decide on her placement and then quickly lobbed the grenades. As she watched, her placement was around ninety percent accurate. Not bad, as she had never thrown an object of such size and weight before. She did a little dance of cheer inside her head when she saw that the bombs had given the agents, Jill, and Deputy Davis the critical minutes for reinforcements to arrive.

While the smoke billowed and blocked the vision of Lark and her companion, Jill took the opportunity to look around her. The seven visitors had all taken cover at the back of their vehicles, giving them, some shielding. In the distance towards San Francisco, she could see a helicopter approaching. This could be the FBI's or the California Highway Patrol's copter coming to their aid. She hoped the copter wasn't coming to Lark's aid.

She turned back to stare at the smoke. She had not seen any movement from beyond her own imaginary line of a smoke barrier. She would not believe that Lark would just pack up onto her helicopter and leave over a bit of smoke.

"What do you think is going on? I have not seen any movement. Is the approaching helicopter friend or foe?" asked Jill of the agents.

"That helicopter is a friend. This time, I'm sure, as we veri-fied that with headquarters. Just as Lark can't see us because of the smoke, we can't see her. Our approaching copter has had a scope on Lark's helicopter and movement. Her friend has been seen arguing with her and trying to get her to get back on the helicopter. She has moved toward her helicopter but has not boarded it yet. If she does get on board and the copter lifts off, we could be at greater risk, as she would have an overhead shot," Agent O'Sullivan explained.

By now, the FBI helicopter had reached the rest stop. Lark pulled a shoulder-mounted missile launcher out of her own copter and turned around to aim it at the FBI helicopter. An Agent inside the copter fired at Lark, striking her on the leg just as she fired. Lark's leg buckled under her, and the rocket went off harmlessly straight up in the air before self-detonating.

The helicopter pilot didn't trust her to not try again, so he took evasive action. He executed a series of sharp curves and dives and landed with the restroom between Lark and the FBI helicopter. The rotor was shut down quickly, and everyone exited the cab loaded with weapon power.

The civilians on the ground were completely wide-eyed over the past ten minutes. Thankfully, none of the civilians had chil-dren with them. One of the FBI agents crawled over to them and spoke with them. He gathered them at the farthest car and stayed with them to provide communication and protection.

The other five agents joined Jill, Deputy Davis, and Agents Brown and O'Sullivan. They had a discussion. The smoke grenades were dissipating, and they had a decent view of Lark and her helicopter. She had not gotten onto her feet after being shot. The FBI used a megaphone to tell Lark and her accom-plices that they were surrounded and to put their hands in the air and surrender.

Instead, Lark had been dragging herself closer to her heli-copter and spoke on her cell phone to someone. Her helicopter blades sped up, and her associates got her inside the cab, and the helicopter took off. The FBI agents decided to give Lark a lead. With the civilians in the area to keep safe, they were better moving this fight to a different location.

Leaving a second agent behind, the other agents jumped aboard the FBI helicopter and took off in pursuit. The FAA had been alerted and was tracking Lark's helicopter. The agent spoke with the civilian group. After collecting names and contact information, he advised the people that they were safe to return to their journeys. Deputy Davis removed orange cones from her trunk and closed the rest stop entry ramp. If Lark and her helicopter returned, the last thing they needed was a new group of civilians to protect.

The civilians departed, and Jill was left with the four FBI Agents and Deputy Davis.

"What do you think Lark's next move will be?" Jill asked then added, "As if she has been at all predictable over the past weeks."

"Let me get a status of where her helicopter is at this point," Agent Lansky stated, as he stepped away from the group to call his colleagues aboard the helicopter. After a lengthy conversation, he returned to the group.

"Her helicopter was found abandoned. There was blood in the interior, presumably from her leg wound. It was a moderate amount, but the agent thought he likely did not strike a major artery inside her leg. As the path of blood stops about thirty feet from the abandoned helicopter, we believe she switched to a vehicle previously parked at the site. I have requested that local law enforcement secure the abandoned helicopter. Meanwhile, the other agents have returned to the air looking for suspicious vehicles."

"Great, she has disappeared again. I was hoping to return home with Deputy Davis. However, with her on the loose, I can't go home."

"Jill, I checked in with Sheriff Arstand, and he indicated that he could spare me for the rest of the day. So, we could wait this out with the hope that the FBI will apprehend her. Agents Brown, Sullivan, and Lansky what are your thoughts?"

"We are in a relatively unsecure location. The rest stop does not provide much cover for any kind of aerial or ground attack. Our nearest somewhat secure location is the Stanislaus Sheriff's station. Given the damage Lark incurred yesterday at Deputy Davis's station, we may not be welcomed with open arms, but we'll be secure at that location. Let's remove the cones and depart this rest stop immediately. I'll take the lead as I have directions," Agent Brown said.

"I'll join Jill and Deputy Davis to provide extra coverage in their car," Agent Lansky said.

The rest stop was re-opened, and the two cars departed for the local Sheriff's station. After following Agent's Brown car for about three miles, Agent Lansky spoke up from the front seat of Deputy Davis's cruiser.

"I believe we have a problem. This is not the way to the closest Sheriff's station. I believe that Agent Brown may be leading us toward the vehicle carrying Lark. I don't see any traffic close to us, which is good. I'll alert the pilot in the FBI helicopter via text that we have a problem on the ground in case Agent Brown is monitoring communications."

"Agent Ortiz alerted me to the possibility that agent Brown may be providing information on Jill's location during our flight to the rest stop. Lark's continued ability to locate the agents and Jill sounded like we might have an internal leak. I watched Agent Brown at the rest stop, and he never took aim against the woman. My attention was not on him while I spoke with the civilians. However, I noted that he did not communicate with or look up the whereabouts of the Stanislaus Sheriff's station. That would not be protocol. Furthermore, I looked for directions myself, and we're not going in the correct direction. I don't believe that Agent O'Sullivan is involved."

"Why don't I call ahead to Agents Brown and O'Sullivan's car and indicate that we're having car problems and to pull to the side with us. I know what is under the hood and can easily disable the car. Depending on how I disable it, I can quickly repair it if we need a fast departure. I'll start slowing down, and then I'll pull over to the side of the road, pop the hood, and quickly disable the car. If we're sure that Agent Brown is Lark's puppet, we could handcuff him to the squad car and take off in the other car until we get some backup," Deputy Davis suggested.

"I'm just re-confirming with Agent Ortiz as to whether we have a problem with Brown. I would hate to leave him hand-cuffed to a car if he's still one of us, a good guy."

Deputy Davis and Jill listened to the one-sided conversation that Agent Lansky had with the FBI regional office in San Francisco. On his end, Agent Lansky mostly said yes or no after describing the current situation. He ended the call and briefed them.

"Agent Ortiz believes that Agent Brown is involved in the crimes. We've been ordered to handcuff him inside the squad car. We'll need to search him for weapons and cell phones prior to locking him in the car. Once we handcuff him, we're to contact Agent Ortiz, who will place a call to the Stanislaus Sheriff requesting backup and giving us a status as to the current situation. Any questions? Then Deputy Davis, let's put your plan in place. Call Agent Brown, slow down, and disable this car as soon as you can. Do you have handcuffs that we can use on Agent Brown?"

Deputy Davis nodded and picked up her phone and called Agent O'Sullivan.

"Agent O'Sullivan, we have a car problem. I'm slowing down and pulling off to the right shoulder. We'll all have to pile into your car, along with the dog, as we head toward the Sheriff's station."

CHAPTER 31

*T*he deputy pulled her foot off the gas and let the car drift to the side of the road. She quickly popped the hood and pulled a few things apart before Agent Brown arrived to look at the engine with her. Agent Lansky casually came up behind Agent Brown. Agent Lansky and Deputy Davis handcuffed Agent Brown. Jill had Agent Ortiz on the cell phone and passed it over to Agent O'Sullivan so that she could hear from her supervisor that Agent Brown was on the wrong side of justice.

In no time, they had a resigned Agent Brown handcuffed and minus his weapon seated inside the Sheriff's squad car. The car windows were partially down, and he was in the backseat unable to get out of the car. Agent O'Sullivan, Agent Lansky, Deputy Davis, Jill, and Trixie all got into the unmarked FBI car. This time they did a U-turn and followed the correct route to the Sheriff's station. According to their GPS, it was twelve miles to their destination.

Agent Ortiz had notified the Stanislaus Sheriff of their pending arrival. Her request for backup could not be met, as the

242

deputies had already answered two serious calls, a domestic dispute, and a bad car accident.

Agent Lansky contacted the helicopter to get a progress report.

"Any thoughts on Lark's whereabouts or what make and model of a car she might be in?"

"We checked the vehicle purchase records of her company. We don't know if she has a company car. If she does, it's likely one of three models, a silver four-door sedan, a large black SUV, or a black Hummer. I can give you the make and models if you spot anybody, but I think it's more important to look for vehicle body types. We believe that there are likely four people in the vehicle. We've swooped down on a few silver sedans and nearly caused the drivers to go off the road in surprise. We're going to fly to your vehicle to give you an escort to the Sheriff's station. We'll then return to the field."

As Agent O'Sullivan looked up through her windshield, she saw the FBI helicopter. It had been a wild day. From the fast departure to drive to the rest stop to pick up Jill, to the hand-cuffing of her partner inside the Sheriff's car, she hadn't had time to process everything. Typically, she would have analyzed how the situation had gone down at the rest stop. She and Agent Brown had been partners for a couple of years. After observing his behavior while locking him in the squad car, she had no doubt that Lark's company had figured out how to exploit her partner.

In the backseat, Jill was composing in her head the email to her friends in Wisconsin and a phone call to Nathan. She rather thought it would be interesting as a bystander to watch how her day had gone so far. Most people would think that it had to be a vivid dream. Surely no small-town grape grower got chased by black ops helicopters in essentially her own backyard. She supposed that it was good that she could maintain a sense of humor about the situation.

They spotted the Sheriff's station up ahead on the right. Deputy Davis escorted Jill and her dog inside the station. There she met Lieutenant Garcia. The Stanislaus County Sheriff headquarters were in a different location. Three uniformed officers as well as a dispatcher stood inside the building. Deputy Davis, in consultation with Agents O'Sullivan and Lansky, concluded that they could leave Jill in the lieutenant's protection with Deputy Davis. The agents would retrieve the Sheriff squad car if for no other reason so that Deputy Davis could get back to Palisades Valley. She handed Agent Lansky the part that had disabled the car with specific instructions on how to do the repair. Agent Lansky was expected back at the Sheriff's station in half an hour.

Deputy Davis briefed Lieutenant Garcia on Jill's case, and the incident that morning at a rest stop in his jurisdiction. As that was state land, he would leave any cleanup of the rest area to the Highway Patrol. Jill was not sure if the lieutenant would have believed her far-fetched story if it were not for the backup of Deputy Davis and the FBI agents.

In the air, the FBI helicopter searched for signs of a car that might contain Lark. On the ground, Agents Lansky and O'Sullivan had reached the disabled Sheriff's squad car containing Agent Brown. He knew that his life with the FBI was over, and he had nothing to lose and much to gain by talking about Lark. He wore a tracker that was monitored. The two agents needed to stop the tracking abilities of the device, but they did not want to lose it as evidence. In the end, they decided to dig a hole and bury it in an evidence bag about two feet down. That would make it harder to detect and yet they could move the vehicles and Agent Brown without the worry of being tracked by Lark.

Surprisingly, although he had been stuck in the Sheriff's squad car for thirty minutes, Lark had not approached the vehicle. Agent Brown was asked why he had assisted Lark. Sadly, it was for money, one million dollars to be precise. He'd figured that he would not actually cause Jill's death. The little information that he provided to Lark about Jill's location seemed minimal when stacked against Lark's helicopter, manpower support, and an arsenal of weapons. Lark would win in the end, and he may as well get paid as a side benefit. As he had nearly died in the explosion at Graeme's, he felt like he needed to find a safer line of work. The payment would ease his transition to a new future.

After that explanation, Agent O'Sullivan was depressed over the lack of ethics of her former partner. She'd liked the guy and now questioned her own judgment about the character of her fellow agent. She would be morose later. Now they needed to find Lark. Agent Lansky headed back to the Sheriff's station with Deputy Davis's squad car.

The search continued for Lark's car. This part of California was primarily farmland, which should have made the search easier for the car, but they had been at it for more than an hour and had not sighted the car nor did they have a sense of its direction. At some point, Lark would need medical care for the gunshot wound in her leg.

Agent Ortiz had been studying Lark's company in detail. It was her conclusion that she leased or owned thirty to fifty helicopters, around three hundred vehicles, had an endless number of weapons and ammunition, and there were multiple company locations across the country. Furthermore, on her staff, she had athletic trainers, martial arts experts, several physicians, a physical therapist, and nurses. It wasn't clear to her if the medical staff was used for deployments around the world or for treatment and recovery of injuries suffered by employees during training in this country. She placed a conference call to others in the air and on the ground.

"Lark likely has an endless supply of transportation options and weapons. It appears she can even get medical care without going to an emergency room that might report her gunshot wound. This assumes that the wound was not severe. We have had experts in the FBI review the camera footage from our helicopter at the rest stop. While there was minimal blood in the abandoned helicopter, we believe that she could be suffering from a mortal wound if she doesn't get care in another hour. The large bone in her upper leg is likely fractured, which will cause internal bleeding inside the thigh," Agent Ortiz stated.

One of her staff members needed her attention, so she asked the people in the field to hold. "Agent Ortiz, we just received a report from a hospital emergency room located forty miles from the rest stop. An unidentified female was dropped off by three masked men in a silver sedan. They quickly exited and were not available to answer questions posed by the staff treating the woman. She's been rushed to surgery, and she's listed in critical condition. She arrived in shock, unconscious, and with a bullet wound in her thigh."

"Thank you, Agent Williams, and please stay in communication with that hospital. I'll dispatch someone there now, and they should arrive within the next within fifteen minutes," Agent Ortiz instructed.

She returned to the conference call with her field team, and she advised the helicopter to head for the hospital.

"I need you to report to Stanislaus Community Hospital immediately. A female matching Lark's description was dropped off by three males who subsequently disappeared. Her prognosis is poor as to whether she'll survive the surgery on her wounded leg. I would like one officer stationed at her bedside or as close as we can get to the surgical suite. Let's quickly get a positive identification on her. I would like another officer to confiscate any video footage outside the emergency room that identifies her and the other three men."

Agent Ortiz called the nursing supervisor at the hospital to inform her of the FBI's interest in a particular female patient and the pending arrival of the agents by helicopter. She also notified Lieutenant Garcia as the hospital was likely in his area.

Twelve minutes later the helicopter landed and unloaded the FBI team at the hospital's helicopter pad. The helicopter lifted off to find parking elsewhere as it could not block any medical helicopters from reaching the hospital. Agent O'Sullivan arrived seven minutes later in her car.

Hospital security personnel met them, and they divided into two groups. One group departed for a conference room outside of the sterile environment of the operating room.

As Lark was considered under arrest, some medical information was transmitted to the agents. She'd arrived in critical condition with low blood pressure and a weak pulse. She was not conscious. She was determined to have a broken femur with internal bleeding from the broken bone and a nicked vein.

"The hospital began providing care to the woman more than an hour after she incurred her injury. That greatly increases the odds that she'll not survive the surgery to repair her leg. Given the excessive internal bleeding and blood loss, her body's natural response would cause it to release proteins into the blood throughout the body to promote clotting. One of these blood clots could cut off the blood supply to the liver, the brain, or the kidneys, which can cause them to stop working. Normally, if we got someone in within an hour after an initial injury, the repair is not that complicated. Right now, the greatest risk to her is blood clots. . . . or if she runs out of protein, bleeding to death," a surgical nurse explained.

The agents sat down to wait. They had a fingerprint scanner to use on the female to positively identify her. To the hospital, she was simply Jane Doe.

In another part of the hospital, the second group of agents reviewed the camera footage from the time that the female had been dropped off at the emergency room. One of the men wore the same clothing as one of the men who had accompanied Lark at the rest stop had worn. They all wore gloves and had ski masks over their heads. Bare skin showed above their gloves but below the edge of their jackets. All three suspects were Caucasian and male. The FBI used facial recognition software to identify Lark's companion at the rest stop. No match had been made to U.S. passport databases. Now an attempt was being made to match it with data from Interpol.

Both FBI teams were at a standstill, hampered by a lack of information. Meanwhile, in the Stanislaus Sheriff station, Jill relaxed when she heard about the condition of the as-yet-to-be-identified Lark. At least she was in custody. It sounded like Lark was fighting for her life in the operating room. Two questions remained for her. Was this Lark? And where were her men, and were they still after Jill?

The nurse returned to the group of agents assembled in the surgery waiting room.

"Jane Doe expired on the operating table. We believe that a blood clot traveled to her heart, where it blocked the blood supply to that muscle. Despite repeated attempts, we could not revive her. Staff members are cleaning her up before we transport her to the hospital morgue. We'll come and get you in about ten minutes when we move her. We can stop at that time and give you a chance to visually identify her and run your fingerprint verification. If she's your suspect, will you take responsibility to notify her family?"

"Thank you. We'll await the opportunity to identify her. If it is our suspect, she has no next of kin that we are aware of, but we'll take responsibility for the notification to her company and the attorney representing her estate," Agent Jackson responded, the leader of the helicopter team.

Agent Jackson updated all parties on Jane Doe's death and sat down to wait. It had been a long day. Ten minutes passed and the nurse appeared to take the agents to Jane Doe's gurney.

Agent Jackson carried an iPad with several pictures of Lark. In addition, it contained the software for fingerprint verification.

"Visually, she looks like our suspect Lark Sumac," He held her fingers to the fingerprint scanner and waited for a match. "Since she did some defense contracting, we know that her fingerprints are in the system."

The iPad beeped and indicated that Jane Doe had indeed been positively identified as Lark Sumac. He wanted to look at the bullet wound but knew that he would be stepping over the line of her medical privacy rights. He'd learn more about the bullet wound by obtaining the coroner's report of her death. Someone pulled the sheet up over her head and continued the journey toward the morgue.

Agent Jackson notified all parties that Lark Sumac was confirmed deceased. That left only one loose end.

CHAPTER 32

*A*gent Ortiz was trying to identify one of the men in Lark's group. Had Lark issued a dying order for Jill to be killed, and if so, were her men going to follow that order? A review of the company revealed that she was Chairman and CEO. A CFO signed tax filings, otherwise there were no other names associated with the company. A search of the media about her company revealed very little data. The company had generally managed to stay out of the news for over twenty years. She would contact company headquarters to see who was in charge in her absence.

In the interim she would have Jill and the dog transported on the FBI helicopter to the safe house. Until she knew the direction of Lark's men, the Bureau would strive to keep Jill safe. She left a message for Agent O'Sullivan, who then contacted her via conference call with Deputy Davis and Jill. Both Deputy Davis and Agent O'Sullivan agreed that Jill should go to the San Francisco safe house. Jill agreed with this as well. Deputy Davis was heading back to the Palisades Valley. Given the uncertainty as to whether Lark's men were still pursuing Jill, Sheriff Arstand was happy that someone else was keeping Jill safe. He had a heck of a mess on his hands to clean up, and it would be weeks before his station was back to normal.

The FBI helicopter landed close to the Stanislaus Sheriff station. Agent O'Sullivan was transporting Agent Brown back to San Francisco to be booked into jail. Jill would have new agents by her side for the immediate future. She gave Deputy Davis a heartfelt hug, as she had done much to keep Jill safe over the past several weeks.

Taking a reluctant Trixie to the helicopter, she climbed aboard with the dog. The agents buckled her into her seat and gave her headphones to reduce the noise and keep her connected to the other agents onboard the helicopter. Trixie was likewise placed in a harness so that she wouldn't be tossed around the interior of the helicopter as it made sharp turns. She barked when they took off, but the first swooping turn had her quickly lying down and looking terrified. It would be a forty-minute trip before they landed in San Francisco.

Jill needed to get word to Nathan. On the advice of Deputy Davis she had powered off her cell phone and removed the battery on the off chance that someone was tracking her movement. She had been offline for about five hours now. If Nathan had tried to reach her and couldn't, he likely would have contacted his friend Sheriff Arstand to see if something was going on. She could only hope that he had gotten lost in an artistic frenzy creating labels and other concepts for his friend in Washington.

When they landed in San Francisco, Jill asked for a few minutes alone on the roof to call Nathan.

"Nathan, how has your day been going so far?"

"When I couldn't reach your cell phone earlier, I called the Sheriff to see if anything was going on. You've had a busy day, and I'm so happy to hear your voice right now!"

Jill gave him a briefing about what had happened over the

past few hours and the fact that Trixie was with her in the safe house.

"I was sort of hoping that you would get lost in your art and not worry about me today. I'm sorry I couldn't contact you sooner, but frankly, we didn't know the extent of Lark's tracking abilities. Given that some of her company's work is done in secret, no one was sure what technological abilities she had. It turns out that she had less technological capabilities and more extortion skills when it came to Agent Brown. The FBI agents are waiting for me down below, and I'm going back into a secure location until we can figure out if Lark's team members are targeting me. I don't know when I'll call you again, but I'm hoping to be completely free from this case within a day."

"Really appreciate the call. I know you have had a rough day. Love you, take care."

"Love you back, good night." Jill ended the phone conversation with a sigh and proceeded into the building.

Standing at the door someone waited to escort Trixie and Jill to a conference room. Inside the conference room, Jill met up with Agent Ortiz and a couple of new agents. She was introduced to the new agents who would be guarding her in the same safe house location across the street.

They had the added complication of taking Trixie outside for frequent bathroom breaks. In the end, one of the staff members was a dog lover who offered to take Trixie home with her. Her husband worked from home, and Trixie would have company all day. More importantly, in the Bureau's eyes, no one would have the distraction of the dog, including Jill herself, if the situation got sticky again.

Agent Ortiz directed a briefing concerning theories about Lark's team members. She had reached out to the Bureau's behavioral analysis unit for evaluation by its experts.

"In addition, I received back from Interpol a facial match for Lark's teammate in the rest stop attack. He was identified as

Arben Frroku, an Albanian national wanted by Interpol for a category labeled homicide committed in other special circumstances."

Jill asked, "What are the special circumstances?"

"According to Interpol, he's wanted for the murder of a police officer, which is a special classification."

Jill added sarcastically, "Great background. Do we have any idea of his loyalty to Lark? Did they have a relationship? Interesting that he's also from Albania."

"He's a bad person otherwise Interpol would not be after him. He's been on the run for nearly two decades. Unless he stands to inherit Lark's company or he's seeking revenge for her death, we think he'll disappear."

"Have the FBI behavioral people been able to speculate about his personal relationship with Lark? It seems that the tape of him at the rest stop and of the men dropping her off at the hospital would tell us something about the depth of his relationship with Lark and possibly point to his likely desire to continue to pursue me versus hiding from Interpol."

"They warn me that with little to evaluate beyond the few seconds of tape we gave them, their accuracy would be very questionable. Thus, they've declined to give us an opinion. So, we have to assume a worst-case scenario that he'll continue Lark's mission until we get sufficient information to the contrary," Agent Ortiz stated.

"Who oversees Lark's company upon her death? Do we know anything about the workings of her company, the Board of Directors? Isn't it privately held? Can we get any information from the IRS about the company?" Jill asked.

"Good idea, Jill. We have also sent an alert to Homeland Security for distribution to all points of exit from the United States. The company has a major office in San Diego. If I were him, I would get in a boat and sail south to Mexico, have some plastic surgery, and re-emerge several months from now."

The FBI needed to collect information about Schmidt Industries. The meeting broke up, and the agents agreed to gather again in a few hours to review information. Agents were available to escort Jill across the street to the safe house. She asked that Trixie be taken outside to take care of business. The agent returned with the dog, and Jill was moved across the street. The employee who was taking care of Trixie would collect her in a few hours.

Jill sat on the familiar couch with her laptop, overwhelmed by a sense of déjà vu. She felt like she was starring in a bad zombie movie. Each time one of the bad guys was killed, another one popped up in his place. She really needed to get some information about Schmidt Industries. She wanted to know that once Arben was captured, the saga of this case would end. She looked at the clock and knew that it was early evening in Wisconsin. She called Marie on the off chance that she had time in the next two hours to assist with research.

"Hey, Marie, how's it going?"

"Jill, I was just going to call you. I just caught your story on the news. Tell me that you're being protected by law enforcement now. Just when I thought that the good guys defeated the bad guys, another bad guy pops up."

"That's funny, I was just thinking to myself that I was the star in a badly-produced zombie movie where the zombies won't stay dead. I'm in the FBI's protection so I can't say much more than that. Do you have time to do a little research right at this moment?"

"I have plans tonight, but your safety is more important. What do you need? I can rearrange my schedule for the evening."

"There'll be a meeting soon to discuss Schmidt Industries. You are the queen of people and company online searches. We are looking for information about the structure of that organization. With the CEO dead, who manages the company now, who are the employees loyal to? We're trying to determine if Lark's team member, Arben Frroku, will continue to make attempts on my life. Whatever you can find out about him or the company in the next hour or so would be more information than I have now."

"Arben who? How do you spell that?"

"Apparently you can see his picture and the spelling of his name on the Interpol site. But it's spelled F–r–r–o–k–u"

"As soon as we hang up, I'll rearrange my evening, and then I'll start with the Interpol site. You know, I love a challenge, and this is likely more exciting than the evening I had originally planned!"

"After the last three weeks, right this minute, I crave a boring life!" Jill exclaimed ending their conversation.

In ten minutes, Marie was searching a number of databases. She was amazed by the lack of information available about Schmidt Industries. She had never seen such little information on a large company. There was nothing on social media; there were no advertisements in well-placed publications, no Wall Street business intelligence on the company.

After another fifteen minutes of fruitless searching, she called Jill. Her call immediately went to voicemail, and she then remembered that she needed to communicate with Jill by email. Marie got a quick response on the lack of any information available. Jill hadn't recovered any information either.

In the end, they decided to stop their search and approach the problem from a different angle. Arben was a smart man. He'd stayed out of police custody for over twenty years. Assuming he would know that his face was captured on camera, he would know that he needed to get out of the U.S. as soon as possible. He had to know that the commercial airports were blocked as were rental car companies and trains.

Canada was a thousand miles away and Mexico was three hundred-fifty miles away. Jill thought that he would likely head

ALEC PECHE

to Mexico. She asked Marie if she had access to boat, car, and private plane data. She did not have access to those databases. She told Marie to give up on the search and have a great evening. The FBI meeting was in about thirty minutes. She emailed Agent Ortiz with an idea.

Agent Ortiz agreed to explore the idea. Using the DMV, FAA, and the California Boat registrations databases, the agent identified Schmidt Industries' vehicles registered in California. It had five helicopters, a jet airplane, and three-light planes listed as belonging in San Diego. It kept them housed on an airfield close to its company building. It also had at least thirty cars and trucks in San Diego and one boat moored at the San Diego harbor.

Arben didn't have a pilot's license according to the FAA. Of course, given that he was hiding from Interpol, it was unlikely that he'd used his real name. He'd not been seen piloting the helicopter. The team assembled at the FBI decided to target the boat at the marina. If he'd driven south directly after dropping off Lark, he would have reached San Diego by now. An agent put a call into the Coast Guard for assistance locating the boat.

The harbor where the boat was moored was a fifteen-minute boat ride from the Coast Guard station. Commander Smith of the station was eager to help and immediately dispatched a crew to check on the location. The crew verified that the boat was gone and that it had been re-fueled within the last hour, judging by the gas pump at the marina. A PIN code had to be used to access the pump so that boats could be refueled at any time of the day or night, and a PIN linked to Schmidt Industries had been used, according to the harbormaster, who had been woken out of a deep sleep to answer Commander Smith's questions.

The San Diego FBI office dispatched officers to embark on the Coast Guard cutter in a search for the boat. They could go some distance into Mexican waters but not all the way to Ensenada, which had a major harbor. They had night-vision goggles, radar, and a few other tricks up their sleeves. They hoped that this was the actual route that Arben had taken to leave the country. It was good practice to look for a boat in the dark, it kept search and rescue skills sharp. The problem was that if they failed to locate the boat, they wouldn't know if it was because Arben had gotten too far ahead of the search or if he hadn't chosen that route to escape the authorities.

CHAPTER 33

$\mathcal{I}$t had not been Arben's lucky day. He'd started off by arguing with Lark about her continued pursuit of Jill. He had lost that argument. The day had really gone to crap when Lark took the bullet in the thigh. At first, he'd thought it to be a flesh wound, but then she'd started fading on the helicopter. By the time they transferred to the car, she was down to single-word responses to his questions. Her last request of him was that he continue her quest to kill Jill.

Her last sentence to him had been "Kill Jill because she is the cause of the decline of Schmitt Industries and Lark Sumac."

A small, quiet part of him had wished that her final words had been 'I love you, Arben'.

Schmidt Industries had no value to him with Lark gone. He knew that he'd been caught on camera and that Interpol was after him. He had no desire to die attempting to fulfill Lark's final wish. There was no upside for him to that wish. He needed to cross the border to Mexico and disappear. Fortunately, he'd several cash stashes across the world and multiple bank accounts. He had always known that he would have to run someday, and that day had come. He'd enough money to be able to never work again. He drove south toward the border. He would be there in about five hours.

The other men in the helicopter had been dropped off at the Greyhound bus depot and were on their way to Los Angeles. Someone from Schmidt Industries would meet them at the depot with their final pay. The helicopter was a loss. Arben was sure that the FBI would confiscate the helicopter.

Five hours later, he reached the San Diego harbor. It was evening and the perfect time to take a small boat south into Mexico. Schmidt Industries kept a boat at the harbor so the company could train for underwater surveillance and rescue. He knew where the spare keys were kept for vehicles, planes, and boats around the world.

He'd not been on this boat before and had to walk around the harbor to find it. He climbed on board. He checked the radar and lights to see if he could see at night. After exploring the boat for nearly an hour, he felt that he had enough lights and instrumentation to safely navigate the Pacific Ocean and make it to Mexico overnight. He started the boat and navigated the harbor, filling up the gas tanks as he departed.

Arben safely exited the narrow waters of the San Diego harbor. He could see the lights of the coast as he followed it south. The boat's GPS and radar indicated the international waters of Mexico ahead, and he would be free. He was headed to the Puerto Salina Marina, which was forty-five miles south of San Diego. As it was nighttime, he was not steering the boat at full speed. He estimated that he would reach the marina well before dawn. He just needed to stay awake in the unending blackness of the ocean at night.

Just then he saw a well-lit boat approaching from the north. Over the boat's loudspeaker came "This is Lieutenant Jacobs of the United States Coast Guard. Please heave to and prepare to be boarded."

The announcement was repeated in Spanish. He figured he

ALEC PECHE

had nothing the Coast Guard wanted, as he wasn't smuggling people or drugs. He put the boat in neutral and waited at the railing for the Coast Guard boat to come alongside.

As the Coast Guard cutter approached, he noticed the FBI windbreakers on some men and knew he was screwed. He could not outshoot all the men aboard the cutter. He didn't know enough about boats to know if he'd the engine power to outrun the cutter. The ocean was too cold, and he was too far from shore to risk trying to swim away. Since he knew so much about Schmidt Industries, he thought he might be able to work a deal out with the prosecutors.

The Coast Guard boarded his boat, and the FBI agents approached him.

"Arben Frroku, you are under arrest as an accessory to the attempted murder of a federal agent. There are likely additional charges that will be levied against you by Interpol. You have the right to remain silent. Anything you say can and will be used against you in a court of law. You have the right to an attorney. If you cannot afford an attorney, one will be provided for you. Do you understand these rights as I have read them to you? With these rights in mind, do you wish to speak with me?"

Arben answered, "I would like an attorney and to work out a deal, and after I have spoken with the prosecutors, I'll be willing to speak."

After a pat-down for weapons and suicide pills, he was silently led to the Coast Guard cutter, where he was seated inside a cabin with his hands handcuffed in front of him. A Coast Guard officer boarded his boat and was prepared to follow the cutter back to the base.

Meanwhile, a call woke Agent Ortiz up from a sound sleep. She was notified that Arben was in custody. She notified her agents and Jill in turn.

Arben was in the custody of the San Diego office of the FBI. The FBI would charge him for his assistance to Lark Sumac at the rest stop. Given the complexities of this case, they needed to buy some time so that the various law enforcement agencies and the judicial offices of the United States could reach a common deal that would bring the greatest benefit to the various agencies, and then there was Interpol.

Arben hadn't requested any deal in relation to the charges against him from Albania. It was the intent of the FBI to fully cooperate with Interpol, but if he knew anything about the political dealings of Schmitt Industries, the U.S. judicial system would be cutting him a deal. The U.S. could not deal away the international charges. He would have to face those after the U.S. legal system finished with him.

The next day, an attorney represented him while he put forth his case. In exchange for spilling everything he knew about Schmidt Industries and Lark Sumac; he would face no charges in the United States. He would, at the end of the case, be placed in the custody of Interpol. This was an acceptable deal to the U.S. Attorney as he'd not killed anyone while in this country.

Over the next several days, Arben gave testimony as to the inner workings of Schmidt Industries. He'd been Lark's lover for nearly a decade and had been privy to all kinds of information about the company's dealings. After weeks of testimony, conversations, and fact-checking, the U.S. was able to take down a huge political machine filled with graft and corruption. Schmidt Industries had its tentacles into several government officials, from county-elected to a governor, in one case. Those tentacles had allowed it to gain contracts that spurred the creation of great wealth.

EPILOGUE

*J*ill and Trixie had returned to the Palisades Valley the morning that Arben was captured. Nathan returned that evening from Seattle. Although he'd been with his favorite client, he could complete that client's work in his home studio. Jill made a personal decision to turn down any cases until the fall. She wanted time to recover from the disruption to her life that the Graeme St. Louis case had caused. She wanted nothing more than to concentrate on her first vintage of Moscato. Her beloved classic Thunderbird had been restored to its customary beauty after a month in the body shop. The car seemed happy with its mid-life facelift.

She'd harvested her grapes, followed her perfect recipe, and had several large barrels ready for a mobile wine-bottling service that would arrive later in the morning. She was expecting a run of a thousand cases. Jill had a marketing plan that should help her sell those six thousand bottles. If she failed, she would never have to buy another bottle of wine again.

She had a website that Nathan had helped her design, consistent with her label. Three wine stores in town were going to sell her wine for her. Nathan had helped her create a display for the three stores that she thought would draw buyers, and the store owners had been pleased as well with the displays. The rubber would hit the road tomorrow when she delivered the display and ten cases of wine to each location.

Life was good. Nathan was a great friend and lover. He'd taken her to that martial arts demonstration just after he returned from Seattle. Jill was so impressed with all the martial arts. At first, she didn't know which one to pick to try and master. In the end, she developed three criteria for the art that she would study. One, she could use it for self-defense, Two, she wanted to avoid injury while learning the art. And three, she could physically continue to practice the art into her 70s and 80s. Tai Chi was her choice. She'd been taking lessons for two months and really appreciated the spiritual side of the martial art. She felt that she could do basic self-defense moves now, and she would study the art for years to come.

After she made her delivery to the three wine stores tomorrow, she was going to go back to consulting and offering others a second opinion on the cause of death of their loved one. She hoped that people had not forgotten her work. By only concentrating on winemaking and the meditation of Tai Chi, she felt renewed and ready to take on the next case.

She and her friends were departing on a vacation in a week to spend some of their consulting money. They were flying to Belgium to explore Jo's ancestry and drink lots of beer. She was really looking forward to the trip with her girlfriends, eating, shopping, and drinking their way across the world.

While Schmidt Industries was primarily concentrated in the United States, the corporation had the same behavior of political graft worldwide. Interpol, like the United States, had worked out a deal for Arben's testimony that made life difficult for other governments. In the end, it was rather ironic that

Arben needed Interpol's protection, as he had a bounty on his head. After a miserable two years of testimony and investigation, a bounty hunting sniper took him out one morning. Fortunately, prosecutors worldwide had what they needed to clean up political graft.

ABOUT THE AUTHOR

About the author....

I reside in Northern California with my rescue dog and cat. I love to travel, play sports, read, and drink wine and beer. I enjoy the diversity of the world and I'm always watching people and events for story ideas.

If you would like to sign up for my monthly blog and announcement of new books, please follow this link: www. alecpechebooks.com.

While you're waiting for the next story, if you would be so kind as to leave a review for this book, that would be great. I appreciate all the feedback and support. Reviews buoy my spirits and stoke the fires of creativity.

Readers that sign up for website receive a free prequel novelette for the Jill Quint Series.

ALSO BY ALEC PECHE

Jill Quint, MD Forensic Pathologist Series

Vials

Chocolate Diamonds

A Breck Death

Death On A Green

A Taxing Death

Murder At The Podium

Castle Killing

Crescent City Murder

Sicilian Murder

Opus Murder

Forensic Murder

Embers of Murder

Ashes to Murder

Damian Green Series

Red Rock Island

Willow Glen Heist

The Girl From Diana Park

Evergreen Valley Murder

Long Delayed Justice

Michelle Watson Series

Now You Don't See Me

Where Did She Go?

How Did She Get There? (2022)

Made in United States
Troutdale, OR
07/22/2024

21481814R00170